MW00901860

"It is TIME."

...again

The
Dragon God

Book #2 of the Horn King Series

BRAE WYCKOFF

To Jessica —

Enjoy the adventure!

The Dragon God

The second book in the Horn King series.

©2013

All characters in this book are fictitious. Any resemblance to actual persons, living or dead is purely coincidental.
All Dragon God characters and their distinctive likeness are property of Brae Wyckoff (author).

Printed in USA

ISBN: 1492996335

ISBN-13: 9781492996330

Library of Congress Control Number: 2013920077
CreateSpace Independent Publishing Platform
North Charleston, South Carolina

All rights reserved. This book is protected under the copyright laws of the United States of America. Any reproduction or unauthorized use of the material or artwork contained herein is prohibited without the express written permission of Brae Wyckoff.

No part of this publication may be reproduced or transmitted in any form or by any means, electronic or mechanical, without permission in writing from the author.

Request for permission to make copies of any part of this work should be directed to the website, www.braewyckoff.com

Editor: Krisann Gentry
Maps created by Michelle Modifica-Nichols
Cover art by Michelle Modifica-Nichols, Jill Wyckoff, and
Sharon Marta of Marta Studios
http://www.martastudios.com

DESTINY

1. The inevitable or necessary fate to which a particular person or thing is destined; one's lot.
2. A predetermined course of events considered as something beyond human power or control.

CONTENTS

ACKNOWLEDGMENTS

My wife, Jill Wyckoff, is amazing! Thank you for your support, your encouragement, and loving me through this entire process. You are such a gift to me…

Thank you Michelle-Belle for reading one chapter at a time and growling at me, not in disdain, but in insistence, encouraging me to have more chapters written. Special shout out to Michelle creating the map of Ruauck-El and the Chamber of Cleansing!

I would like to give a huge thank you to the Rancho Bernardo Writer's Group for their amazing critique of my book. I can't say enough about you all, but three of you stood out as the greatest influence of my work…Peter Berkos (Academy Award Winner and Author), MJ Roe (Author), and Terry Ambrose (Author).

Thank you to my Dungeons and Dragons family. We have had some great adventures. Thank you Eric for inspiring the wickedly fun Dal-Draydian.

Thank you to Tom Modifica Jr. for creating a wonderful character—Trillius Triplehand.

Steve Maddox… "It's lonely at the top."

And this book wouldn't be as good as it is without my wonderful editor, Krisann Gentry!

The Heroes of Ruauck-El

Bridazak Baiulus – An orphaned Halfling (AKA Ordakian or Dak, for short) who was the Carrier of the Orb of Truth and the leader of his friends, Spilf, Dulgin, and Abawken.

Spilfer Teehle – Spilf is also an orphaned Ordakian that Bridazak and Dulgin found on the streets of Baron's Hall and have travelled with for years. He is in search of his family.

Dulgin Hammergold – This red-bearded surly dwarf is stubborn and always looking for a fight, but deep down he has a heart of gold and will do anything for his friends. He favors an axe that was gifted to him by his father.

Abawken Shellahk – He comes from the Province of Zoar in the East. Abawken was led to find Bridazak and protect him. He is a human fighter that wields a magical scimitar called the Sword of the Elements.

Raina Sheeldeen – Raina is an elf mystic that was lost for centuries to a curse called The Burning Forest. She is a powerful wizard that fights alongside a Dwarven King named El'Korr.

El'Korr Hammergold – El'Korr is the older brother of Dulgin and was also lost for centuries within The Burning Forest curse. He is now the King of the remnant of dwarves fighting for freedom against the Horn Kings.

Rondee the Wild – Rondee is a Wild Dwarf of the Smasher Clan and is the bodyguard of El'Korr. Wild Dwarves release wild magic that is not always beneficial to themselves and others around them.

Xandahar Sheldeen – Xan is an elven fighter cleric that has lived over 700 years. He is a great and powerful healer. Raina is his sister.

Jack – A rescued teenage human boy trying to find his way in the world.

The Villains of Ruauck-El

King Manasseh – A evil human who lived over three centuries and was the ruler of the Northern Kingdom. He was known as the North Horn King.

The Dark Lord – This deity is the ruler of Kerrith Ravine, a doorway to the underworld.

Reegs – Shadow creatures that are demonic spies for the Dark Lord. Reegs are to report their findings to the Dark Lord and are spread throughout Ruauck-El.

Vevrin and Veric – Human Mystic brothers of rival Horn Kings. Vevrin served Manasseh in the North. Veric serves Ravana in the West.

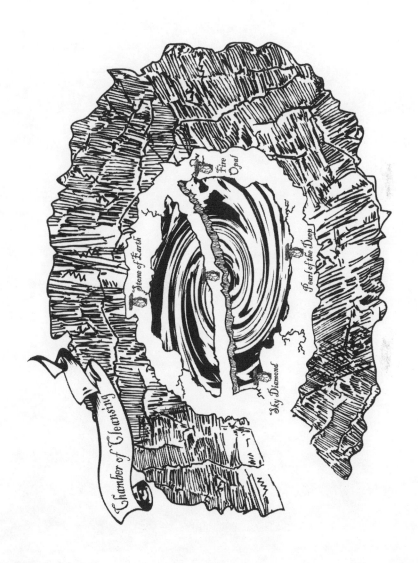

PROLOGUE

The Remnant

The stout dwarf stood at the ridge, overlooking the valley. Smoke billowed into the overcast sky from several locations in the distance. His dark eyes focused under the brim of his thick eyebrows. A shield rested against a rock within reach, the leather straps on the inside were worn and stained with blood. His attention from the scene far away was diverted when the clanking of armored footsteps were heard from behind.

Without turning, the dwarf spoke, his voice a deep, husky tone, "What did you find, Shem?"

"Still only rumors, my liege. King Manasseh has fallen, by all accounts."

"How is this possible? The most powerful Horn King suddenly falls and no one knows why?"

"No confirmation yet, but some fleeing the area to the south have spoken of dwarves holding up within the Moonstone Mountains and calling anyone and everyone to band with them."

"Moonstone Mountains? There are no dwarves in that area. We can't move on rumors alone, Shem. Find someone who has a first hand account."

"It might not be anything of importance but one of our patrols picked up a human cook along the north ridge."

"A cook? Do you long for human prepared food, Shem?"

"Of course not, Bailo. I have been told he was Manasseh's personal chef at a hidden castle close to the border of Kerrith Ravine."

Bailo squinted as he turned to face Shem. Bailo's long black braided beard reached his armored gut.

Shem nervously spoke, "I know that it is not what you were expecting, so I won't bother—"

"No," Bailo interrupted. "Bring me this human cook. I wish to speak to him directly."

An unshaven human, escorted by four warrior dwarves led by Shem, stood before the imposing Bailo, whose two prominent scars—one on each side of his neck—melded into his wrinkled skin. His dark brown eyes bore into the scrawny human who wore grey breeches and a dirtied white tunic.

Bailo asked, "What is your name, Human?"

The man answered, in a raspy voice, "I'm called Valcod."

"And what is your profession, Valcod?"

"I'm the personal chef to King Manasseh. At least I was."

"Tell me what happened, Valcod." Bailo looked at each of his men and said, "No harm will come to you."

The human peered off into the valley below, the black smoke rising at several towns. "You don't know?"

"Speak!" Bailo ordered.

"King Manasseh is dead. The towns and cities are now under martial law, or in some places civilians have taken over. It's chaos down there. Most assuredly the other Horn Kings will come. People are fleeing to the forests and mountains until things settle down."

"Where is your proof, Valcod? Something is clearly happening, but dwarves and elves have gone into hiding and to show ourselves to humans is dangerous."

"Are you their leader?"

"I ask the questions, Human. Give me proof."

Valcod only returned silence. Bailo looked to Shem.

"All he had was this." Shem produced a corked vial filled with a black fluid. Bailo reached for it and inspected the contents.

"What is this, Valcod?"

"Just an ingredient of mine that I like to use."

There was an awkward silence and then Bailo responded, "Good. I'm hungry. Prepare me some food using your ingredient."

Valcod chuckled, "I have nothing to make for you."

"Well, I'm thirsty then, Valcod. This should do fine. Dwarves love dark brews."

Shem stepped forward, "My liege, it could be poison."

Bailo glared at Valcod, "Wouldn't be the first time I drank something I wasn't supposed to."

Valcod, stoic in his stance, did not say anything. Bailo uncorked the vial, giving sound to a hollow pop as it was released. The dwarf slowly brought it to his lips, locking his eyes on the human, who claimed to be a chef of King Manasseh. Bailo tilted the glass and the black substance began to edge closer to his mouth. Valcod's hazel eyes didn't blink, though he held his breath. At the last instant he halted Bailo, "Stop!"

Bailo instantly lurched forward and grabbed the human's tunic with his free hand while lowering the vial away, "Who are you?"

The human sighed and finally admitted, "I am a former royal guard of Manasseh."

"What is this that I almost drank? Poison? On your life, you had better speak!"

"Nay, it is not poison. It was taken from the Pool of Recall within Manasseh's tower at Black Rock Castle."

"What is this Pool of Recall?"

"You can see past events through the eyes of the one you name."

Bailo peered at Shem and then handed him the vial with the cork. "Keep it safe."

Valcod brought the dwarf's attention back, "I am looking for refuge. I have experienced the hand of an evil king and I wish to be free of any future evil king's which are coming."

"You speak of the East and West Horn Kings."

"Indeed. Once they verify Manasseh's death, then the inevitable will happen. I brought the water from the Pool of Recall to secure safe passage by revealing the truth of what actually transpired."

"What did happen?"

"An army of dwarves attacked his castle, led by a mystic."

"Dwarves? Are you certain?"

"Yes, I saw them with my own eyes."

Shem spoke, "Dwarves don't have mystics, Human."

"It was an elf mystic."

Bailo glanced to Shem, who returned the look of concern.

Valcod continued, "I heard some of the men speak of her being a Sheldeen Elf."

Bailo stared deeply into Valcod's eyes, "Show me how to use this Pool of Recall. I need to see with my own eyes what you speak of." Bailo then turned toward Shem and whispered, "Call a meeting with the other leaders."

Three dwarves gathered by a small fire, well hidden within the mountains. Howling wind resounded outside their boulder-protected location. Four stone markers, dwarven language carved on each, stood towering above them at the center.

A deep maroon-colored beard dangled from a dark-brown eyed dwarf who leaned against one of the markers, arms crossed over his barrel chest. Another dwarf, massive in girth, and an orange and grey beard matching the width of the clan member, sat on one of the benches between the upright stone pieces. The third and final dwarf huffed loudly as he slung his braided brown beard over his left shoulder and asked, "What is taking so long?"

The fat dwarf chuckled, placed his right palm out, and said, "Cough up yer gold, Kog."

He pulled out a small pouch and tossed it, "Here ya go, Brewtus. Got me again, dammit."

The third dwarf stood dumbfounded at the transaction that revolved around him and responded, "Your incessant gambling is a disease to our race."

Brewtus scoffed, "Our coffers grow while yours diminish, our sweet Hahlid of the Redheart."

"You dare speak of my surname in jest? You Bluefists are the reason we stay separated as clans."

Brewtus grumbled as he stood in anger, "Time for me to shut your mouth."

Hahlid roared and charged, slamming into the gut of Brewtus, who did not budge. Brewtus brought his clubbed fists down on top of Hahlid and dropped him to the ground. Kog laughed heartily in the background.

A booming voice coming around the bend halted them all, "Enough!"

Each of them turned and watched Bailo enter the confined meeting area.

"About time, Bailo," Brewtus said as he sat back down.

Hahlid stood and then made his way to his bench.

"Why the meeting?" Kog asked as he sat.

Without a pause, Bailo answered, "El'Korr has returned."

Each of them shot puzzled glances at one another.

"You speak nonsense, Bailo. He fell in the crusade against Kerrith Ravine."

"I have seen with my own eyes, and that is not all."

"Speak Bailo, before I charge you to step down," Brewtus announced.

"The entire crusade survived. They unleashed their fury upon the doorstep of King Manasseh, defeating him, and now reside within the Moonstone Mountains amassing a new resistance. Raina also lives."

"How did you come by this information?"

"Shem, bring it in!" Bailo called.

Shem and another dwarven warrior walked in together, each carefully holding the end of a small basin as they came into the area.

"What is the meaning of this?" Kog stood.

"My brethren, the time has come. You will each see firsthand what has transpired, and know what I speak is truth."

The basin, filled with the murky water of the Pool of Recall, was placed in the center of the meeting. Shem and the warrior exited without a word.

"Place your face into the water as you think of El'Korr, and you will see what has transpired."

Each clan member did as instructed. Brewtus stood upright, black water trickled down his face as he stared intently at Bailo. The overweight dwarf stumbled away in shock as Kog was next. They waited until the final leader of dwarves witnessed the fall of Manasseh at the hands of El'Korr Hammergold and Raina Sheldeen.

Bailo said, "It is time to gather the Remnant, unite the clans, and march to Te Sond."

1

Old Friends

Abawken closed his eyes and breathed in the arid air, sensing his prey was close. The Sheltothii ritual was as ancient as the realm of Ruauck-El itself, and was the foundation of the desert ways. At the age of Ragiil each youth was tested—sent to hunt the deadly Chuulkath within the sand chasms of the far East. The desert nomad, wrapped in ceremonial linens from head to toe, held his gleaming scimitar, and thought, *"Wait. Let it come."* His instincts and training melded together as this life and death ritual unfolded.

Waves of sweltering heat intensified in the deep maze of canyons. The desert wind sent dune sand from above cascading down the brittle walls, sounding a bit like rain. He veered away from the shadier spots, staying within the sunlight. *"It is close. Be patient,"* he reminded himself. Then he heard it. He froze in place, breathing silently as he focused in on a slight clicking sound, masquerading itself from behind a stream of pouring sand. The time of the Kemsing, full sun, when the sharp lines separating shade from light would begin to dissipate, was seconds away. Only the light of day would reveal the Chuulkath, but he would have to be close to it before the sun waned and the shadows returned.

As Abawken took another step closer, focusing straight ahead, his left arm dipped within the edges of the shade; before he'd even noticed, the claws of the creature dragged him into the pocket of darkness as deep as twilight. He swung his sword but the pawed hand grappled his arm and

1

smashed it up against the rocky alcove, forcing him to release his weapon. It plopped onto the sandy floor.

Abawken wrestled with the mythological desert creature, fighting to bring it into the light, but the strength of the beast was far beyond his own. He had to stay alive long enough for the sun to be at its zenith. Precious seconds elapsed while the Chuulkath lifted the human into the air and slammed his body into the rocky wall. Sand enveloped him; the volatile terrain exploded on his impact. The creature would remain blurred, its form undefined, as long as it stayed within the shade. Abawken kicked as instinct directed, but missed. Then the human's legs were swept out from under him and he fell back into the soft sand. His lower body was still in the shade, but the brilliant sun blinded him briefly as he looked up. He felt it grab his legs and pull him back. Still disoriented, he managed to snatch his scimitar as he was dragged, and swung once again. This time he connected, and was released. He arched his back and quickly flipped up to his feet acrobatically.

The sun repelled the shadows away and the last sliver of shade quickly faded. It was at this instant that Abawken reached inside. His hand caught hold of it and he held on, gritting his teeth, struggling against the fight. Then it appeared before him. Abawken tackled the creature to the ground, pinning it below him. The golden fur of the sphinx and the pearlescent claws glistened in the sun. It was forced to relax within the daylight and succumbed to the human. He stared into the yellow cat eyes of the malevolent face and watched as it transformed slowly into a female human visage. The lioness body remained.

Abawken demanded, "Give me my name!"

It struggled at first and then calmed, but did not answer him. Then it smiled and the smell of lilac encompassed Abawken's senses—a smell that did not belong in this scenario. One he recognized from his past.

He shook off the confusion of the aroma and pressed down harder, "You must, as per the Sheltothii Ritual."

"Get off me," the female answered in perfect common.

Her comment jarred his senses. "What did you say?"

"I said, get off of me ya blundering fool!"

Bronze hair transformed to scraggly red strands and rich, yellow eyes became muddy watered orbs. The smell of the desert, and the overwhelming lilac, gave way to the stench of an old burnt out campfire.

"Am I interrupting something?" Spilf peered out from a hole in the wooden floor boards to the sparse room.

Abawken retreated hastily from Dulgin and looked around his surroundings. He was back inside their small hideout. The dusty, windowless, and barren space, big enough to stash only their meager belongings and bedrolls to sleep, brought him back to their reality of being cooped up here, hiding these last few days, in wait for their contact to bring them the information they needed.

"What happened?" Abawken asked.

"Listen here, Stubby! This human is crazy," Dulgin pleaded with Spilf while ignoring Abawken's question.

The ordakian's eyebrows rose, "Sure Dulgin, whatever you say. Anyway, Bridazak is waiting for us at the tavern. He made contact with Scalve. Remember to put on the oversized cloaks to hide yourselves. See you there," Spilf finished and the top of his brown, messy hair disappeared back down the dark tunnel underneath the foundation of their makeshift home.

"What happened?" Abawken asked again.

"You were having a bad dream so I went to wake you, then you attacked me, dammit," Dulgin responded as he stood. He pointed his finger at the human, "Don't do that again."

"I never planned on it in the first place, Master Dulgin. My apologies."

"What was that all about anyway?"

Abawken was not quick to answer. "You're right. It was a bad dream."

"Well, that is the last time I try to wake you. I will let your nightmare resolve itself next time."

Abawken didn't respond, as his thoughts of her had captured his mind. He walked to the other side of the room, facing away from the dwarf and closed his eyes to calm his nerves. "Kee vuulaun," he gently whispered.

"What did you say, Huey?"

"I need to pray, Master Dulgin."

"Well, hurry it up, I want to get out of this shady town before someone in our past finds out we are here. Baron Hall holds the best of scum and villainy."

Abawken closed his eyes as he knelt by a lit candle, his elevated palms resting on his thighs. Giving thanks to God for all he had been blessed with, a smile began to form on his face. He recalled Mistress Raina, and their many meetings together in the Moonstone Mountains before he departed.

They had grown fond of discussing intellectual tidbits, and the histories and customs of their home realms. He chuckled to himself, remembering her strict corrections every time he mispronounced an Elvish word she was teaching him that day. He'd always been drawn to her strong leadership, but noticed a softness when they were alone he had not seen. The more he thought of Raina, the stronger he could feel the emotional link she had taught him to establish.

Dulgin shook his head and began to gather the dark brown cloak to cover himself. He whipped it around his shoulders; it made a sound like a flag unfurling.

"You done, Huey?"

Abawken sighed, his focus broken. "It doesn't look like you're giving me much of a choice."

"Ever thought about talking to God while movin?" Abawken stood, turned to face the dwarf, and grinned. "What are you smiling about?" Dulgin's eyes squinted.

"Just thinking about the past and now the future, my friend."

"Yeah, well hopefully the future holds a bar-fight and plenty of ale," he licked his lips, "and it doesn't have to be in that order."

Abawken grabbed his oversized cloak and slung it around his shoulders. He tucked his sheathed scimitar inside and then pulled the hood to drape over his head, concealing his face. Dulgin retrieved his dwarven battle-axe from its place against the wall.

"Time to get out of this shack we've been holed up in. C'mon, I can smell trouble." Dulgin jumped down into the narrow tunnel—the only way in and out of the confined, dilapidated hideout.

Abawken followed closely behind. "I think you are smelling yourself, Master Dulgin."

"Where are they?" Bridazak asked."

"I think Abawken was showing Dulgin some new moves," Spilf coughed. "They'll be here shortly. Where is Scalve?"

"He is collecting a debt. He said he would be back with the information."

"Bridazak, would you look at all those leather purses out there. These drunks are just asking for someone to come along and take them off their hands. Don't you think it is weird that we don't have that desire to steal any longer?"

"Well, I would say, that makes you an honest thief."

They chuckled and continued to watch the tavern patrons. Their table was positioned by the back wall to give them the best vantage point. The crowded bar was filled to capacity. Metal steins of mead clanked throughout the tavern, which was in full swing. Scraggly, thieving humans dominated most of the establishment, while some of the half-orc race, the meat-headed muscle type, occasionally showed up. This breed of half-human, half-orc originated in Baron Hall. The Baron, an evil human who enslaved warrior orcs and bred them with his slave concubines to procreate the brutes, formed his own small army over time, known as the Headbashers.

"Why did you pick the Bog, of all places, to meet Scalve?"

"What better place to make Scalve feel comfortable? He knows our history with Dorg and his gang, so it makes sense we do this under Dorg's very own nose."

"You are taking a big risk my friend, but I like it."

"Don't you worry Spilfer, I have taken care of everything. Scalve will get us what we need and then we will be out of here."

Spilf nudged Bridazak to alert him of Dulgin and Abawken's entrance. The cloaked duo made their way to the back table.

"You know you two ordakians stand out like a gnome's sore nose," Dulgin commented as they joined them at the table.

"That's what I told Bridazak," Spilf jabbed his friend in the shoulder.

"Don't worry. It's all under control. Once we get the map from Scalve we will be on our way to find Spilf's parents."

"Why do we all need to be here, Master Bridazak? It seems we will stand out even more as a group."

"Scalve insisted. He never deals with anyone he hasn't looked in the face. Plus, you have the loot we are trading with. Did you bring them?"

"Yes, I have the gems."

"Are you sure you want to part with them for my sake? Maybe there is another way," Spilf asked.

"It's fine. Any wealth I can offer in the way of finding your family will be yours."

"My deepest thanks, Abawken."

"Ever going to tell us where you got those beauties from?" Bridazak asked.

Abawken remained silent, and Dulgin piped up, "Good luck cracking this Huey. I've been asking since we met where he got that sword of his and he has yet to explain that supposed gift."

"Now is not the time, Master Dulgin."

"Yeah, when is the time? Now you suddenly have a small pouch of diamonds as if you plucked it from the royal treasure itself. I've never seen their like before. They're not from this region. Where did you say they came from, Bawky?"

"Dulgin, it's not gemology time. I agree with Abawken, now is not the place. Once Scalve gets here then I need you all to follow my lead. Understand?" Spilf and Abawken nodded. "Dulgin, do you understand?" Bridazak asked again.

"Yeah, I get it. Now, where is this Scalvey fella?"

"He just entered," Spilf pointed.

"Okay, all of you be quiet and let me do the talking. I'm mainly referring to you, Dulgin."

"I get it. You do the talkin and I'll do the fightin."

Scalve approached. He was a scrawny looking human of average height with gangly arms and brown short hair, whose only real distinguishing features were bad hygiene, and that he was missing his entire left ear. The heroes scanned their contact intently, noticing the leather armor underneath his beige pants and tunic and dark brown cloak draped down his back. They knew a weapon could be easily concealed, as there were none out in the open.

"Well met," he bluntly announced as he joined them at their table.

"We are all here, per your request."

"Good, I always want to know who I am doing business with. Speaking of business, do you have what we discussed?"

"Yes. I take it you have what we need?"

"You are correct." Scalve drew forth a folded parchment from within his tunic.

Bridazak nodded to Abawken, who withdrew a small pouch containing the diamonds. Scalve inspected the goods without taking them out to display to the world. Bridazak took the leather parchment and lowered it to his side to take a quick glance. They both were satisfied.

"So, when will your other ear fall off?" Dulgin blurted.

"I'm sorry, forgive my friend here," Bridazak tried to parlay the insult.

"What did you say?"

"I'm sorry, let me talk into your good ear. Wait, which one is that?"

"Oh brother," Spilf sighed.

"Enough, we both got what we wanted so let's part ways before we get to a point we can't back out of," Bridazak motioned with his hands out to try and keep them separated.

"This just makes things a lot easier," Scalve said with a smirk, raising his hand to signal someone.

"What does that mean?"

A squad of the Headbasher Gang entered the Bog tavern, answering the question. They shoved the other patrons aside to clear a path. Stepping through the doorway last came the infamous Dorg, the Baron's right hand thug. The greasy haired, half-orc leader had broken pieces of banded mail armor crusted with dried blood dangling from him. Bridazak focused on the unforgettable deformed and jagged teeth protruding from the sides of his snout-like mouth. He was the ugliest out of his entire entourage.

Silence fell upon the establishment and Dorg's thunderous boot steps echoed off the wooden floor boards as he moved toward the heroes in the back.

"You traitorous bastard!" Dulgin spat at Scalve.

"It's business. Dorg has quite a bounty on your heads." Scalve stepped aside and made his way to the exit.

Bridazak whispered to his friends, "Stay calm. Trust me."

Dorg's voice crackled, "Well, well, well. Look what the trolls dragged in."

There was no rebuttal, only a calm grin from Bridazak. Dorg scoffed, "What, no funny comments from the halflings? Let's see here, we have Bridazak, Spilf, the ugly red-bearded dwarf, and a newcomer." Dorg yanked the hood away from the newcomer's face and growled, "What's your name, Human?"

Pulling back from Dorg's bad breath, he answered, "Abawken."

"That's a funny name for a human." Laughter erupted from his goons behind him in support of their master's comment. "You're not from around here. Where are you from, Human?"

Abawken glanced at Bridazak who gave him a slight nod to go ahead and answer.

"I come from the province of Zoar to the East."

"Oh, we have a foreigner in town boys!" Another eruption of laughter heightened. "There is a foreigner tax here at Baron Hall. Isn't that right, boys?" Snarls and nodding heads responded to Dorg's question.

"Bridazak, I've had enough of this!" Dulgin said loudly, staring down the half-orc.

"Oh, finally, I was wondering how long it would take before the dwarf came around. I was getting bored with the human."

"Dorg, it was an accident those ten years ago. You can't still be upset after all this time?"

"Upset, Bridazak? You think I'm upset? No, on the contrary, I'm so very happy that you all decided to come back to the Hall. When Scalve told me you were in town, I was overjoyed. In fact, the Baron is preparing a feast in your honor as we speak. Isn't that right, boys?" More chuckles and snorts resounded.

Bridazak calmly replied, "Well, that is good to hear. I'm looking forward to catching up with the Baron after all these years. Is it alright if I invite a few guests?"

"Guests? Why sure, I wouldn't have it any other way," he grinned.

"Good. Dulgin, do you mind sharing your thoughts about Dorg's mighty fine tavern he has here?"

"Yes, enlighten me, Dwarf."

Dulgin pushed his chair back and stood, planting his hands on the table. He stared deeply into Dorg's recessed eyes. "The Bog is a great name for this place," he started off. "It stands for a 'Bunch of Garbage,' and I'm here to take out the trash."

Dorg guffawed, "There's the dwarf we remember." Then, quickly twisting his face into a scowl, he snarled, "I'm going to savor the years of torture in the dungeons awaiting you."

Dorg moved toward Dulgin but Bridazak suddenly stepped between them and whistled loudly. Cloaked patrons at several tables sprang to their feet and revealed their faces. A huge, seven-foot tall human wielding a gigantic maul with an arm's length anvil at the end rose and stepped forward as their apparent leader. Muscles bulged out from his leather armor draped with animal skins, and fur boots to his knees. His steel grey eyes glared through his thick blondish brown hair at the half-orc leader.

"Bridazak, my debt is paid," his deep voice resonated throughout the room.

"My thanks, Griplock. You have my gratitude for coming all this way in from the tundra, my friend."

Dorg and his gang were completely surrounded by the barbarian tribe that had infiltrated the town—they were long time rivals over a deep family grudge lasting many years. Explosive attacks at any given moment between the two factions were common.

Dorg spun back on Bridazak, "You will pay for this."

"Have a nice chat with my invited guests. Give my love to the Baron," he mocked.

The heroes moved quickly out the back door. They heard angry, muffled words exchanged that escalated into an all-out brawl. Shouts from fleeing patrons, mingled with the sounds of chairs toppling, tables crashing, and glass shattering.

"I love the sound of a good bar-fight," Dulgin said.

"Well played Master Bridazak. How did you know we would be set up?"

"C'mon, we can't expect to come to the Hall without someone recognizing us. It was inevitable. Just glad it worked out."

"I hope this map is something we can work from to find my village," Spilf chimed in.

"We'll find it."

"Can we go back and join in the fun?" Dulgin pleaded.

"Perhaps next time, my friend."

"I will remember you said that."

They moved further into the shadows of the town—heading for the outskirts of the open tundra beyond. Suddenly, Abawken smelled the scent of lilac. It stopped him dead in his tracks. *"She is here. She is following me,"* he looked around nervously.

"Abawken, what's wrong?" Bridazak asked.

"Nothing. Let's go."

2

Tales of Power

Raina stood before a basin filled with water atop a pedestal, formed from the Moonstone itself. She was thankful to have the privacy of her brother's home nestled into the rock cave away from the hustle of El'Korr's troops, outside building barricades and exercising their military skills. A library of ancient tomes surrounded her. After the fall of Manasseh, she had taken it upon herself to investigate all that had transpired in Ruauck-El since her centuries-long captivity in the curse of the Burning Forest. With knowledge, she would increase her power to protect the realm and its citizens, until they could be brought into the Holy City.

People from all over the nearby realms had come in with reports of tyrant leaders—formerly Manasseh's troops, attempting to establish power holds over communities and regions, aiming to fill the gap the evil king left behind. They needed a plan, and she sought to understand the happenings in the other three horns, to determine the best course.

She leaned low, the tip of her nose almost touching the calm water, and whispered, "Show me what I need to see."

The water rippled and images began to replace her reflected face, revealing four colored stones, no bigger than the size of a man's fist. The first was as white as snow, with dimpled glints of scales. Next, was an emerald green that seemed illuminated from deep within. Another was red which glowed like a metal ore in a blacksmith's fire, and finally a black stone. It was dark as night, but soft like a raven's wing. The ripples churned and flashed to another scene; a mystic in dark robes with gold stitching, bearing the emblem of the West Horn King. He was standing before a monstrous black dragon Raina recognized; it was the same one who had captured Bridazak and delivered him to King Manasseh on top of his tower. Her thoughts churned like the water in the basin as she held tightly to the rim.

"What are you up to?" she whispered.

She refocused when two green scaled dragoons dragged King Manasseh's lifeless body into the scene, laying him before the black monster. The vision then ended.

"Very interesting," she contemplated. "Four stones and a fallen king. What do they mean?"

For the next several hours she scoured through the books and parchments strewn about the room. Xan had kept a grand collection over the centuries and there was much information to be gathered.

"What do we have here?" she said aloud. She read the passage in the book entitled *Tales of the Ancients*, "The ancient dragons searched for ways to prolong their spirits and worked with a human wizard of unknown origin. The wizard promised the old wyrms of the five colors that their spirits could be harnessed into younger bodies and they could live through eternity. However, he betrayed them and harnessed each of their powers into his own spirit. The wizard was known as the Dragon God, but was destroyed. Magical items pulling from the power of the natural elements of water, earth, air, and fire were created. When the age-old races banded together, bringing the antiquated heirlooms and combining the energy contained within them, the artifacts activated and opened a powerful portal, summoning the Dragon God against his will and casting him into it, to bring an end to the calamitous uprising." Raina suddenly stopped as the next sentence spoke volumes. "The evil power of the wizard and the dragons were then separated and scattered throughout Ruauck-El in the form of the five colored stones."

"Five colored stones," she whispered. "They have four. They are looking for the fifth stone, but what does Manasseh have to do with this?" A flash of realization hit her.

Xan suddenly entered the room. The door was partially blocked with stacks of books and a couple of rows fell over with his sudden intrusion.

"What did you do to my library?" he exclaimed.

"You won't care once I tell you what I have found, my brother. Come, we need to speak with King El'Korr."

She whisked past him as he stood in the entryway looking around the disheveled room; his cherished collection of manuscripts tossed feverishly. Shaking his head, he closed the door and said under his breath, "Raina, this better be good."

"Get your boys over that ridge and secure that location!" El'Korr demanded, pointing to an area on the wooden table, covered with maps.

"Yes sir!" the dwarf warrior responded as he back-peddled out of the room.

Raina and El'Korr, along with several of his generals, had spent time strategizing the best recourse for handling their growing numbers—thousands of remaining dwarves, elves, ordakians, and humans had come to them, seeking to serve the ones who had brought down Manasseh. The Moonstone Mountains were fine for training, but it would soon be unable to contain their masses or allow for a defensible position.

Geetock, a wild dwarf and longtime general under King El'Korr, stroked his knotted graying beard, and asked, "I know you are keeping the ranks busy here, so what is the real plan?"

El'Korr's left eyebrow rose, "Very perceptive, Geetock. I'm planning on moving everyone to a place called the Shield, northwest of here. I need you and Rondee to coordinate with the others to get ready for the march, within days."

"That is a lot to do in a short period of time."

"Once the other Horn Kings verify Manasseh's fall, they will begin strategizing their takeover into the North region. We can't stay here. Moving to the Shield can give us a better defense and give us more time to gather strength."

Geetock nodded his approval and said, "We will make it happen, my Malehk."

"I know you will, my friend. Find Rondee and get him in here. I need to get him updated."

"Yes sir." Geetock exited just as Raina arrived.

"Raina! Where have you been?" El'Korr was surprised to see her in such a flustered state.

13

"Researching."

"What information did you find?" El'Korr noticed Raina's uneasiness. "You are troubled, and that makes me nervous."

"I wish I carried happier news," she responded.

"Clear the room!" El'Korr waved his arm in a sweeping motion.

Several wild dwarf sentries moved out of the room. Xan closed the door behind them and then turned to join Raina and El'Korr.

"What is it? I'm trying to secure the north ridge from those moonstone rock creatures."

"They are the least of our worries," she responded.

El'Korr glanced over to Xan, who shrugged. El'Korr was now concerned, as Raina did not get frazzled easily.

"A mystic of the West Horn is working with the black dragon, the same one who captured Bridazak and Xan," she started her tale.

Xan shifted uncomfortably as he remembered being held hostage in the mouth of the beast.

She continued, "They are gathering the powerful dragon stones."

Silence engulfed the room. El'Korr's bushy orange eyebrow shot up on one side and he examined the tense posture of the mystic, noting her anxiousness. "So? I'm not following what that means exactly."

"There are five colored rocks, each representing the dark dragon colors. Five ancient wyrms are held captive inside each of them. Once combined, under the right conditions someone could harness their powers and bring them back." She stared at them to get some reaction, but the room remained silent.

"I'm still not following you. How do some crazy stones give me any reason to jump?"

"Where were these items placed, Raina?" Xan interjected.

"They were scattered across the realm and no one knew their location."

"Well, there you have it. It appears it will take the mystic and the dragon quite a long time to gather their precious stones." El'Korr shifted to the maps on his table, "Now in the meantime, it will take us a few more days to finish our training here before we march." El'Korr looked up with excitement on his face, "Our new base will—," he stopped short as he glanced back to Raina, her scowl communicating clearly. He cleared his throat, scrunching his brows as they wrinkled. "I guess I missed something."

"I said *were* scattered. They have gathered four of the five stones." She let this information hang in the air.

"Well, do they know where the fifth is located? If they don't, then it could take quite some—"

Raina cut him off, "They also have the body of King Manasseh."

"Now why would they need that foul corpse?" El'Korr blurted in disgust.

"I asked the same question, and I have surmised that Manasseh knew the location of the fifth stone."

"But he is dead, and that knowledge died with him. There should be nothing to worry about, right?" El'Korr asked.

Xan, realizing what his sister had discovered, interjected, "The power of a black dragon combined with the dark magic of a mystic might possibly be able to bring back the dead."

El'Korr paused. "That changes things. What do you suggest, Raina?"

"We need to find the elements originally created to destroy them."

"Great, now it's a mad search for things we know nothing about," El'Korr responded.

"On the contrary, someone does know about the elements and their locations."

"Who?" Xan quickly asked.

"I read of a Captain Yasooma. His life was dedicated to finding these elements in hopes of protecting the realm against anyone seeking the power of the five dragons."

"Wonderful. Where is he?"

"He is dead, but I am certain he would have left behind some clues. The information we need from a long-dead man will be much harder to gather, when compared to what our enemies may already have, if they were successful. We are running out of time and we must go now."

"Where do we start this search then?" El'Korr questioned.

"The great city of Tuskabar on the west coast, where he is buried," she replied.

"Very well then, I will arrange for my men to hold the fort while we investigate. Rondee will accompany us."

"My apologies King El'Korr," Raina stated cryptically.

"Why do you apologize?"

The female mystic began her spell.

"Raina! No!" Xan countered, but it was too late.

Rondee burst through the door to see the swirling vortex of shimmering silver and gold energy. "My Malehk, de mosh teph me!" The wild dwarf dove into the dissipating remnants and was swallowed up just in time. The warped window of brilliant colors closed behind him and the crackling power sealed in an instant, leaving behind a low rumble of thunder in the distance.

Raina, Xan, and El'Korr found themselves standing inside an old wine cellar. Wooden aged barrels were lined up and stacked on either side of them. A musty smell of fermented alcohol assaulted their nostrils.

"Where are we?" El'Korr growled at Raina.

"Tuskabar."

Suddenly, Rondee materialized and fell from above, landing on top of El'Korr. A clattering of armor sounded from the impact.

"What in dwarven hell!!?"

"Malehk El'Korr rocks sembe float?" Rondee said in his bizarre verbiage.

"Du-maerde! Your rocks are going to be floating if you don't get off of me." El'Korr yelled angrily as Rondee helped him up, but then controlled his emotions and spoke calmly. "Raina, I understand you mean well, but I prefer to be asked to go somewhere and not forced."

Xan stepped between them and tried to calm the situation, "She knows you better than any of us, and I suspect she teleported us now instead of waiting for you to plan out your departure. Apparently, this couldn't wait."

"My brother speaks the truth. I'm afraid we are called once again to protect the realm, but not with an army in tow."

"What am I to do with you? Do you realize I was in the middle of planning a march to the Shield?"

"Yes, and last of my discoveries, that I hadn't yet mentioned, is the location of the banishment portal for the Dragon God, which is at the very same place you named."

El'Korr paused and then sighed, "Rondee, contact Geetock with your telepathy power and have him move the army to the Shield. Let him know that we are apparently on a side mission, and we will meet them there."

3

Separate Paths

Flaming torches atop long poles lit the trail for the unit of approaching dragoons. These creatures with the lizard-like heads spoke in a slithery language of their own—a race born from a mysterious lineage of dragon kin. Two of the dragoons dragged a human corpse by the arms. The sound of the cadaver's black leather boots sliding along the cold stone floor echoed off the tunnel walls. They soon entered a large chamber where a monstrous black dragon, perched in the shadows atop an immense, worn stalagmite, awaited them. Attending the dragon was a human mystic adorned in black robes, clutching a jade staff topped with a ruby inset. The hooded wizard nodded as the dragoons plopped the body face down at his feet. They flanked their master, the dragon, and stood at attention.

"Are you powerful enough for this task, Mystic?" the booming voice of the dragon demanded inside the mage's mind.

"Barawbyss, I taught my brother everything he knew. Manasseh will give us our information; that is certain."

"Very well. Let the ceremony begin."

The mage pulled back his hood. His pale skin glowed in this dark chamber, emanating a soft light through the black tattoos covering his bald scalp. Dark circles surrounded the deeply sunken eyes on his colorless face. He waved his staff over the corpse of the fallen King Manasseh and in a raspy arcane language, began to chant, the right side of his upper lip curling and revealing rotted teeth. "Shuul fha-té. Cal odem she et-kal." His ruby crested staff began to glow brighter with each spoken word over the lifeless body. Slowly, Manasseh levitated and rotated until his face pointed to the ceiling. The chanting continued, "Telhal vatcu shadhal!" The dead man's mouth opened wide.

The black dragon expanded its wings and leaned its head low. The toothy maw slowly opened and a single drop of saliva fell into Manasseh's open-hanging jaw.

"Kobess-cay zesheil," the mystic touched Manasseh's chest with the tip of the brightly lit ruby as he finished his incantation. A surge of power, accompanied by a loud humming noise, jolted the corpse, which shook violently as a low gurgling sound rumbled from deep inside his gut and a foamy froth erupted from Manasseh's mouth. The light dissipated and Veric backed away as Barawbyss retracted his wings and lifted his head.

Manasseh's body continued to convulse; his long jet black hair flew wildly around his face with each violent rotation of his neck. Then all motion suddenly stopped. The body slumped and went limp.

"Can you hear me?" the mystic bent over to ask.

The blue lips of the corpse moved slightly as his dry voice replied in a hoarse whisper, "Yes."

"What is your name?"

"Manasseh."

The wizard righted himself and addressed Barawbyss, "It is complete."

"Not until he gives us the answer we truly desire, Veric," the dragon answered in his thoughts.

"Yes, of course," the mystic leaned back toward Manasseh. "Where is the blue dragon stone?"

Manasseh's body jerked, but he gave no answer. It was as though he was somehow resisting.

"Where is the blue dragon stone, Manasseh?" he asked again more forcefully.

Refusing to answer the question, he only replied, in a raspy, guttural tone, "I want revenge."

Veric paused, looking to Barawbyss. The dragon glared back at him, *"You will continue, Mage."*

"It is too dangerous to have him return."

18

"You made your deal with me, that is no concern of mine. Continue!" he roared inside Veric's mind.

Veric bowed low and turned again to Manasseh, "You will have your revenge, if you give us what we want."

Manasseh slowly turned his head toward Veric and growled, "Bring me back first."

"You can only name one soul. From whom amongst the living do you seek revenge?"

"Bridazak!"

Bridazak pointed to the old, edge frayed map, and asked, "Does any of this look familiar to you Spilf?"

He studied the markings, shook his head and said, "I just don't see anything that stands out. I'm sorry."

Dulgin growled, "Great! That's wonderful, Stubby. We risk our necks for this map and—"

Bridazak held up his hand to stop him. He turned his back to the group, closed his eyes and silently prayed. He spun back a second later, a glint in his eyes.

"We obviously need to try something a little different."

"What is your meaning, Master Bridazak?" Abawken inquired.

"Yeah, what do ya mean 'different'?"

"Spilf, I want you to sit down with the map and ask for guidance on where to go."

"Guidance?"

"Maybe there will be an impression or an instinct that comes when you concentrate. Let's just try it. We have nothing to lose."

Spilf sat as instructed, while the rest of them watched. Dulgin skeptically squinted, crossing his arms across his barrel chest.

The ordakian closed his eyes and began to focus on the memory of what God had shown him. It played back vividly in his mind. His mother was hit by the arrow and fell into the cold water. She pushed the canoe with all her remaining strength and told him to never come back and look for them. Tears were visible on Spilfer's face as his friends continued to watch him relive the painful past he had forgotten—until God in the Holy City had shown him the memories he had lost.

Spilf then recalled the mist hovering over the lake engulfing him and the small vessel. While his eyes were still closed, an image of the map he held burst into his mind like a flash of light. He opened his eyes and without hesitation, pointed, "It's here."

Dulgin barged forth, "What!? Let me see." Spilf's finger indicated a spot on the parchment that had no lake. It was a small area nestled at the base of the mountains. "There's nothing there, ya blundering fool!"

Spilf turned to Bridazak, "I did as you asked and I feel it is there. I can't explain it."

"Well, that's good enough for me, my friend," Bridazak reassured him.

"What? You are going to follow this ridiculous eye-closing, finger-pointing, Ordakian-guessing? This is dwarfshit!"

"Dulgin, please calm down. We promised Spilf we would do what we could and all we have is this. Let's make an adventure out of it, shall we?"

"Adventuring is one thing and sightseeing is another!" Dulgin stormed off, mumbling more obscenities under his breath.

Spilf shook his head, "You'd think meeting God would have changed even *his* heart."

"Oh, his heart was changed," Abawken responded, "Dulgin cares for each of us more deeply than before. His reconciliation to his brother and father, after hundreds of years, has undoubtedly disturbed some buried emotions and he is most likely a bit out of practice at letting those concerns show in any way other than dwarven anger."

Each of them nodded in agreement before returning their attentions to the map.

"This location Spilf indicated will take several days to get to. Be mindful of our rations. There are no roads out here, so this map is a vital source," Bridazak said.

At the break of dawn, the campfire, which had burned through the night, mingled the scent of charred wood with the refreshing brisk air of the new day. The heroes awoke and studied the rolling, treeless plains around them. In the distance, a maze of mountain ranges soared into the clouds. Throughout the rocky terrain were hundreds of bodies of water; some small, some vast. This area, known as the Endless Lakes, had notoriously taken the lives of a few travelers trying to navigate its seemingly peaceful but secretly deadly domain. This beautiful scenery was more dangerous than many creatures of the realm; some fell victim to the poisonous liquid appearing as clean as a fresh spring, others had died when drawn to the mesmerizing black-as-night waters, ready to swallow any passersby. It was easy to see why so few had ever seen this place, and how unknowing visitors could meet an untimely end.

Bridazak looked beyond the glistening lochs and toward the base of the looming crags, hopeful for what they would discover tomorrow. A soft breeze washed over their camp and he closed his eyes. He smiled as he thought to himself, *"Yes Lord, it is time."*

4

Captain Yasooma

R aina led their small group through the bustling streets of the busy
trade capital, Tuskabar. Her emerald robes fluttered behind her as
the others tried to keep up. The Heart of the West, as the high-
walled city was called, was largely considered the most important city of
the civilized realm. It consisted of over three-hundred thousand hardy
souls, mainly humans, which made the two elves and two dwarves rushing
through its roadways stand out even more than they might have usually.

Coastal cliffs along the north ridge of the bay formed a natural wall,
where a famous landmark, Ravana's tower—called the Ten-Heads—impos-
ingly stood. Resembling a tall scepter with nine pointed spires surrounding the pinnacle, the tower ceaselessly watched over every district and ward
within the walls of the city. Raina began to tell her comrades the tale of
Ravana, a powerful mystic and the daughter of the insidious West Horn
King, Oedikus. She has never yet been seen by any subject of the land, as
legends say she remains in her tower, growing her skill and magical attain-
ment. As for their king, the citizens see him only when appearing before
them each month at the moon festival, on a high balcony.

"You seem hurried?" El'Korr asked Raina, hoping their pace might
lessen for a moment.

Without looking back or stopping, she replied, "It is long since I have
visited Tuskabar. I sense a change and fear my presence might alert the
reigning monarch."

"You mean the West Horn King?"

"When I knew Ravana, she was ruthless and calculated. At the moment, I sense a great deal of preservation and animation spellwork in the air here. So, yes," Raina paused, "the West Horn King, in a manner of speaking."

"How much further, then?" he asked as he stared over at the tower with a new concern in his voice.

"We are here."

The heroes turned the corner and found themselves looking into a cemetery. Even though it was mid-day, the tombstone grounds still held a lingering coastal mist woven throughout the generations worth of graves. There were too many monuments to count; the cemetery's unordered rows extended beyond their line of vision.

Raina explained, "Captain Yasooma's tomb lies within. It is here I expect we will find information for the whereabouts of the fifth stone."

"This will take us days to locate," Xan proclaimed, dismayed.

"No. It will be sooner than that, my brother."

Closing her eyes, Raina raised her hands, splaying her fingers wide, and mumbled the words of the arcane. She ended her incantation, opened her emerald eyes, and smiled, pleased at the accuracy of one of her favorite help-ing spells. It was a smile that Xan had not seen for quite some time—he whispered a quick thanks to God for reuniting them.

"It is this way," she entered.

The adventurers followed behind Raina as her magic spell lead them deeper into the maze of final resting places. They wound their way amongst the varied stones carved with epithets to the dead, whose long-past depar-ture was evident by the faded etchings. Many headstones had broken cor-ners or were listing into the soft earth. Statues adorned the entrances of the larger crypts; holding swords or a candle to signify lighting of the way for the departed.

El'Korr stared at one of the statues they were passing. Its cracked face, chipped nose, and missing arm, now laying nearby and grown over with moss, sent shivers up his dwarven spine. "This place is creepy."

Raina quickened her pace. They rounded a large gnarled tree with wispy leaves that drooped down low to the ground. A slight breeze rustled through, and the smell of wet wood permeated the air as they shuffled around the knotted base and found themselves standing before a large iron gate.

"This is Captain Yasooma's tomb," Raina declared.

The adventurers stared in amazement at the thick iron-gate, guarding the largest monument they had seen. The side of the tomb was painted with a mural depicting crashing waves, ships with tall masts, and various battle scenes—tales from the late captain's life, no doubt. Bronze statue guardsmen held swords, crossing one another, overhead. Weeds grew in the open area surrounding the ancient residence and thin, leafless vines stretched along the base of the burial chamber. A stone door was barely visible at the top of the stairs. The group heard faint cries echoing from below, and they noticed the gate was ajar.

Xan whispered, "We are not alone."

Raina and the heroes moved closer to the iron fence for a better view. There was something in the shadows, at the top of the stairs, but they could not see what it was. As Rondee pulled the iron-gate slightly open, it dragged through the overgrown weeds and creaked loudly. Immediately, the crying stopped. For a moment everyone froze in position until Rondee continued opening the gate wide enough for all of them to enter. Suddenly, a hooded figure burst into the light and dashed to the left, attempting to escape. Xan and El'Korr gave chase. They caught the mysterious individual trying to climb over the fence, who quickly turned on them, brandishing a dagger. The elf and dwarf backed away.

El'Korr held his hands open in a sign of peace, "We mean no harm." The figure relaxed a bit, so El'Korr questioned, "Why are you here?"

The hooded one slowly removed his head covering. The heroes were surprised to see he was just a teenaged boy, his unruly brown hair tousled by the hood, his eyes darting from one person to the other and back again—confused and frightened.

His voice trembling, he said, "I should be asking why are you here."

Raina walked toward the young boy, "We came to pay our respects to Captain Yasooma."

He glared into her face, pointing his dagger at her in an attempt to halt her approach. The boy growled, "He is nothing but trouble."

"Why do you say that?" Xan asked.

"He placed a curse on his family. Death is all he has left behind." His voice trailed off, and he flipped his dagger in his hand, pointing it toward himself.

Raina quickly uttered a single word, "Thairmo!" The child's blade instantly became hot in his grip and he let go. El'Korr and Rondee grabbed him so he would not run away or try to hurt himself. He did not resist.

"You are a mystic?" he reveled in awe.

"Yes. Now what is your name?"

"Lufra."

"Well met, young Lufra. My name is Raina. This is my brother Xan, and my dwarven friends, El'Korr and Rondee."

"I've heard of dwarfs, but I've never seen one before. The elves have travelled through periodically down at the docks, but never dwarves. You truly are hairy creatures."

"Why did you try to hurt yourself, and what is this curse you speak of?" Raina diverted him back with her questions.

"I'm his great, great, great grandson," he said, motioning to Yasooma's tomb. "I came here to find out why the curse was placed on our family, but the tomb is sealed just like my fate," he replied solemnly.

"What makes you think like that?"

"Because of what has happened in my life. My mother died when I was born, and Father was killed on the docks in an accident. I have no more family."

"No other relatives?" El'Korr asked.

"All dead."

Xan reached out and lifted the young boys head to look at him, "I have a friend that once told me a curse is meant to be broken. Perhaps we can help."

"He angered the sea gods. There is no way to stop it. My dad warned me of the curse and told me there was nothing we could do and that it was our lot in life. I must now accept my destiny."

"Now that is just a bunch of gnome-riddled nonsense. We will open the tomb and the truth of the past will be revealed. You can be certain of that and nothing else. Will you help us, young Lufra?" El'Korr held out his hand to Lufra and the boy grabbed hold of it.

Rondee held the torch up to read the etching on the door.

"Beneath the waves I lie;
break the surface to rise again."

"Do you know what that means Lufra?" Raina asked.

He shook his head.

"Klello, me Malehk," Rondee said.

"Klello? What is that?" Xan asked.

El'Korr answered, "It means clue." He read aloud the writing on the door, 'Beneath the waves I lie; break the surface to rise again.' I saw waves on the mural outside. Perhaps there is some deeper meaning to the pictures," El'Korr finished.

While inspecting the chiseled impressions, Lufra spotted something amiss and pointed it out to the others.

"You have a good eye, young lad. Take a look, Raina. This particular crest of the wave seems isolated from the others."

The elf mystic ran her fingers across the smooth carved mural. Raina moved her hand along the edge, and closed her eyes as she released the magic that coursed through her body. A hidden button within the image was revealed. She pressed it in and a loud click startled everyone. The stone door of the front entrance opened with a loud grinding sound. They quickly moved to the doorway leading into the ancient tomb of Captain Yasooma.

"Make yourself useful lad, and hold the torch," El'Korr stated.

"You want me to go in there?" His voice turned suddenly shrill.

"Time to face your fears. We will be with you. Now stay behind us in case we run into any critters."

"Critters?"

El'Korr pulled out his dwarven war hammer, unslung his shield, and entered the tomb. "Rondee and I will lead the way; our dwarven eyes can see well in the dark."

Rondee walked passed Lufra and pulled forth a tiny golden mallet. The young boy's forehead wrinkled in contemplation of the wild dwarf's toy weapon. Xan then caught his attention; the sound of steel being pulled from its scabbard—a longsword.

"Lufra, you go next," Raina said. "All will be well."

She guided him with her hands to turn, nudging him forward. As they descended the stairs into the dark, cold tomb, the flickering torchlight created long shadows and danced off the smooth stone walls. El'Korr's magical plate mail clanked with each step he took downward. When the heroes stepped onto the chamber floor, a fine dust of many ages was stirred, giving witness that no one had been in the tomb for years. A sarcophagus rested in the middle. Statues depicting military seamen at attention lined the perimeter walls. The group fanned out and surrounded the resting place of Captain Yasooma.

El'Korr said, "I've been in many burial sites like this one and I'm not a novice at recognizing a potential threat. Rondee, watch those things while we investigate."

"What is he talking about?" Lufra whispered to Raina.

"He is referring to the statues."

"What about them?"

"Some places have dark magic that will cause the inanimate to become animate."

"You mean the statues could come alive?"

She nodded, "Do not worry; you are safe with us."

Suddenly Lufra thought the statues were moving. Fearful, he whipped the torch around crazily creating frightening shadows.

El'Korr grabbed his shoulder, "Calm yourself, and bring the light closer."

Lufra gulped and nervously moved toward the stone bed in the center.

"What are your thoughts Xan? You have been too quiet," El'Korr said.

"There are no markings to indicate a curse, but I have a strange feeling of heaviness. I suggest caution."

"Telling a dwarf to be cautious is like telling a Baruvian cat to take a bath. How about Rondee and I slide the lid off and see what we are dealing with? Everyone ready? Lufra, step back."

Xan shrugged, "Why not?"

El'Korr nodded to his trusted protector, Rondee, "Try to be, cautious," he scoffed.

Rondee grinned, revealing his yellowed teeth, and then began to push the stone cap. The sound of grinding rock echoed in the chamber and then finally the weight of the lid tipped off the other side; one end rested on the ground and the other leaned against the stone coffin.

The adventurers squinted while Lufra shuddered at the sight before them—the remains of the famous Captain Yasooma. He wore a regal white uniform, and his arms crossed over the sabre laid on his chest. The skin of the cadaver was a withered, bluish grey, and its face was sunken with teeth that protruded from curled up lips. A look of pain distorted his deathly features. The chamber filled with a putrid smell of decay.

El'Korr said in disgust, "That's not only the body. The stench of a demon is here."

The heroes waited, deathly quiet, staring at the corpse in the sarcophagus.

Lufra pointed, "Did you see that? The sword." He stepped forward and suddenly a quick gust of whistling wind fluttered the flaming torches and a slithery, raspy voice crackled from the shadows, "Who dares to enter my domain?"

Every one of them was jolted as they turned this way and that, their glances darting around the shadowy tomb.

El'Korr, making light of the matter, taunted, "Well, looks like we have a hider. Come out and reveal yourself; we are not leaving."

Beads of sweat formed on Lufra's brow; he was visibly shaken. He looked to Raina with wide eyes; she placed her hand firmly on his shoulder, and nodded to calm him.

Xan stepped forward, placed his blade tip on the ground, and knelt down on one knee, "In the name of all that is good, in the name of all that is pure, we banish you from this place!"

From the shadows came a howling shriek. At that moment, Xan was hurled backward by an invisible force into the wall. He fell to the ground grimacing in pain, his sword clattering beside him on the stone floor.

"Don't do that again, Elf," the whispery voice crackled.

Rondee assisted Xan to his feet and retrieved the elf's weapon as El'Korr insisted, "Show yourself, dark spirit."

In answer to El'Korr's demand, the invisible demon's whistling wind once again hurled Xan, this time with Rondee, through the air and slammed them both into the wall, with their arms and legs hanging like rag dolls. They fell to the rough floor, grunting and fighting for air. They crawled on all fours to stand with the others.

El'Korr turned to Raina, "We could use some help right about now."

The powerful Sheldeen elf mystic said, "I can help once I see what it is. Get it to reveal itself."

"That is what I'm trying to do."

Throughout the bizarre happenings, Lufra, shaking and gasping for every breath, stared down at his deceased third generation grandfather. He was overwhelmed by a vision which overlapped his natural sight. He watched as incorporeal waves began washing over the cadaver before him.

He could almost hear the lapping, and smell the sea salt, but then the clear water turned to an inky red.

He was snapped back to reality when Raina grabbed his arm and cried, "We need to leave."

The teenager resisted and pulled away, "No! I have to do this."

Raina watched as Lufra approached the corpse of Captain Yasooma. She started to follow him, when suddenly the impact of the powerful force of the demon pushed her away. A loud ear-piercing screech filled the room and the heroes winced in pain and covered their ears.

Unphased, the boy turned quickly to El'Korr, "I need water," he cried. "Water?"

"Yes, do you have any?"

El'Korr took a vial of holy water from his pouch, Lufra grabbed it, took off the cork and poured the contents over the corpse. As the blessed liquid touched the withered body, a ghostly plasmatic hand formed and immediately wrapped its fingers around the throat of Captain Yasooma. El'Korr stared in disbelief.

"It turned red," Lufra whispered in realization. "My blood. It's my blood we need!"

Without hesitation El'Korr understood what Lufra was saying. He drew his dagger to cut the boy's hand and draw the blood needed to complete the ritual. However, before he could carry out his intentions, the beast of darkness manifested on top of the tomb. It swung its skinless red arm covered in purple veins mightily against El'Korr's face; sending him sprawling across the floor. The creature whirled to face Lufra; the hideous monster's razor sharp blackened teeth extended from a snarling snout. He sneered at the boy, his elongated jaw nearly touching the nauseated young man.

"You lost your inheritance, child," the scratchy tone of the demon said. "You will be forever mine."

Although Lufra was in near shock, he was aware that he had not completed his mission; his blood must mix with the holy water he had poured on his grandfather's corpse. Determined to complete his commitment, he steeled himself and then slammed his jaw down on the rough stony ridge of the sarcophagus, opening a wound that spurted his blood against the screeching beast and onto the deceased Captain Yasooma.

At that very moment, a blinding light burst forth from the tomb, consuming the vile creature whose screech grew to a guttural roar that pained the ears of the heroes until the beast of darkness dissipated and the wrenching sound faded away and there was silence. With the creature gone, the spectral hand also vanished from around the Captain's neck.

The heroes gathered silently around the ancient crypt and saw that the countenance of Yasooma's gnarled face had changed to an expression of peace.

"How did you know what to do?" Xan questioned the young man.

Lufra pointed into the sarcophagus, "I don't know. I think maybe he showed me."

At that moment, an apparition appeared in the tomb; an angelic being with beautiful, unfurled white wings that turned blue at the tips. A bright aura glowed in and around its face, shielding it from scrutiny. Standing eight feet tall, the muscular seraph wore a silver kilt that reflected the flickering light in the tomb. Gold straps crossed over his shoulders down its midsection to connect at the waist. Each piece linked together to form the shape of an arrow.

It spoke in a deep, powerful, melodic voice, "Heroes of the realm of Ruauck-El, you have defeated Niberius, a fallen one assigned to the Yasooma family. It is my honor to fill the open position as the Yasooma family's guardian." He turned to the child, "Approach, Lufra."

The boy looked at the others, who nodded for him to obey the command. He took a step forward. The angel of light reached down into the sarcophagus and retrieved Captain Yasooma's pristine weapon—a sabre. The curved, single edged steel blade sparkled. Gold etchings were engraved from top to bottom. As the celestial being held the sabre, a sizzling sound came from the weapon as the letter 'Y' became engraved by unseen hands on the large guard over the hilt.

The angel then turned to Lufra, "Your courage has conquered evil, and so it will be with this weapon. Receive your inheritance."

He held out his open palms, and the blade came to rest on top of them. He felt the magic pulsating through the weapon—a blessing instead of a curse; something he had never felt before. His bloodied face instantly healed and tears flowed down his cheeks.

The guardian bowed deeply, and then vanished. Each of the heroes gathered around Lufra and embraced him.

When things had quieted, El'Korr said, "Raina, we still need to find the information about the elements, but there is nothing else here."

"I have my grandfather's journal," Lufra chimed. "It contains notes about strange gems and other cryptic writings. I kept it in hopes of finding a way to break the curse, but the journal was beyond my understanding, and I never found the items he spoke of. I even tried to burn it, thinking it was the bane of all that has happened, but it would not burn."

"Can we take a look at it?"

"Of course. Heck, you can have it."

"We are most indebted to you," Raina said sincerely.

The heroes emerged from Captain Yasooma's resting place. The stone door closed behind them as they headed to the docks.

Fifty yards away, a darkly cloaked figure wearing two sheathed swords on his hips asked, "What are your orders, Veric?"

"It appears we have other guests who are interested in our little bauble. This might work out better for us. We will hold, and let this group do all the work."

"Hold?"

"Yes, this might be the group my brother spoke of, instrumental in Manasseh's fall. If that is the case, then we must be mindful of them. Rest assured, your pay will be the same, Daysho."

5

Saybrook

The breathtaking collection of waters at Endless Lakes were as different from each other as Ordakiankind was from Dwarf or Human. One body of boiling water bubbled turbulently, stirring up sediment and releasing mildly poisonous gas into the air. An adjacent shoreline surrounded a glacial lagoon that crackled with the movement of its frozen glaze. A third water basin lay dormant with hardly a ripple across its surface. The natural elements existed in concert.

Bridazak studied the beautiful phenomenon, and saw a scenario that spoke to him of the warring nature of the races of Ruauck-El. He looked at the creation of this world through different eyes, having returned from the Lost City, and the unique formations of the land spoke to his soul. *"You are truly amazing, God. This world you have created is beyond imagination."*

His thoughts were jarred when Dulgin pointed to the ice-covered lake and asked, "What is that?"

Abawken investigated the location the dwarf pointed out and saw a strange object under the surface. He drew his scimitar from its scabbard. The magnificent, gold and platinum curved blade, which was razor sharp at the front edge and five inches across at its widest point, was inlaid with jewels. Swirled etchings laced the metal from top to bottom. The human whispered a single word, "Esh." Placing the point of his weapon against the ice, it sizzled and melted through the frozen thickness. Steam escaped as he carved a hole large enough to free the object.

Dulgin laughed, "Good job, Huey, you found wood."

Abawken retrieved it, "Not just wood, Master Dulgin, but a sign."

The dwarf's bushy eyebrows shot up in surprise and the ordakians quickly gathered around Abawken to get a better look. Emblazoned across the arm's length, damp wood in faded paint, they struggled to make out the lettering.

Dulgin read aloud slowly, "S-a-y-brook."

In unison, Bridazak and Spilf responded, "Brook."

A puzzled look engulfed Dulgin, and then he glared at the two child-like daks. Bridazak and Spilf were holding in a burst of laughter. Their faces were turning red, eyes squinting, and their lips were tightly pursed.

"What are ya up to, ya blundering fools?"

Unable to contain themselves any longer, laughter erupted from the ordakians. They held their stomachs and doubled over while the dwarf's skin on his face matched the red beard and hair in uncertain embarrassment.

Abawken watched the interaction of these old friends and smiled. These lifelong comrades had allowed him to become part of their family. He thought about the years ahead of them all, and his smile departed as he remembered his limited years as a human, in comparison to his companions superior longevity. His mind flashed back to the library in the Moonstone Mountains, when he asked Raina how to say the word 'old' in the elven language. He whispered the word, "ahn-keth," to himself.

Dulgin smacked him on the shoulder to get his attention. "Stop day-dreaming, Huey. I asked ya question."

"Oh, I am sorry, Master Dulgin. What did—"

"Ah, nevermind, let's go!"

The ordakians were still giggling while walking ahead. Dulgin emphasized each step with a stomp of frustration as he knew he was part of a joke. Abawken quickly followed. Bridazak paused to study the map and then glanced up to the mountain range that rose before them.

"We've been out here for days. How close are we?" Dulgin asked.

"I estimate that the location Spilf pointed out is within that grove of trees." He nodded toward the pine forest.

The thick green spires sprawled out to either side and ran several miles deep to the base of the rocky crags. Suddenly, a chilling gust of wind blew through the trees, the tops swayed and the smell of sap engulfed the heroes.

Dulgin scoffed, "Well, it won't take us long to figure out there is no lake in there. Stubby remembered a lake covered in mist. Why are we even here?"

Bridazak smirked, "We are following—"

"Yeah, I know, following the mystical-prayer-finger on the map thing."

Spilf sighed, "He's right, Bridazak, there can't be a lake here. The trees are thick from here to the mountain. Maybe we should look elsewhere."

Dulgin relented, "We are here now, Stubby, so let's get a move on. We can salvage this yet by having some cooked meat. There is no lake, but I am damn sure there must be an elkhorn or two in there."

When the four of them stepped foot into the edge of the tree line there was a discernible shift in the atmosphere around them. Now under the pine canopies, the environment had changed from what they saw before entering. The birds sounded different, the smell of sap changed to wet wood after a rainy day, and a lingering fog weaved through as far as the eye could see in the dense foliage.

"Whoa, what just happened?" Spilf asked while raising his hands.

"I'm not sure, but I feel different," Bridazak responded.

Without a word, Abawken stepped back to the open tundra. At that moment, the air around them wobbled as though an invisible force field of magic had been activated.

Bridazak called, "What did you sense, Abawken?"

"I'm uncertain of your meaning, Master Bridazak."

"You stepped back to other side, so you must have felt something."

"I do not remember what you say I did."

The three of them on the inside of the field looked at one another, contemplating the phenomena.

Spilf burst out in realization, "This is why I lost my memory. This field of energy somehow blocks memories and that is why I could never find my way back."

Everyone nodded. Abawken stepped back through to join them.

"Welcome back," Bridazak said.

"Strange, it feels like my first time entering."

"What is this place?" Dulgin asked, scrutinizing the shadowy realm while pulling out his battle-axe.

Before anyone could answer, the adventurers heard the terrified scream of a small child. Abawken darted in the direction of the cry with his sword in hand, and the others followed hastily. Abawken emerged from the forest onto a misty lake shore and skidded on the pebbled shoreline. Another scream alerted him and he instantly veered in its direction.

Spilf and Bridazak burst through the brush next and halted suddenly when they came into the clearing. The sound of lapping water hitting the pebbles triggered recessed memories inside Spilf's mind.

He whispered, "I remember."

The fog hovered upon the loch, giving its rightful name—Misty Lake. Bridazak stood in awe beside his friend.

"This is it Bridazak. I'm home."

Dulgin charged through the tree line and stopped in his tracks at the sight of the body of water.

"Well, I'll be a bearded-babbit, there is a lake here after all." The dwarf smiled and smacked Spilf's shoulder. "Which way did Huey go? I don't want him to have all the fun if some critter is about."

Bridazak pointed the direction and Dulgin stomped off; the loud crunch of the small worn stones with each of the dwarfs steps resounded.

"C'mon, Spilf," Bridazak tugged him.

Another scream, more intense than the previous, rang in their ears. The daks were now chasing after Dulgin, who was following Abawken's footsteps along the shoreline.

The human moved swiftly, out-distancing his friends with his long strides. Again, he heard the cry; it seemed to come from within the trees. He charged back into the forest and shortly came upon a clearing. He was shocked to see, in the center, a young child tied down on a wooden altar. The small boy, who looked about two, was stripped of all clothing but caked in dirt and mud, with well defined tracks of tears on his face. He whimpered and sniffled when Abawken appeared. A snap of a tree branch and the roar of an unknown animal caused Abawken to spin and face the sound. Snorting and bellowing came from within a dark, shadowy section of the forest, and then the creature rushed toward Abawken and entered the clearing.

The brown furry beast was easily double Abawken's height, and resembled a baboon. It reared up and brought its powerful arms to beat its chest. Immense fangs of misshaped sizes protruded from its jaw. Its eyes glowed with territorial anger. Abawken stood between the child and the enraged creature.

The monster lunged and Abawken flew into the air, flipped over, and then landed perfectly behind it, ready to do battle. The beast snarled, stopped short and spun to attack again, but at that moment the child screamed. With a roar, Abawken's opponent changed his intention and headed for the child. The fighter knew he could not reach the boy in time. Abawken had thought the creature would continue to attack him but saw his mistake unfold. The huge ape reached for the toddler but before snatching the boy, Dulgin burst through into the clearing, and swiftly severed the creature's hand with his mighty axe. Blood gushed out and it wailed in pain. Abawken slashed it across its lower back with his scimitar. It arched backward in agony. The dwarf swung another devastating blow into its leg. Raw, pink flesh opened and more blood oozed. It fell to the ground prone.

Bridazak and Spilf arrived at the clearing. The mortally wounded creature labored to breathe as its vital fluid continued to spill from its wounds.

Dulgin stood proudly over it, and said, "Bad monkey." The dwarf's axe came down and cut off the head.

The ordakians moved quickly to untie the child. They instantly spotted dry blood covering the wood framed altar.

"This is a sacrifice location," Spilf realized.

"Who would do this?" Bridazak asked.

With tears streaming down his face, the child pointed into the forest and said, "Home."

The smell of burnt wood coming from the village dwellings wafted through the dirt pathways. Dilapidated structures resembled playhouses for human children. Repairs to the original wooden homes did not match the original engineering, and time had not been kind to this hidden community. A sense of depression and despair weighed heavily upon entering the area. A group of bone-thin women sat outside weaving baskets, while another group prepared meager amounts of food. Dirt smudges covered their faces and arms, aged feathers were woven in braids of hair, and they wore matted animal hides. When the heroes came into view, the women abruptly stopped their daily duties and huddled together in fear.

"Yep, this is definitely where the child lives. Dirty and sorry folk," Dulgin grumbled.

"This *was* my home," Spilf said, "but I don't see any ordakians."

"Perhaps someone here knows what happened, Master Spilf."

"Where are the men?" Bridazak questioned.

Abawken carried the boy. An old woman, with a wrinkled face, grey scraggly hair, and an eye, milky-white with blindness, hobbled toward them.

Her scratchy voice spoke, "What have you done? You have brought us ruin."

"Look here—" Dulgin began, until being cut off by Bridazak.

"We are looking for the ordakians, like us, that once lived here."

Abawken held the baby toward the woman, "And we are looking for the mother of this child."

"What is done is done," she resigned, and then pointed to a large leather tent, animal hides of various coloring stitched together forming the walls and roof. The shelter loomed before them, and a light pillar of smoke rose from an opening on the top. It was the largest structure in the small village.

Suddenly, the faded orange animal skin at the entrance flapped open and an imposing man stepped out. He paused a moment, his sallow green eyes glaring menacingly at the strange intruders. His frame reached higher than six feet with his large headdress. He wore more clothing than anyone else in the village: a tanned hide wrapped around his waist, with a beartock skin that draped over his shoulders descended to the ground and fur boots with the bones of small beasts dangled from the high tops. Each step he took toward the heroes caused the bones to clack like a wind chime.

Other tribesmen funneled out of the tent behind the apparent leader holding spears and axes. A lone woman emerged, and instantly burst into tears at the sight of the child. She tried to run toward Abawken but she was held back by two strong members of the tribe. All she could do was yell, "Ky!" Her arms were stretched out as she cried.

The village leader barked, "You must take the boy back now before it is too late."

"Why are you sacrificing your children?" Bridazak asked bluntly.

The man turned his head slightly to see the reaction of his people, but quickly countered, "Our ways are not your ways. You don't belong here and you bring my tribe danger."

"Danger from what?"

"We must satisfy the Thaloc. It is ordained by our god."

"You talkin about this, Chiefy?" Dulgin unslung a large blood-soaked sack he had over his shoulder and flared the content before them. The head of the monster rolled out and landed at the chieftain's feet. Its black lifeless eyes stared at him. Everyone gasped. The mother broke loose and sprinted to wrap her arms around her son.

The chief shouted, "Defilers! You have angered our god!"

His followers brought their weapons up to bear and stood ready to attack. It was apparent that they were uneasy about the confrontation, as the heroes had just destroyed what none of them thought possible.

Bridazak held up his hands to placate the building anger. "We only want information about the ordakians that once lived here. We don't mean anyone harm."

"I know nothing of your kind. You must leave and never return."

The mother whispered to Abawken, "Take my son. His fate here is to die, but you can save him." He looked at Bridazak who overheard her plea.

Bridazak addressed the leader, "What is your intention with this boy?"

"It is not your concern. Now leave before more blood is shed."

Dulgin stepped forward, "That sounds like a threat and dwarves don't take kindly to that."

The chieftain brought up his arms and then waved them in a circle. His armed followers began to fan out and encircle the heroes.

"Good, I was getting tired of talkin," Dulgin said.

"What is our play here, Master Bridazak?"

"Our play is to have a lot of widows," the dwarf scoffed.

"There are answers we still need to find that are here for Spilf," he whispered back to Dulgin.

Bridazak was at a loss on what to do next. This misguided tribe's death was not the answer. He silently prayed for help, and a single word came to his mind—*challenge*.

Just as the custodian of this community was about to order his men to attack, Bridazak stepped forward and shouted, "I challenge your god!"

Everyone froze, eyes widened, and several gasps resounded around the adventurers. The ordakian stunned the overseer and his followers took a step backwards in slight fear of the statement.

"Bridazak, what are you doing?" Spilf whispered.

"What element is your god known for?" he continued without acknowledging his friend.

"Thahaal is a fire god."

"Then this will be a fire challenge. You will call upon your god and then I will call upon mine."

"How do you know of our custom?"

Bridazak didn't respond to his question, "If your god wins, then we will leave and never return, but if my God wins then you will turn from your wicked ways and stop your sacrifices."

The chieftain squinted his eyes. He walked toward the ordakian and leaned down, face to face. "When my god wins then you will be sacrificed, and your friends will leave never to return again."

Bridazak looked at his cohorts who were shaking their heads pleading with him to refuse.

He turned toward the tribe leader, "Agreed."

6

A Pinch of Luck

"There she is. *A Pinch of Luck*," Lufra pointed to the journal sketch and then to the ship before them. The four mast warship, standing tallest amongst the hundreds of various vessels anchored inside the confines of Tuskabar Harbor, bore a long oak bow, which featured a figurehead carved in the image of the legendary Delphin, its spiraled horn projecting out like a spear. The square gallery at the stern and the symbol of the creature of the sea were the most distinguishing features of the mighty galleon. Several men worked on the rigging woven through the spruce pillars, others unpacked supply crates on deck. Sounds of sloshing water slapping against the hull, twisted ropes tightening and loosening in the endless tug of war of the ocean tide, and flocks of white and grey seabirds squawking above, stood second against the unmistakable smell of the salty sea water and gutted fish.

"Impressive," El'Korr whistled.

Rondee and El'Korr walked to the edge of the wooden ramp and halted. Xan and Raina followed with Lufra right behind them.

El'Korr called to the top of the steps, "Permission to board!"

A dark haired man with a frizzy beard and wearing a sweat stained shirt looked over the side and yelled back, "Who's askin?"

"I'm El'Korr and we wish to speak with your captain."

"I'm the captain," he quickly responded.

Raina stepped forward and snapped, "Maybe someday you will be captain, but not before Elsbeth says so."

The bearded man's face reddened and he bit his lip to fight back a rebuttal. At that moment, a female voice called, "Alright, Skath. I will take it from here."

A woman jumped down from a plank of wood dangling from the side of the ship where she had been working with two deckhands scraping barnacles off the hull; she was half-elven. Her beige leather pants and scuffed black boots showed how hard she worked, but her light green blouse with frilled cuffs, shoulder-length, tied back hair, and dove-like brown eyes only displayed loveliness. She was petite in her five-foot frame, but her walk and mannerisms showed she had experience. A sheathed rapier hung from her belt.

"I heard rumors of your return, Raina, the Sheldeen Mystic." She brushed a strand of brown hair away from her face.

"Captain Elsbeth, I presume."

She nodded, "Permission to board granted. Let's talk in my private quarters," she motioned them aboard.

Elsbeth gestured for everyone to sit at the mahogany table. Her cabin was stark, compared to the cluttered feel of the rest of the ship, and smelled of rich tobacco. Only a few baubles of interest adorned the walls, one being a painted portrait of Captain Yasooma. His manicured beard and piercing blue eyes stood out prominently, and a peculiar bronze medallion with a symbol of a galleon riding a wave dangled around his neck.

"I would like to introduce you to my crew. This is my first mate, Skath Steel; I believe you all met." Pointing to a man to her right, she said, "Second mate, Myers. Next to him is Anders, our priest, and last, but not least, Urlin Thoom, our wizard."

Each one nodded as they were announced by their captain. Urlin stood and stared intently at Raina. The frail, clean shaven young spellcaster seemed nervous. His light brown hair was cut in a bowl shape and his plain tan robe would suggest at first glance that he was a monk.

"Mistress Raina, it is an honor," he said shakily.

Raina slightly smiled and nodded in acknowledgment of the respect Urlin had shown her.

"Before we begin, I wish to pray, with your permission captain," Anders the Priest indicated.

"Of course," Elsbeth responded.

The dark blue robed man bowed his head and began, "Dear God, Creator of the Seas, we thank you for the blessings you provide. The oceans belong to you and we ask for protection and guidance." He suddenly began to cough violently. His face turned a bright red and his fisted hand covered his mouth as he continued to hack. "Excuse me." He stood up and hobbled out of the quarters.

"My apologies," Elsbeth said. "We are honored to have you aboard *A Pinch of Luck*, but we are unsure as to the nature of your visit."

"We are in search of Captain Yasooma's ship, *The Wave Rider*," Raina spoke.

A slight scoff came from the half-elf, "That is impossible. It sank centuries ago."

"There were items on board that we seek, and we would like you to take us to it."

"No one knows the location where it went down."

"No one but you, Elsbeth," Raina quickly corrected.

There was a pause while the captain stood and turned to look out the back window. She leaned against the sill and spoke softly, "Yasooma was a great man. He helped thousands of people in his life and accomplished much, until he changed, suddenly. He spent the rest of his career in search of fabled elements—a path that I did not champion after his passing. What makes you think that I can show you this location?"

"You were there; you and Yasooma were the only survivors," Raina's announcement lingered before she continued, "And you wear his medallion underneath your clothes."

Elsbeth turned quickly and studied Raina. "You are indeed a powerful mystic," she took in a deep breath, "and who is this that holds the Captain's sword?"

"Lufra Yasooma," the boy answered with pride.

Elsbeth raised her eyebrow and smirked, "Indeed."

Raina brought everyone's attention back, "Powerful forces have risen. They have four of the five dragon stones and have most likely acquired the location of the fifth. We know from his journal that Yasooma had finally gathered the elements necessary to destroy the stones, and that they were last on board *The Wave Rider*. The medallion you wear will show us the location. We are asking—"

Skath interrupted, "Is it true that King Manasseh has fallen?"

"Yes, 'tis true," El'Korr answered. "My army attacked Black Rock Castle. His power source was uprooted. We expect war will ravage the North after the other Horn Kings assess the truth. The borders will fall. I would like to get back to my *men* as soon as possible, so we wish to leave immediately," El'Korr finished, still cranky with Raina for dwarf-napping him.

"You said *they* have four of the stones; who are *they*?" Elsbeth asked.

"A mystic from the West Horn, in league with a black dragon."

"You speak of Veric," Urlin jumped in.

"That name doesn't sound familiar," Raina responded.

"Veric is the brother of Vevrin, King Manasseh's mystic."

"Vevrin is now dead. Thanks to my own brother, Dulgin," El'Korr stated.

"It was known that they were sworn enemies. Vevrin of the North and Veric of the West, but—"

"Go on Urlin. Tell them what you saw," Elsbeth gave permission.

"We were off the coast of the Singing Rocks. I was testing out a new spell on the upper deck during the night watch, which gave me the ability to see far leagues off, even in the dark. It was there I witnessed two robed individuals off in the distance, standing on the water, conversing."

Lufra asked, "Wait, you mean they were actually standing on water? How is that possible?"

"Wizards, young Lufra," Xan responded, "Let us listen. Go on, Urlin."

"One wore red robes and the other black. I couldn't make out their faces but it was obvious they were working together, as they concluded with an embrace. They disappeared. I have only shared this with my captain since suggesting such a thing openly would bring certain death, if they were to find out."

"You are on an isolated ship in the Great Illustrya ocean. What makes you so frightened?" questioned Xan.

With a troubled expression, Urlin continued, "Spies are everywhere, and if one were to overhear my knowledge then I would be silenced quickly, along with everyone else around me."

"It is alright, Urlin," Raina acknowledged, "It makes sense now. Veric knew that Manasseh had the knowledge of the fifth stone's location, so he made a deal with his brother in hopes of Vevrin finding out where it was."

"What do these stones actually do? We have far more serious issues with the Horn Kings than some rocks," Skath chimed.

"The Horn Kings will look like a calm day on open seas compared to what will be unleashed on Ruauck-El," Raina responded.

"Unleashed?" the captain questioned.

"The power of the stones will summon the five dragon spirits and set loose the Dragon God. It will control all the dragons in the realms and reign terror on everyone."

Raina's words soaked in and there was a long pause.

Captain Elsbeth stood, leaned forward and said pointedly, "Tomorrow, we set sail."

7

The Challenge

"What in orc hell are you thinkin, Bridazak?"

"I don't know, Dulgin. It just came to me. I believe God gave me this task."

"This *task*? What exactly does that mean?"

Without answering, Bridazak walked toward the wicker door.

Dulgin snapped, "Where do you think yer off to, ya blundering fool?"

"I'm gonna check on Spilf," he answered as he left the room.

"Yeah, sure, just leave why don't ya!"

Abawken stepped in front of the dwarf to take his attention off of Bridazak.

Dulgin's rant continued, "What's your stance on this, Huey? You've been very quiet at a time Bridazak could use some of that wisdom you like to tell me all about."

The tall fighter moved to a small window and, because ordakian structures were not designed for the height of humans, bent down to peer through the opening. He turned to the dwarf and motioned him forward, "Take a look."

Dulgin looked to where he pointed. He saw the tribesmen in the center of the village preparing two wooden altars; one was a simple pile of wood, forming a teepee, obviously meant for Bridazak's use. The other was an elaborate structure, upon which the women stacked hundreds of tiny skulls; the remains of their children. As they carried out the macabre ritual, they chanted an eerie song; asking their god to recognize their previous gifts and to bring favor upon them.

"That is why Bridazak is doing what he is doing, and this is why we need to support him more than ever."

Spilf sat at the lake's edge and slung flat rocks across the surface. The fog hovered over the body of water and captured each stone the ordakian threw. The sound of the rapid splashes skipping across the surface faded as the crunch of worn pebbles under footsteps approached him from behind.

Without turning his gaze, Spilf said, "This was my home once."

"We will find your parents, Spilf," Bridazak responded.

"Do you really think this tribe knows something?"

"I don't know, but we need to find out."

"And finding out means challenging their god?"

Bridazak sat next to Spilf, "I think the challenge goes beyond us. These people are lost in their own world and have let something terrible misguide them."

They both stared out onto Misty Lake and listened to the gentle lapping water hitting the shore.

"This is where my mother pushed me out in the canoe. Why aren't they here, Bridazak?"

"They must have escaped at the same time you did, and never came back."

"Do you think this memory energy field caused them to forget about me?

Bridazak paused. "Spilf, they never forgot about you. Even you yourself knew deep down inside that they were out there. I'm sure they remember you."

"I still have hope, Bridazak. I just thought they would be here."

"Hope is good. We are going to need some of that real soon." Bridazak stood up, "I'm going to check on the 'wood stackers' as Dulgin is calling them."

"I love that dwarf," Spilf smiled; his eyes remained on the lake.

The sun shined brightly when the four heroes stood before the two wooden altars erected for the challenge. A dozen warriors stood shoulder-to-shoulder around each of the structures, humming a low dirge and swaying side-to-side in rhythm. The chieftain, with red stripes painted on his cheeks, yellow on his forehead and nose, orange streaks on his arms, and black tribal markings on his chest and stomach, waited for the appropriate moment and then raised his arms above his head and declared, "Our fathers and oldfathers taught us the ways of our tribe, Yavakai. We will honor them once again in the tradition of Arati, the Flame of the Sky. Our god has never lost. I remind you now of the names who have bowed before our god. Lovakee, Hurroon, Azbon, and Bimola—all were challengers, and all are only spoken now to glorify the mighty Thahaal. Our great sun lord has given us our customs, our ways of life, and our harvest of children to continue to gain his favor."

Dulgin nudged Abawken, "Too bad we can't feed this Huey to the monkey we killed and see how he likes it."

The chief yelled, "Let the challenge of the gods begin!"

His followers immediately shifted from vocalizing the low hum, to uttering a cadence of several repetitive grunts, like thuds of a beating drum. The women of the tribe danced out on the dirt forum and added to the initiated rhythm with high pitched shouts.

Again, the leader raised his hands and the sound dwindled back to shallow guttural grunts. Turning to Bridazak, he began again, "You have challenged our mighty Thahaal and he has accepted. Once the all-powerful Thahaal sets fire to the altar, then the ordakian is to be sacrificed to satisfy Thahaal's anger."

Bridazak stepped forward and shouted above the commotion, "When my God smites my wood with fire, then your people will turn from Thahaal and worship my God—and you will never sacrifice innocent life again."

The chieftain glared and then grudgingly nodded. "Let it be so."

Two tribesmen grabbed Bridazak by the arms. Dulgin raised his axe and started toward Bridazak and his captors, but Abawken stopped him.

"It will be okay, Dulgin," Bridazak reassured his friend. "He said He would never leave us nor forsake us. Do you remember?"

The two brutes dragged Bridazak to a wooden pole, a short distance from the prepared altars, and tied his hands and feet. Then they pulled out a dagger and held it to his throat. The cold steel made him flinch.

Spilf held his breath and thought, *"I can't lose the family I have known in pursuit of the one I lost. How did it come to this?"*

Dulgin whispered to Abawken, "If they kill Bridazak, this village will be destroyed with or without your help, so help me God."

The painted chieftain raised his hands in the air and his subjects began their eerie chant once again. He circled the shrine of wood and children's skulls.

"Oh great Thahaal, hear us! Oh great Thahaal, send us your fire! We give you thanks for bringing your people to this place. You have surrounded us with your protection in the secret mist; those men who rejected your gift or leave your provision are outcasts never to return, banished, forever separated. You have tested us in this time with shortage of food, but we are faithful to your ways even now! See our offerings and bring your burning judgement on these challengers." His pleas continued for a long while until the zeal of the dancers and bowing villagers lessened to shuffling and a murmur of unintelligible prayers.

Bridazak's eyes raked across the village of a desperate people in search of something to ease their suffering, and he felt overwhelmed with compassion for them. The jangle of ornamental animal bones and horns hanging about the village sounded like wind chimes. The old skins the village clothed themselves in were bleached and worn, and, he noticed, repaired one too many times. The cryptic story the chief had told suddenly made sense. Still tied to the post, Bridazak called out, "Everyone! Your Thahaal is the cause of your lack of food. He is the cause of your men who hunt and never return. Can your god not hear your cries?"

The tribal leader shot a menacing glare at the ordakian and then turned back with renewed strength. "Oh great Thahaal, this defiler mocks you and we ask for retribution. You have only taken our men who are not worthy. Send us your mighty power and set this altar ablaze for all to see your greatness."

Bridazak pleaded, "It is not about power of summoning fire, but instead about providing for those in need. You silently pray in your hearts that he would answer you with food, but he does not come. Why? Where do your prayers and sacrifices go?"

Dulgin turned to Spilf, "Be ready, Stubby. Our fearless leader is riling this Chiefy up and I expect trouble soon."

"Yeah, that's what's scaring me. What is he doing?"

The sun had blazed through the day, but now it steadfastly dipped lower in the horizon. With no godly response from Thahaal, the chanting song barely dwindled on, but it had lost its fervor.

Bridazak began again, "Don't lose heart, Yavakai tribe! The true God of everything has heard you, and will answer you with the return of the elkhorns," Bridazak smiled reverently, compassion in his eyes.

A scream of utter rage came from the chieftain. He fell to his knees while lifting his arms in worship of his deity. His tribe also followed his lead and began shouting. Their cries echoed through the village in audible waves, undulating in tones from low-pitched groaning, to high, emotional screeches.

Bridazak noticed others within the congregation exchanging glances to one another and he pressed on yelling above the chant, "How did I know of the elkhorn herds vanishing if not told by my God? I don't understand why your deity does not answer you."

The tribe leader became more outraged and his voice intensified.

As the sun's last rays disappeared over the looming mountains, the Chieftain ended his chanting and stood. He waved off the guttural moaning and then silence fell on the village.

He slowly approached, and whispered to the dak, "Your god will not answer you, of this I am sure. I look forward to your death."

"I have a request," Bridazak said in a dry, cracked voice.

"Go on, what is it?"

"I would like some water."

The chieftain nodded to a warrior, "Bring him water."

"No, not for me."

"What, then?" the Chieftain snapped.

"I want a ditch dug around my altar, and I want you to pour four jars of water over the wood."

There was a long pause as the face painted leader stared into Bridazak's sincere eyes. He scoffed and backed away.

"Do as he says!"

The tribesmen ran and dug an arm's length ditch all the way around the wooden tribute. Others gathered four huge jar pots and filled them at the lake, pairs of women lifting the heavy load. Once the trench was in place, they began to pour. The water ran down the wood and slowly leaked into the freshly dug dirt gulley.

Dulgin called, "What are ya doing, ya blundering fool?"

Spilf added, "You're soaking the wood!"

Bridazak smiled at his friends and turned back to the chief, "What is precious to the Yavakai tribe?"

He sneered back, "The elkhorns are prized amongst our people. The horns symbolize our god's favor and strength." He pointed at the tribal tent that was encompassed by the aged and cracked bone of the animals that once roamed freely through the woods.

"Where have they gone? You have not seen any for years and your people starve."

"Our god wants to see our faith. We will not waver." The chief turned toward his people, smirking, and raising his hands in victory. "You see this man-child has no power to summon food that only our god can provide us with."

Just then a low whimper of an animal echoed from the hut the heroes had occupied. A hush fell over the gathered. The leader squinted at the wicker doorway, and then his eyes flared wide when the antlers of an elk-horn suddenly materialized and pushed open the entrance and pranced out into the sunlight. The gasps of the tribe rose as a single chorus. They watched this crucial resource that they had longed for years to see, as it slowly approached the altars, seemingly oblivious to the people surrounding it.

The chief yelled, "This is a sign from Thahaal. He has answered us!"

The animal moved to Bridazak's wood pyre and laid down at the base. The ordakian turned to watch the villagers' response.

The chief spat, with spite in his voice, "One elkhorn will not feed our tribe, half-man. This is a fire challenge and your altar still drips with water."

"You look worried, chief. Perhaps we should douse it with more water to make sure."

"Are you done delaying the inevitable, ordakian?" the Chieftain mocked.

"More water, please."

He stared at Bridazak and then nodded to his warriors standing at the ready.

Within minutes, water now trickled in all directions out of the muddy trench. The wood was soaked and continued to drip, all the while the elkhorn remained peaceful at its base.

When the moat was full, Bridazak began his prayer, "God, let these people know that you are the true Lord of Ruauck-El and I am your servant. Let them know that I have done these things because you told me to do them. Let them see your Truth so these people will know you, and they will serve you and no other."

No one moved. Every breath was held, waiting in suspense. The chieftain turned to Bridazak with a wicked smile of victory—but stopped suddenly as the brightest of lights filled the sky. Everyone tried to look but it was so brilliant they had to bring their hands up to cover their eyes. A low rumble was heard, and it began to intensify, as did the light. Fire came down from the air. It burned up the wood and the water instantly evaporated. The roar of the beam of fire sounded louder than the rushing of a raging waterfall.

The tribe's leader turned toward Bridazak, fully enraged. He withdrew his ivory horned dagger and screamed through gritted teeth as he approached, "No! You will die for this!" He raised his weapon to strike the halfling.

A tentacle arm of a scorching ray still surrounding the altar shot out from the pillar of fire, engulfing the tribe's chieftain. He instantly melted like candle wax. Then as quickly as it came, the flame vanished. The crack of a lightning bolt rattled the village and then left them all in silence.

Bridazak's altar was annihilated, and the village leader was a pile of ash at the ordakian's feet. From the smoke, the single elkhorn that was summoned pranced out and bounded through the crowd unscathed. Then another bolted forth from the smoke, and soon an entire herd poured out and ran into the forest. The heroes spotted the wobble of the energy field as it broke down; the colors of the sunset became more alive and vibrant. The mist on top of the lake dissipated and everyone witnessed hundreds of elkhorn come to the water's edge and drink before darting into the treeline one by one.

The tribe dropped to the ground in fear and cried out, "The Lord who Bridazak follows, He is our God forever!"

Bridazak's friends rushed to surround him. They quickly untied his ropes from the wooden post, and then embraced him. No words were exchanged. They stood silently together, aware that the power of the true God had been shown this day in this tiny village of Ruauck-El. The entire tribe worshipped the new deity, some even bowing toward Bridazak.

Spilf sidled up to Bridazak and whispered, "How did you know?"

"They told me."

"They?"

Bridazak swept his arm from left to right, across where his altar had once stood. "Yes, don't you see them?"

Suddenly, four glowing orbs of silver light appeared and the heroes' mouths opened in awe. Each orb of brilliance expanded and then dissolved to reveal an angel. The villagers continued their praise, unaware of the beings. A soothing aura surrounded the angels of light and prevented the adventurers from seeing any detail of their faces or clothing; shimmering eight-foot tall shapes were all they could make out.

A booming voice filled the air, "Heroes of Ruauck-El, your Father has answered your prayer and this community has been saved. Blessings upon you, who are highly favored."

Then, the angels' light became bright, casting a silver halo, and as quickly as they arrived, they disappeared before their eyes.

The mysterious woman tracking Abawken watched from the shadow of the woods, witnessing this unspeakable force. *"Who is this ordakian that can summon the power of gods?"* she thought to herself. She had risked much entering the mysterious memory loss field, uncertain of the true ramifications of what would happen when she left, but her need to fulfill her contract and capture her prey was more pressing. It mattered little now, since the power had somehow been dispelled.

A group of elkhorn suddenly leapt over her and the bush she hid behind. The forest was overrun with the animals. She said under her breath, "Abawken, you have surrounded yourself with powerful friends, but eventually you will be alone, with or without my help, and then I will bring you back to my fold." She half-smiled and continued, "Another visitation in your dreams is warranted, my friend." Abawken would submit to her wishes, but first she needed to rest in order to summon the power necessary for the supernatural feat.

There was a huge celebration in their honor that night. The heroes sat on wicker mats while the people of the tribe danced around the large fire pit in the exact spot God had struck earlier. Drum beats and well-timed grunting gave the rhythm needed as men and women stomped around. Joy and smiles were seen on everyone's faces. The adventurers were admired and throughout the evening, women and their children, of all ages, brought them hand-made gifts and food. When the meal was set before them, Dulgin wrinkled his nose and whispered, "It smells like dirt."

"Quiet, be respectful and pretend you like it," Bridazak responded while smiling at the next person delivering and nodding his head in thanks.

The ordakian agreed with Dulgin, it had the strong aroma of rich soil. They proudly served portions of a freshly slaughtered and charred elk-horn, alongside their traditional staple—a sticky brown rice flecked with herbs and served upon tree bark. Bridazak pinched off a small amount of rice with the meat, and stuck it inside his mouth, politely smiling as he chewed. The women watched him eat and were pleased by his response.

"By the looks, I'd say you hated it," Dulgin whispered back with a slight smirk.

Bridazak replied, "It reminds me of Dwarven mead. You will like it."

"Really? Why don't I believe you?"

"It's true Dulgin," Spilf said as he swallowed his portion in discomfort. "Definitely Dwarven mead."

"Abawken?" Dulgin looked for the human's opinion, not trusting the Daks.

"Master Dulgin, I think this will certainly put hair on your chest. I'm not familiar with the taste of this mead you speak of."

"Well that is good enough for me." Dulgin dove into the pungent smelling meal. He turned his head slightly sideways as he contemplated the taste, crunching on the still-firm rice. Bridazak and Spilf winked at one another. Then Dulgin glared at Bridazak. Anticipating the dwarf's anger, the ordakian was ready to scurry away, but a smile broke through the red, bushy beard instead.

"Smells like dirt, but it tastes great! Now this is what I call comfort food."

Bridazak, Spilf, and Abawken shrugged and shook their heads in disbelief.

"Are we sure this tribe doesn't have dwarven blood in them?" he mused as he scooped another helping and bobbed his shoulders up and down to the drum beats.

As the celebration continued, the children approached the heroes in single file and placed white petaled flowers on the ground before them. Mothers, watching the little ones perform the ritual, smiled or wept with joy, knowing their children were safe and now had a future. During their presentation, the rhythmic drum beat diminished to light taps of a wooden mallet on a hollowed tree trunk and the dancing suddenly ceased.

An old woman, ushered carefully by two tribesmen, approached. Bridazak watched with his friends standing beside him. The dak tried to ignore the stares of the people and remained focused on the elder approaching him. She looked into his compassionate, teal eyes, her one milky white eye contrasting sharply against her spotted dark one. The wrinkles on her face spoke of her experience, and the hardship she had endured as the eldest amongst the community over the years. There was pain buried within her, but at the same time Bridazak saw hope returning; she seemed to walk taller than she had when they first arrived.

She shakily extended her hand and grabbed hold of Bridazak's. He gently gripped her leathery hand and smiled. She turned toward the gathered, while at the same time lifting his arm up with hers, a triumphant symbol that caused the tribe to engage in a high pitched hooting.

Her raspy voice escalated into a sharp shrill, hushing the crowd instantly. She spoke, "Our prophets of old spoke of the season of change to come in the silent days. We have seen, on this day, their words come to pass." More hooting resounded and then died back down. She continued after lowering Bridazak's hand, releasing her grasp, and then stepping forward. "It is time to cast our former beliefs of our fallen god and take hold of the new and true God we have seen this day. No longer will our children suffer." The women nearby clutched their babies tighter upon her words, remembering the horror of their past. She continued her speech, "It will take us time to adjust to this change and it will require us all, not just me, to answer to the truth of what we have seen today. In repentance of our past, we will celebrate each sacrificed child, one a day, until all have been recognized, in order to repent, and honor the true God. You have heard my words, now let it be so." The hooting deafened the heroes and the woman turned and motioned for another to join her.

A mother with baby in arm, the same child the heroes rescued, came forward. She sheepishly smiled as she approached. A hush fell as they considered her toddler to be special; the first boy saved from the old, evil tradition.

"Thank you, Bridazak," she said.

"You are welcome. What is your son's name?"

"Kaiym."

The crowd watched in silence as Bridazak walked closer to the roaring fire and turned back to the mother and son. In a loud and authoritative voice, he said, "This child's very name means life. Your future leader resides inside Kaiym. Raise this little one as a symbol of what happened this very day. Teach him the ways of the true God, through loving one another and helping those in need. Blessings from Heaven will continue to rain on your village. Celebrate each year in remembrance of this day of redemption."

The tribe instantly fell to their knees and bowed to their future leader; the boy named Kaiym. The mother held her son high into the air and looked around in amazement. Bridazak then walked off into the shadows of night, already beginning to pray in thanks. He may not have the orb anymore, but God's voice really was still with him.

"How does he know these things?" Dulgin asked.

There was no response. The old woman with one blind eye came forward and walked toward Spilf.

"I have something to show you child-man. Come with me."

Spilf looked to Dulgin and Abawken and they both waited for his decision. Spilf stood and the three of them followed her.

"What is this place?" Spilf gently touching the faded pigments on the stone wall of the cave she led them into. The pictographs depicted a lengthy history.

Dulgin and Abawken held torches inside the small alcove nestled inside the granite of the mountain.

The aged woman limped forward and pointed, "It's a timeline of events. This is when my people invaded your village."

Figures of humans with bows and spears were attacking. Then she indicated the Thaloc creature and a dome encompassing the forest. They saw other depictions of importance for her tribe but then spotted a small creature with hair on its face.

"What is that?"

She pointed at Dulgin.

"Dwarves?"

She nodded, "The stories as told from generations say they tried to trade with us, but we sent them away and considered the bearded-ones to be a bad omen."

"How does this help us?" Spilf asked.

Dulgin responded, "It means there are dwarves around here and it is possible that your village sought refuge."

"Which direction did the dwarves come from?"

"Along the mountains to the west, beyond the old settlement Saybrook. Before the fall of our people and the vanishing of our men had begun, there had been expeditions, and they discovered altars two days travel from here. Perhaps they belong to the bearded-ones." Dulgin blurted out in realization, "Brook, I get it! Say-brook!" Dulgin finally understood the joke the ordakians had shared at his expense.

A spark of excitement came over Spilf and he smiled at Dulgin and Abawken, too eager to even tease Dulgin. He took off back to the village, yelling, "I need to tell Bridazak!"

"Dwarves leave markers for their kind to find, but outsiders won't know what they have discovered. Dwarves don't openly announce here we are," Dulgin said to Abawken.

"If nothing else, it has given our friend hope. Looks like we have a new direction to go now." The human fighter followed after Spilf.

The old lady hobbled after Abawken but was stopped suddenly by Dulgin.

"Do you by chance have any more of that delicious rice food we had earlier?"

8

The Great Illustrya Ocean

A *Pinch of Luck* was never so lively as it was in the open ocean under full sails. Each member of the crew masterfully manned his post and attended to his duties, while below deck, Elsbeth pointed out the locations on the old sea map in her private quarters.

"It will take us three days to get to the Singing Rocks," the captain explained.

Raina and El'Korr nodded, understanding their passage through the Great Illustrya Ocean—named after Illustrya herself, who travelled these waters for centuries in the Unknown Age—would take some time.

Elsbeth continued, "Then at least two more to get to Pirate's Belly. We will restock there, and then head out to the Whispering Sea. Captain Yasooma's compass will lead us to his sunken ship."

"Pirate's Belly doesn't sound good to me," El'Korr responded.

"We will be fine. I know the locals, and have built a relationship over the years that will garner us safe passage."

"If you say so." The dwarven king shifted uncomfortably in his seat. He was not accustomed to being off land as it was. Adding pirates to the mix was not his favorite idea.

"Come, let us get some fresh air," she motioned them with her hand toward the exit.

El'Korr, Raina, and Captain Elsbeth stepped out from her cabin. The salty air filled their lungs. The ship crashed through the rolling hills of water. Heavy ocean spray showered the crew who worked the rigging to perfection. The sails flapped incessantly, adding to the unfiltered chorus of the unsettled white-capped ocean. Skath and Myers called out orders to the men as needed.

Suddenly, Rondee the Wild ran past them, draped himself over the ship's railing and barfed last night's dinner into the angry sea.

"Will your friend survive? This is only day one," Elsbeth asked.

"Dwarves are meant for mountains, not the sea."

"My priest, Anders, has a remedy. Take Rondee below deck."

El'Korr made his way over to his dwarven protector, who moaned in discomfort. Rondee grabbed his King's beard to look him in the eye, and said, "Te dufett."

"Nobody is dying today my friend. C'mon, my loyal Bodyguard. Let's get your stomach back in order." El'Korr hauled Rondee away.

While Xan and Lufra began to explore the deck, Raina ventured, "Captain, now that we are alone, what can you tell me of the elements that Yasooma had collected on his ship?"

"I was wondering when you were going to ask. I can tell you he was a very private man. The elements became an obsession of his. I'm not sure why, but then, I suppose every man has a quest in his heart to make his mark in this world. I do know that he had acquired two of the elements before becoming captain of *The Wave Rider*—the Earth Stone, and the Fire Opal. In our travels he discovered the location of the third element—the Pearl of the Deep. We headed out to the Whispering Sea to recover it, and that is where the sea gods swallowed our ship. It was—," she paused, recalling the terrible details. "It felt as though the ocean rose up against us. I blacked out and woke aboard a pirate ship alongside Yasooma, but I was the only true survivor. Yasooma became a shell of a man, damned his life, and brought a curse upon his family. We lost everyone, and it haunts me to this very day. Heading back there is not something I ever imagined I would do. Perhaps it is my destiny—" her final words trailed off.

Raina could see the pain in Elsbeth's eyes as she recalled the event. She had mentioned three elements, but Raina knew there was a fourth, due to Lufra supplying her with Yasooma's personal journal—the Sky Diamond. "Come, half-sister, you have seen and experienced much to bring this heavy sadness you carry. I will share with you a story of hope about a prophecy, an ordakian, and the Orb of Truth." They stepped back into Captain Elsbeth's private cabin and closed the door.

As El'Korr made his way below deck, taking Rondee to the priest, he wove his way through rows of hammocks swinging back and forth from jumbled ropes attached to wooden columns. Some were occupied by snoring sailors resting before their shift. The stench of old sweat and salty fish permeated the air, and the beating thuds of the ocean against the ship's hull with every dive resounded in the ears.

They approached the stern and heard the voice of Anders the Priest conversing with a sailor who had suffered a gaffing injury to his left shoulder. Rondee's arm hung over his king's shoulder as he stumbled along. Anders noticed the dwarves approaching.

"Well sailor, be more careful next time. You could have lost your arm. Now go and get some rest. I will inform Myers of your modified duty."

"I can see why the captain named the ship *A Pinch of Luck*," El'Korr said in jest as he set Rondee down on a wood chair.

"It looks like your green friend can use some of my Gut Check remedy, as the boys like to call it." Anders stood up and spoke to Rondee, "Listen my dwarven friend, if you feel the need to purge then use the bucket next to you."

The mere mention of vomiting caused the warrior to lurch for the container, into which he deposited chunks of partially processed food. A strong smell of fish and alcohol assaulted their nostrils. El'Korr and Anders turned away in disgust, their faces sour.

"Looks like he experienced an old sailor initiation last night."

"He was drinking with some of the men," El'Korr acknowledged.

"Yeah, well, they weren't being sociable. It is their way of welcoming a newbie, but he should take it as a compliment."

"Let's not let Rondee know about it. He might not see it that way," El'Korr whispered.

They brought Rondee, who was moaning and holding his stomach, to a sitting position. His finger-length beard had vomit residue streaming through and dripping onto his leather hide armor.

The priest withdrew his pouch and produced a stringy substance resembling tobacco. He stuffed the concoction into Rondee's mouth, and maneuvered it to rest along his jawline; it bulged out his left cheek.

"Rondee, make sure you don't swallow any of the juice. Spit as needed into the bucket. Your stomach will settle within the hour. Do you understand?"

The dwarf attempted to speak, "Fluffy chuckemba clouds," and then slumped back into the chair. Anders then began to speak a blessing over him.

"To the God of the seas and of our hearts—" he began, but then stopped as the strange coughing returned.

El'Korr squinted and then noted this was the second time Anders had a coughing fit. He suddenly realized that the attacks happened only after the priest began to pray.

"I could probably help you out with your cough." Anders put up his hand to keep El'Korr from approaching as he continued to hack loudly.

"It is my infliction to bare and I am grateful to be chosen," he sputtered.

"Chosen? You feel God has given this to you then?"

Anders cough subsided, "But of course. How is one to have their faith increased if not tested? You being of the cloth should know this."

"A father tests his child, yes, but in order to increase the strength of faith. Our God whom we both serve, I do not believe would cast such a burden on one such as yourself."

Anders stared deeply into El'Korr's eyes and said, "Well, to each his own. I have accepted my fate and embrace it as a gift."

El'Korr was going to respond but Rondee moaned loudly, holding his stomach, as the ship continued to sway back and forth.

"Will he be alright?" El'Korr asked.

"He will be fine and should be back on his feet in a couple of hours. I will watch over him."

"Thank you for helping my friend." The dwarf walked away.

"That is good Lufra. Well-done," Xan stated while parrying his sabre.

"My father taught me a few things before the curse killed him."

"Now let's work on your defense."

"I'm ready; show me what you've got," the energized boy readied himself.

Xan didn't hesitate to come in swinging with his longsword. He gave Lufra two easy swipes to block, setting him up for a swift, harsh, swat on the rear by the flat of his blade. The teenager reached quickly for his rear-end, rubbing it, and his face contorted from the sting. Several sailors laughed heartily at the elf's education for the child.

"I'll have to remember that one," Lufra stated.

"It's all about feeling and instinct, not memory. You have to know your opponent's next move before he does."

"How do you do that?"

"It takes time and practice. Lots of practice."

"How long did it take you to learn?"

Xan chuckled, "A good hundred years." The elf swung his blade again and Lufra jumped back out of the way.

"I don't have a hundred years Xan."

"Then you had better learn quickly," the elf smiled and moved into the proper posture again. As the brilliant orange and pink sunset pushed aside the light of day, the metallic clashing of steel against steel continued to ring from the deck of the galleon.

"Trillius," a female gnome whispered.

"Shhhh. Stop using that name. Someone might hear it."

"Sorry, Silly Samuel. Is that better?"

"Shhhh. I'm trying to listen through this damn creaky wood," he responded.

No taller than a barrel, the gnome had his ear against the ceiling planks, focusing on the muffled voices coming from the captain's quarters above. The silver-eyed creature mashed his face into the ceiling while balancing on the thin, makeshift scaffold inside a storage room. His dark hair lay in wisps around his tiny ears, and his rotund grey nose was smooth like lamb skin. The sniffer was the pride and joy of all gnomes, like the beard on a dwarf, and this gnome had much to be proud of.

"They mentioned Pirate's Belly," he said softly.

"Good, that is where we can get off and disappear."

"Wait! Ah, dammit, I missed the next place they were going. It's your fault, Sugar, if we miss something good."

"Don't call me Sugar. And you know I don't care for all that thieving stuff you do."

"Yeah, I know. You're a nature-gnome."

"We need to get off at Pirate's Belly. This is our chance to escape and leave your—"

"My *what*, Rozelle?" he focused in on her meaning.

"I was just referring to your past is all. I didn't mean to offend you."

"Yeah, right. Are you sure you're a gnome? I've never heard of one taking up the druidical profession."

"Well, let it be known, that I'm trying to change the profiling of our race to a more noble impression."

"Somehow I don't think saving nature is gonna change anything."

"I don't share your—"

"Shhhhh. I hear the mystic talking now with the captain."

Rozelle held her breath. She was the same height as Trillius. Her rosy cheeks brought out the beige color of her large nose. Ashen locks weaved in and out of her long, birch bark colored hair, complimenting her attire. She wore a green skirt and soft velvet green blouse. Brown boots and a belt finished off her ensemble.

Trillius plucked his ear away with a smile on his face.

"What is it?" she asked.

"Have you heard of something called the Pearl of the Deep?"

"No. Why?"

A mischievous grin and a raised eyebrow alerted Rozelle.

She glared back at him in understanding, "We are not getting off at Pirate's Belly, are we?"

9

The Singing Rocks

On the third day out to sea, the routines on board *A Pinch of Luck* kept their journey moving smoothly. Xan continued to train Lufra in the art of swordplay, and the boy showed natural skill and growth. Raina shared many stories with Captain Elsbeth; her half-elf counterpart offered more historical background, explaining some of the time Raina spent as a captive inside the Burning Forest. Rondee the Wild was learning the ropes, literally, from the crew, who at one time jokingly hoisted him into the rigging high above the deck. El'Korr noticed Anders the Priest seemed to be avoiding him whenever he approached. Some of the more superstitious sailors associated Anders coughing spasms with strange happenings aboard the ship and became spooked. Several men reported that some of their small trinkets and belongings, like single socks, or mementos from past voyages, had gone missing. First Mate Skath and Second Mate Myers began an investigation.

Rozelle lobbed a shard of a pearlescent shell at Trillius, "Why do you continue to steal this worthless stuff?" she chided.

Trillius, who was sitting on top of a bag of grain, caught it, looked it over, and mumbled, "I don't know. I'm bored."

"Stealing is a sickness, and you've got it."

"I'm not sick. Being cooped up in this hell-hole ship with *Nature-girl* is more than a manly-gnome can take," he countered as he jumped off his grain perch.

"Don't give me that. You love the fact that you have two Horn Kings looking for you. All that attention. It's *all* about Trillius," she jabbed.

"Stop using my real name," Trillius said through clenched teeth.

Rozelle snapped, "Why? Are you afraid someone will come down here and find they have the Great Trillius?!" She narrowed her eyes and tightened her jaw, hurt by his sharpness toward her.

After a long pause to assure himself that no one heard her outburst, Trillius smiled and said smoothly, "You are kind of sexy when you get angry." As he spoke, Trillius walked seductively toward Rozelle.

She smirked, "Why do you do that?"

"Do what?" He moved closer to her.

"That silly walk."

"Oh, you mean this?" He laughed and spun around on one heel, placed his hands on his hips, and gyrated from side to side.

Rozelle giggled, "Stop it, silly." A blush spread across her face.

Trillius had her right where he wanted her. He slowly shuffled closer, but before he could take her in his arms to kiss her, she stiffened and said, "Did you hear that?"

"Unbelievable. No, what is it now? Last time you needed to check on that old man's garden that wasn't being attended to properly."

"It's...singing."

"I don't hear anything except my hope being squashed, *again*." Trillius leaned against a barrel, crossed his arms, and pouted.

"What are you talking about? I hear women singing."

At that moment, they heard the muffled call of the sailor on watch in the crow's nest yell out, "Ahoy, approaching the Singing Rocks!"

Captain Elsbeth studied the cathedral-like rock formation jutting up above the ocean's surface, situated starboard of the galleon, from her place on deck. Towering swells of water formed into waves and engulfed the many reef outcroppings, sending mountains of furious white frothy foam high into the air. The booming bombardment of breakers assailed the ears of the crew as shifting tides receded, revealing the barnacle covered black rock and numerous alcoves and caves. Then the sea rushed in at a greater speed than it had earlier subsided. Above the din, a melodious choir of female voices carried by the wind encircled the vessel.

"What causes this?" Raina asked, joining the captain.

"The legend of the Singing Rocks comes from the Unknown Age. The story speaks of a Beruvian slave ship and its captain being infected with the Sea Fever. The captain went mad and slaughtered the female elven slaves, thinking they were spies. His ship crashed on the rocks at this very spot and everyone aboard died. The legend tells of how the elven spirits sing their story to passing ships."

El'Korr nodded, "Very interesting, Raina, do they sing in your language?"

"I can't make anything discernible from it, but it is beautiful. It does remind me of home."

Elsbeth added, "There is another facet to their song."

"Oh, what is that?" El'Korr asked.

"Hidden within their history is a warning. The fallen elves sing an alert to the captains of passing ships, of spies aboard their vessel. I have personally never had a spy aboard to confirm—," Elsbeth froze and then suddenly frowned, "It appears there is a first time for everything."

"What is it?" Raina asked.

Elsbeth called out, "Skath, Myers, follow me!"

The first and second mates hustled by her side as she strode to the stairway leading below deck. Raina, El'Korr, Rondee, Xan, and Lufra followed. Elsbeth seemed to know exactly where she was going as she walked rapidly to the unknown destination. She kicked open a wooden door and stepped into a small storeroom. In a swift fluent action, she withdrew her rapier. Skath and Myers followed suit and drew sabers, waiting for her command. The room showed no movement amongst the stacked barrels and bags of grain. There was a long pause as the three surveyed the room, the creaks of the weathered galleon were the only discernible sounds.

"I know you are here. Reveal yourself," the captain demanded.

Raina spotted a blurry shift to her left. She cast a spell, pointing her staff, and releasing a command word, "Voshnu." In an instant two gnomes appeared. Raina had dispelled their chameleon-like illusion. Skath and Myers moved to apprehend the intruders.

"Not them!" Elsbeth said. Her eyes were focused straight ahead. "The gnomes are stowaways, not spies."

Suddenly, a once unseen, two-foot-tall creature with a tail, became visible on top of a barrel. The shimmering magic faded as it dove behind a crate.

Skath turned to the gnomes and barked, "What did you bring aboard our ship!"

Trillius stepped forward and began to weave his story, "Well, that hideous beast captured us and forced us onto your ship. We are so thankful you rescued us. We've been stuck in here for days, and—"

"Shut it gnome, before I cut out yer tongue!"

"Skath, hold your position!" Elsbeth commanded. "I can sense that thing is still behind the crates. Advance."

The wild dwarf tossed the wooden containers aside. He spotted the reptile-like tail as it hurriedly slithered away. Rondee pointed out the direction, and Skath maneuvered to the other side and began tipping crates.

"You have it pinned," Elsbeth cried.

Everyone stood at the ready. The tension mounted as the barrels were moved aside one by one. When only two remained, Rondee nodded to Skath, coordinating their next move. Together they snatched a barrel away from the wall. Immediately, a large rat screeched, darted between their legs, scurried through a cracked opening, and disappeared into the hull.

"It's only a rat," Skath shrugged.

Rozelle stepped forward, "That's no rat, it's a shape changer. Trust me, I know. I'll get it." She instantly morphed into a large rodent and chased after it.

"Rozelle. No!" Trillius pleaded.

"What is that thing?" El'Korr exclaimed.

There was no response as they listened to the hurried scratching claws of the metamorphic animals battling within the walls of the ship.

The two creatures scampered through the narrow, damp, and moldy hull. A strong musty scent filled the passageway. Rozelle moved with ease as she stayed on top of the spindly tailed intruder. There was a slight turn, and then suddenly there was nowhere else to run; a wide and reinforced beam cut off access from going any further. The spy turned on Rozelle, hissed, revealed its sharp fangs, and glared with glowing red eyes. Rozelle skidded to a halt.

"You have nowhere else to run," Rozelle squeaked in her new rat language.

It screeched back a response, the tone stronger, "They will smell your rotting body inside this ship for days, druid."

"I'm not looking to harm you. I just want to talk. Let's work out this misunderstanding."

The vile rat lunged for Rozelle. They tumbled together. She extended her legs and claws to try and keep the feral animal's distance. One of its claws raked across her stomach and then grabbed hold of her neck with its razor sharp teeth. Screeches of pain echoed through the ship.

Rozelle morphed once again, this time into a large snake. She wrapped her new, long and slithering form around the rat, attempting to squeeze the life from it. Growls of pain came forth from the rodent at Rozelle's surprise counterattack. It managed to scratch its way free from her grip. She quickly coiled into a defensive posture.

It attempted to get around her, but Rozelle snapped and pushed it back, blocking its escape. Feeling trapped, the mangy rat attacked relentlessly, and Rozelle was unable to react quickly enough in her snake form to defend each strike. Rozelle knew she couldn't defeat this creature as a reptile.

The spy hissed as it lunged in with its claws but was surprised once again by the clever druid as she morphed into a black cat—the clear rival to the entire rodent family. Startled, it backed away from the vicious feline retaliation. Rozelle confidently approached in her new body, her feral yellow eyes glowing in the dark. The fur on her back rose and she hissed, revealing her sharp, white teeth.

The rat tried to change back to its original size but was unable to do so, backed into the corner of the confined area. It was desperate to get away. Rozelle moved in for the kill. Her senses were heightened and she could smell fear. It didn't take long for her to swipe the rodent a few times with her paw and then grab hold of it with her teeth at the back of its neck. She tasted blood and felt its body go limp.

A sleek black cat emerged from the opening that led back into the storeroom with the rat dangling from its mouth. Skath and Myers pointed their swords. Everyone was speechless, waiting to see what was going to happen.

Rozelle laid the rodent on the ground. It suddenly materialized back to the two-foot tall creature they had originally seen. Rozelle then shape shifted back to her gnome stature and joined Trillius, proudly clutching his arm.

"What is that thing?" Captain Elsbeth questioned.

"It's called a devling," Raina responded.

"A what? I've never heard of such a thing. Why is it on my ship?"

"It is following *us*," Raina said. "Devlings are used by mystics. Apparently, someone is keeping an eye on us."

"What are we to do with the gnomes?" Skath asked the captain.

She eyed them carefully before responding and then walked closer.

"What were your intentions, little-ones?"

Trillius quickly chimed, "We overheard Raina speaking of 'the Pearl of the Deep' and thought we could...help."

"When did you hear this?" Raina questioned.

"Well, before we even came aboard this ship of course, otherwise, how would we have known which one to hide out on?" Trillius smiled, thinking his ploy had worked. He looked around the room confidently at each of the heroes.

"Put them in the brig," Captain ordered.

Trillius' expression changed to shock, "What? Surely helping you kill a spy should garner some leeway?"

"I think not," Skath said as he grabbed the gnome.

"Captain Elsbeth, I wish to hire these gnomes," Raina stated.

Everyone froze and looked confused. El'Korr, Elsbeth, and Trillius simultaneously exclaimed, "What?!"

"We are in need of someone of their caliber. Yasooma did not keep things out in the open, so I suspect we will need some skullduggery skills in acquiring the items."

Trillius stumbled over the words, "Yes, skull-doog-eerriie skills." He then whispered to Rozelle, "What does that mean?"

"She said you're a thief."

"And now it seems it is a paying profession," Trillius responded. He turned back, "I require ten percent value of all the loot we partake in on our little excavation."

A low growl alerted Trillius, and he turned to look over at El'Korr. The dwarf glared at the gnome and, to Trillius's eyes, he seemed to resemble a fire giant with his orange hair and beard ablaze. "Or whatever you deem is fair," his voice a higher pitch.

Captain Elsbeth began to walk out of the hold, "As you wish Raina, but I ask that all items are returned to my crew and any further 'skull-doogery' that happens aboard my ship will be your responsibility."

Raina nodded in acknowledgement of Elsbeth's demands. Skath and Myers followed their captain and headed back to the deck. Xan, who had kept his charge out of the way until he knew it was safe, now allowed Lufra to enter the room to get a better look at the creature and the gnomes.

There was a short span of silence as everyone looked each other over.

"I'm Silly Samuel and this is Rozelle."

"You look familiar to me," Xan professed while scrutinizing Trillius.

"Seen one gnome, seen 'em all," he laughed.

"A druid, I presume?" Raina said.

"Why yes I am," Rozelle proudly stepped forward.

"You were very lucky to take on a devling by yourself and live to tell about it."

"If you say so. It tried to revert back to its original shape but it was too small of an area. I guess it was stuck as a rat."

"Well, I don't know about you all, but I sure could use some fresh air," Trillius began to walk toward the door.

"Where do you think you're going, Trillius?" Xan asked, emphasizing the gnome's true name.

He turned back to the elf and began to respond to the question, raising his hand with his index finger in the air. "Well, I—" Trillius held his gaze and froze in place as he realized he was caught. "Dammit!" he brought his hand back down, taking in a deep breath and then exhaling. "Rozelle, maybe one day you will understand what it is like being famous. It's lonely at the top."

10

Dwarven Clues

"This must be the place the old villager woman spoke about," Dulgin announced.

They studied the slightly tilted granite column, towering above the heroes, adorned with carvings of dwarves and ancient symbols. The old marker stood at the base of a sheer-faced cliff. Prairie weeds dotted the area while fragments of sharp chipped rock littered the ground.

"Do you know what it means, Master Dulgin?"

He studied it for a moment and then said, "It's old."

Spilf scoffed, "That's it? I thought you knew a lot of history."

Dulgin clenched his fist, "I know that you are going to be *history* in a second, Stubby."

"Spilf, have Lester and Ross check it over," Bridazak jumped in.

"I don't think there is anything here, but it's worth a try." Spilf withdrew his simple leather wrap and revealed his rusty thieving tools. Lester and Ross were once a sacred secret to the Dak, but since their heroic escapade with the Orb, Spilf had shared the mystery with his comrades, including 'Grumpy,' as Lester and Ross had titled Dulgin. The brothers appear not as rusted items, but instead truly as magnificent magical instruments, pure bronze in color with enlarged round eyes, but only to whomever wields them. Lester and Ross blinked often throughout their use, adding to their innocent appearance, as they telepathically linked minds with their owner.

"*Hello Master, so good to see you again,*" Lester chimed in his metallic sounding, slightly echoing voice.

Ross' greeting was high pitched and squeaky, "*Hi Spilf, I just had an amazing dream.*"

"*You can dream?*" Spilf quickly formed the words inside his mind.

"*Yep, and it was a good one.*"

There was an awkward silence for a few seconds before Lester yelled, "*Well, what was it?*"

"*What was what?*"

"*Your dream, you pick-head!*"

"*Oh, you do care about me after all, Lester! I knew it even though you said awful things to me those hundreds of years ago when we were trapped inside that scary coffer in the lair of—*"

"*Would you shut up and just tell us your dream for a lock's sake.*"

"*Yeah, okay, the dream. Well, it had a beautiful golden lock that gleamed my reflection and I don't know where you were Lester, but I was in charge this time and I had this mechanism figured out. It had never been opened by anyone, as it was legendary. It was constructed inside a monstrous stone door. Come to think of it, I can't remember who my master was during this dream. Oh well, it doesn't matter cause I opened it and I was the hero.*"

"*What was on the other side of the door?*" Spilf asked.

"*Beats me, but wasn't that a good one, Lester?*"

"*Yeah, great. Remind me not to ask you about your dreams next time.*"

"*Okay, I will.*"

Lester changed the subject, "*Master, what can we pick for you today?*"

"*I want you both to try to find something hidden amongst this old dwarven marker.*"

"*Easy enough. Okay Ross, let's do our thing.*"

"*Oh no, not dwarves,*" cried Ross.

Spilf maneuvered his magical tools from top to bottom and circled the ancient pillar, until his trusted items alerted him by revealing hidden writing. The mysterious gold lettering running straight down the frame of the granite, materialized before his eyes. "*Can you read it?*" Spilf questioned.

"*Yep, we can read it, but are you sure that is a good idea?*" Lester inquired.

"*Yeah, reading the 'Grumpy' language is never a good idea,*" Ross added.

"*Guys, I need to find my parents, and this could help us.*"

"Master, I'm sure it is not important. Dwarves are barbaric and brutal, probably a warning to stay away from their gold."

"Yeah, they are a scary race, just look at Grumpy, he has that nasty scar on his face, you know, the kind that you just can't stop staring at but you also want to look away. Oh no, I'm looking at it now. He has me under his ugly web of ugliness, Lester. Help me."

"Just read it!" Spilf charged.

Lester and Ross quickly mumbled through the guttural language, but nothing happened.

"Master, I detect an enchantment which requires a dwarf to speak it aloud."

"Lester, how do you know that?" Ross asked.

"I'm using my pick-brain, Brother."

"Wow, I'm impressed."

Spilf ignored Ross and Lester's bantering and turned toward his awaiting friends. "There is a dwarven language magically hidden, but they think it needs to be read aloud by a dwarf."

Everyone turned to face Dulgin. He quickly put up his hands, "I don't see nothin to read."

"I have an idea," Bridazak smiled.

"I never like those kind of smiles you give," Dulgin responded.

"Well, it has everything to do with you, my dwarven friend."

"That is what I was afraid of. What is this idea?"

"Well, you are going to hold onto Lester and Ross so you can see the writing and read it to everyone."

"What did he just say?" Lester charged.

"Spilf, send us away, I can't hear this. I want to go back to my golden lock dream."

"What happens when I hold those things?" Dulgin cautiously asked.

"It is harmless. You will have a telepathic link with Lester and Ross. It will only take a minute and then you can give them back to Spilf."

"It better be harmless. I don't like all this magical shenanigans."

"Spilf, please gift Lester and Ross to Dulgin."

Spilf heard the crying and screaming pleas from his trusted picks and looked forward to the interesting encounter forthcoming. "Dulgin, take care of them," he said as he handed them over. The mind link faded with their combined yelling of, *"No!"* as he passed them to the dwarf.

Dulgin's mind instantly flooded with the echoing cries of Lester and Ross inside his head. The once rusty, non-impressive tools now shifted to the illustrious crafted animated items only revealed to the one who owned them. The oversized eyeballs of the picks stared in pure horror at the situation as they gazed upon the burly, red-bearded giant.

He spoke aloud and held them out away from himself as if the distance would lessen their voices, "Keep it down ya blundering fools!"

"Use your mind Dulgin," Spilf said.

"He doesn't have a mind, Spilf!" Ross yelled.

"Ross, Spilf can't hear us, we now have a new master, the dwarf."

"We are doomed, Lester!"

"Would you two pick-squeaks shut your metal mouths. I don't like this anymore than you, so let's get this over with."

"Lester, did Grumpy, I mean—Master, say something intelligent?"

"Yes Ross. Let's do our job and show him what he needs to see. Master, move us closer to the stone structure so we can show you our discovery."

Dulgin did as instructed, holding the tiny tools as best as possible in his ruddy and battle-hardened hands. Bridazak, Spilf, and Abawken smiled and nudged each other at the sight of him wielding Lester and Ross in an awkward fashion, unaccustomed to such items of finesse.

Dulgin saw the dwarven writing flare to life before him and then read it aloud, "Mey sheiz temmey denohrt tasheiz burs lhaz kelohrt markul hallazku sekk frukat." The rest of them waited for the translation, but Dulgin seemed shocked by what he read.

"What does it mean, Master Dwarf?"

He looked at each of them with concern and said, "My crest will announce my arrival, I'm a symbol in battle and I defend all who seek shelter."

"It's a riddle," Lester announced inside Dulgin's mind.

"I love riddles," Ross followed.

Dulgin mentally responded, *"It is not a riddle to dwarves."* He then handed them back to Spilf.

"That could be a lot of different things," Bridazak said. "Any ideas?" he looked around.

"Maybe a flag or a sword?" Abawken ventured a guess.

"Or maybe armor," Spilf added.

"It's a shield," Dulgin announced, matter of factly.

Everyone nodded as it made sense. "This is an ancient dwarven proverb, but only used by the frost dwarves of old," Dulgin continued.

"Here we go. It is history time once again," Spilf said.

"This is not just any shield my friends, this is *the Shield*. We call it te Sond."

As he spoke the name in his native tongue, the cliff rumbled and began to shake, first gently and then more violently. Rocks tumbled down, bouncing off boulders and impacting one against the other with a clattering of stone against stone.

The group moved quickly from the area, covering their heads for protection.

After much shaking and buffeting, the cliff-side groaned loudly and the air was filled with the sound of granite grinding as the bluff wall ripped apart and formed an opening revealing a small pathway of rough stairs leading into the mountain.

Everyone watched, dumbstruck by the magical feat they had just witnessed.

"I guess you figured out the answer to the riddle, Master Dulgin. And it looks like we have a new direction to head."

"You don't understand," Dulgin stated, "This is the Shield, the same location that my brother El'Korr is bringing his army to."

"Are you certain?"

"Bridazak, this is the Shield."

"Then it appears our fates are entwined more than we thought."

Spilf peered into the open cliff. Cold air embraced the adventuring dak. Rough cut stone steps went up beyond his vision, "Where does this go?" his voice echoed.

"Up, ya blundering fool. Let's go."

11

Pirate's Belly

The heroes gathered on the deck when the crow's nest called out, "Pirate's Belly ahead!"

Their ship sailed onward toward a massive, sheer faced cliff wall. Protruding volcanic rock caught incoming swells of water that washed over the top and then receded back to start the process all over again. Elsbeth stood resolute, holding the wheel as her vessel continued to glide forward. El'Korr exchanged a concerned look with Xan, who raised an eyebrow.

"Do you know something we don't?" Xan asked his sister, noticing she seemed amused.

"It appears we will be going through it," she stated calmly, not taking her eye off the spectacle.

Rondee rubbed his eyes and blinked frantically, and then positioned himself between his King and the impending disaster. El'Korr asked, "How are you going to protect me from this, my friend?" Rondee shrugged.

"Half sails!" Skath ordered. The crew moved quickly and efficiently and the speed of the ship lessened. Elsbeth turned the wheel slightly and moments before an impact, the optical illusion of the jutting cliff was revealed; the slight shift in angle unveiled an enormous cave entrance beyond. The hidden cavern swallowed the ship and the bright blue sea quickly transformed into a turquoise green. The sounds of the open ocean faded away.

Trillius yelled from the railing of *A Pinch of Luck*, "Trillius has arrived!" His voice echoed off the walls. Trillius glanced back and was startled to find El'Korr standing right behind him, arms crossed over his armored barrel chest, and glaring at him. The gnome flashed a fake smile and then went to stand next to Rozelle, as if she would protect him somehow.

Fingers of light from small openings above reached down and touched the water, revealing the deep colors of the calm ocean. The humongous pirate harbor catered to over forty docked or anchored ships of various sizes. Most impressive were the intricate docks themselves—multi-level platforms and walkways weaved back and forth along the rock wall of the cave, rope and wood, appearing a chaotic, jumbled mess, but actually quite functional, connected it all together. Small vessels littered the lower wards that jutted out just above the waterline, while large galleons lined tall stilted docks toward the center of the lair. Lit torches adorned the edges of the railed walkways. A glow permeated from deep within the cavern beyond the docks, and soon the heroes could see a main street that shot straight back into the rock.

"That is the Alley," Captain Elsbeth announced.

"Looks like fun-land to me," Trillius chimed.

"Not a chance, Gnome," El'Korr quickly retorted. "You are staying on board with me."

He pouted, "Great, fun-land just turned into boring-land."

The Alley was comprised of vendors, shops, taverns, and repair services; provisions could be found there to meet any traveler's needs.

"How is it that they allow you entrance, Captain? This is not a pirate ship," Raina asked.

"Let us just say, it can be good to know people."

Urlin Thoom, Elsbeth's mystic, stepped out of his cabin and approached. He had not been seen for days as he studied his books within his quarters. "Are you ready, Captain?"

"Yes, you may proceed."

He stepped back and closed his eyes as if going into meditation. Lifting his robed arms, he waved them around slowly and mumbled words of the arcane. Suddenly, everyone felt a noticeable shift in the movement of the galleon. It was now under Urlin's control.

"So this is how you dock instead of anchoring," Xan stated.

"Yes, I don't like ferrying people back and forth. It makes things much easier."

The large ship slid into its spot along an open part of the railing. Elsbeth's crew quickly threw out rope lines and tied it down, using the many bollards. Shouts and hollers from old friends began to spark up between other crews aboard neighboring ships and along the docks.

Captain Elsbeth said, "We will restock and depart first thing tomorrow morning. I would suggest not leaving my ship on your own at any time. Pirate's Belly goes by its own rules—there are none."

A horn trumpeted from within the cavern. It was a deeply resonating sound. Cheers began to escalate from pirates aboard other ships and those working on the docks.

"What is happening?" Lufra questioned.

Captain Elsbeth looked portside, "That sound heralds their fearless leader's return."

A galleon, slightly larger than *A Pinch of Luck*, came into view as it entered the vast chamber. Its flag did not bear a pirate symbol, but instead a red rose. Within minutes it cruised into port and docked adjacent to them on the other side of the pier. It was quickly tethered and Elsbeth's crew mingled with the newly arrived shipmates. The heroes gathered on the railing looking for the commander of the vessel.

Raina stepped toward Captain Elsbeth to ask if they would be able to meet the Pirate Governor of the unusual settlement, but Elsbeth turned to face the opposite direction and smiled broadly, giving Raina her answer. The mystic began to turn with Elsbeth in expectation of the forthcoming introduction.

"You've brought guests to Pirate's Belly," a mysterious, smooth voice came from behind the adventurers. Startled, the other heroes turned.

Before them stood an impressive pirate, who wore dark blue velvet pants, black boots, and a white, billowy, long sleeved shirt with frills around the cuffs and collar. His greatly plumed hat, along with the downward tilt of his head, concealed his face from view.

"May I introduce you to my acquaintances? These are the ones responsible for the demise of King Manasseh," said Elsbeth.

"We are honored to have such heroes among us. My name is Romann de Beaux. Welcome to my humble home." He pulled off his maroon hat and bowed elegantly. The swashbuckler stood back up, displaying his pale face, with eyes that swirled red and blue like a whirlpool. His smile revealed pearly white teeth with two prominent fangs.

The group of heroes were wise enough not to insult the creature by announcing their surprise aloud. That is, all of them, except one.

"You're a vampire," Trillius chimed in awe.

"Forgive—" Elsbeth began, but Romann held up his hand to stop her.

"And what is your name?" he asked. He kneeled down as if talking to a child.

The gnome answered tremulously, "My name is Trillius."

"Ah, yes, of course. Well little-one, since we are being candid, I will call you *Snack*." Romann lifted his lip slightly to reveal one of his fangs while emphasizing his last word. Trillius back peddled away and clung to El'Korr. The dwarf was pleased, as he knew this encounter would keep the gnome on board the ship.

Romann stood and reached into his hat. A light glow shone out from the brim of the magical item as he pulled out a long-stemmed red rose, "From one captain to another." He gave it to Elsbeth. She took it, brought it to her nose, and smelled the fragrant flower.

He then motioned toward his ship and offered, "I would like to dine with you and the elves this evening aboard *The Rose*," he hesitated a moment, then added, "unless of course your dwarvenkind would like to join us as well."

El'Korr spoke up, "We appreciate your invitation, but my bodyguard and I have urgent matters to attend to this evening, and plan to stay aboard."

"But of course, I will accept," Elsbeth responded with a smile. She looked to Xan and Raina's nods, adding, "We look forward to it."

"As do I." And with that, he suddenly evaporated into a white swirling mist and vanished.

Trillius began to breathe heavily, and then with excitement called for Rozelle.

"What is it?" she responded.

"Do you know what this means," he said, still gasping for air.

"What?"

"I just met a vampire and lived to tell about it."

"Oh, brother," she began to walk away.

"My reputation is going to soar! Woo-hoo!"

El'Korr pointed his finger in Trillius's face, "Listen here, Gnome-skull, you are to stay on this ship or I will hand deliver you to that vamp myself."

Trillius fearfully smirked and then gulped.

Although Pirate's Belly appeared to be cloaked in perpetual night due to the lack of natural light allowed within the confines of the massive cavern, even during the midday sun, it was quite apparent that the evening had arrived. The Alley became much louder as raucous men partied with bottles of booze in one hand and flirting bar maidens in the other. Crewmen moved in packs and clashes between rivals occurred frequently. Music echoed out of the many taverns and increased in volume each time a door swung open.

Raina and Xan accompanied Captain Elsbeth to Romann's ship, looming across the dock from them, while the other heroes remained on board *A Pinch of Luck*, with plans to finish inventory, send runners out for final supplies, and then enjoy an evening of drinking. Being in such a harbor meant everyone's favorites were readily available—a rare treat.

As they walked, Raina commented, "Vampires usually isolate themselves. I'm curious how he came to be the captain of a ship, and furthermore the leader of Pirate's Belly."

Elsbeth replied, "I apologize for not preparing you. Romann de Beaux is a different individual. Before he transformed he was a great hero of these oceans, and actually fought against the pirates as a military patrol ship for the West Horn King. He adventured with a group called the Company of the Rose—saving damsels in distress, helping the less fortunate, and killing evil creatures of the realm—until he was betrayed."

"So it is revenge he seeks?" Xan stated.

"That is uncertain; he is indeed a private individual, but I do know he enjoys his solitude on the ocean aboard his ship. Pirate's Belly is a place he can gather information and keep track of his enemies, though he has few."

Suddenly, a gurgled scream jolted them from their discourse. They watched as a group of sailors from the Alley threw a corpse into the water below, yelling pirate obscenities and spitting at it, "Suck blow-hole, Deemmot!"

Raina brought everyone's attention back to their discussion, "And how did you meet Romann de Beaux?"

"Anyone who has a ship will eventually meet him. As it turns out, he fancies elves."

"Hopefully not because of our blood," Xan's face soured a bit.

"No, not because of that, otherwise, I would not be here. He connects with our kind because of our natural longevity and our ability to carry a meaningful conversation. It's hard for a vampire to have many friends when his soul is eternally damned, and the humans he knows tend to live less than a century."

"Dwarves live long as well, why only elves?" Raina questioned.

"I believe it is the candor and roughness of their kind that deters him from any real friendship. He has a great deal of respect for their race, though his intensified sense of smell makes it hard for him to be around anyone who has enjoyed dwarven mead, even if it has been awhile since their last taste."

Xan added, "It might be something else he is smelling."

They chuckled as they arrived at *The Rose* and were escorted to Romann's private cabin. Candle sconces hung on the dark mahogany walls. Paintings depicting ghost ships on dark seas hung between the sconces. There was no bed in his quarters; he spent his sleepless nights moving silently and watchfully about his ship. This night, an ornate, coal-colored pearl table with a red rose emblazoned on the top was their dining destination. Romman sat in a leather chair at the head. His silky, sandy-blonde hair draped perfectly down to his shoulders. Three other chairs surrounded the dining table. Platters of grapes and cheeses sat on top with uncorked bottles and golden goblets. The sweet aroma of Elven wine brought back intense memories of Raina and Xan's gatherings in the High Elven courts in the days of old.

Romann stood as they entered, "Welcome. Please come in and sit."

"Thank you for having us, Captain," Raina said.

"Would you care for some wine?"

"Why, yes. We couldn't pass up Elven wine." Raina reached for a bottle but before she could grab hold, it suddenly levitated and poured in her chalice on its own.

"I prefer unseen servants, to keep our privacy. A handy spell that I like to conjure. I'm sure you can relate, mistress Raina?"

"Of course," she smiled.

The wine bottle moved magically along the table, pouring its red liquid into one goblet and then the next. A second bottle, different than the first, poured a substance, thicker in viscosity, into Romann's chalice, and only his.

"I'd like to propose a toast." Everyone raised their golden, gem encrusted, goblets. "To future endeavors and new friendships." As he drank, his eyes closed and his lids fluttered in delight of his drink.

Elsbeth asked, "How have the seas been treating you?"

"Ah, small talk. How quaint, but I would like to hear about the Pearl of the Deep, and your quest for it."

Xan coughed a little bit. Raina set her drink back on the table and responded, "Have you heard of the Dragon God?"

"Oh, that sounds menacing. Do tell; I love a good story." His eyes glowed with intrigue.

Rozelle emerged from the deck below and spotted El'Korr, Rondee, and Lufra admiring the construction of the pirate's cove.

"Have any of you seen Trillius?" she asked.

El'Korr turned and responded, "I'm sure he is around here somewhere."

"I've looked, and now I'm a little concerned."

"He wouldn't leave the ship, not with that vampire's threat lingering." He paused, "Or would he?"

"My guess is he went in there." She pointed to the Alley.

"Damn that infernal gnome," El'Korr said through gritted teeth. "C'mon, we need to go get him."

Trillius moved easily within the shadows of the street. Drunken pirates gathered near several fire pits, singing songs with their arms draped around cackling women. Others stumbled in and out of the many taverns that adorned the Alley. He had to pick the right establishment as this place was a one-stop-shop. After several minutes of studying, it came down to two: the Fish Head or the Peg Leg.

"Such original names for pirates," Trillius mocked under his breath. An eruption of cheers came from the Fish Head. "That's the place."

He weaved through the throngs of humans dressed in an assortment of non-matching clothing, pick-pocketing a few of the drunken humans as he waded deeper into the tavern. Most of them didn't notice the three-foot gnome; the ones that did couldn't believe what their scar-covered, inebriated eyes were seeing. Trillius quickly discovered his target—the high-rollers table of Pirate's Belly. He watched them play a few hands to understand the game they called Bottoms Up. Then he jingled his leather pouch to check that he had enough. It would do.

Four colorful individuals sat at the table holding cards. To Trillius' right was Scurvy Joe, a bony pirate with a bright red bandana covering his head and a skinny body that didn't match his scratchy voice. The second at the table was called Tigg. He had multiple earrings in both ears and a large silver nose-ring. His dark head of long hair mingled with his wooly back hair that seemed to sprout out from behind his leather vest. The third was known as Patch. A faded seashell tied with hide straps around his head covered his left eye. His brown hair and short stubble beard reminded Trillius of an illustrated pirate out of a book he'd once seen as a child. The last was the largest of the group. He was called Big Jack. His head was shaved, and a scar ran down the left side of his face, from above the eye to the lower jaw. He chewed on tobacco, spitting the sickening spittle into a mug on the table.

Trillius made his way toward them; bolstering his confidence, he thought, *"You can do this, Trillius. You just met a vampire."* The four men had just finished a hand. They glared at the approaching gnome.

The shouts and laughter of the crowd dwindled as Trillius asked, "Is there room for one more?" He then jingled the coins and set his money pouch on the table, which was of such a height that he could just barely peer over.

"I don't be seein any harm in havin one more at th'table," Big Jack said in a deep voice.

The gnome climbed onto a chair and smiled at each of them, his face barely showing above the table surface. Several bystanders from the gathered crowd started laughing at him openly. A barmaid from somewhere shouted, "What are you sniffin at with that nose?" This caused a huge outburst of laughter. Trillius felt a sudden chill crawl up his spine at the thought of what kind of disease he would catch staying too long here.

"I'm here to learn how to play cards," Trillius said.

Big Jack chuckled, "Oh, ye'll be learnin how t'lose at playin cards t'night, little-one."

Trillius' gold and silver pieces slowly dwindled as he lost one game after the other.

Scurvy Joe asked in a raspy voice, "You ready t'cough up th'rest o'yer coin an hand't over t'me, ya lilly livered gnome?"

"I think I'm ready for a comeback and to teach you boys about gnome-economics."

Tigg scowled, "nome what?"

"Nevermind. It is beyond your great intelligence."

Patch slapped Tigg on the back and guffawed, "I think he just insulted ye, ye ol sea dog."

Tigg spun around pointed a long finger at Patch and growled, "Don't ye be touchin me again, one-eye."

While the others were distracted, Trillius slid his dexterous hand into Big Jack's belt pouch and lifted a small, smooth, spherical object. He kept it in his clasped fist as he said simply, "I just hope none of you is cheating me."

With that, the drunken pirates eyed one another and leered at the largest pile of money, currently held by Big Jack. Trillius, who had positioned himself to sit between Big Jack and Tigg, hopped down from his chair, "I'm gonna get a drink. Would you boys care for another?" Trillius made it over to Scurvy Joe who was on the other side of the table when Big Jack barked, "Get aft in yer chair gnome. No one leaves th'table. We be havin wenches t'shag yer drinks."

"Hey, my stack of money looks a little shorter!" Trillius pointed to his spot across the table.

All the players turned their heads to look and while they were distracted, Trillius planted the small pawned object, which he noticed was a pearl, into Scurvy Joe's pocket.

"No one has touched yer coin. Now get aft in yer seat!" Big Jack ordered.

Trillius quickly lifted his hands in surrender and walked back, "Fine."

"Now deal the cards, Tigg!" Patch demanded loudly.

The game resumed and Trillius won the next several hands, until his pile of coins was the largest on the table.

More mugs of grog were delivered and the tension rose.

In the next round, Trillius delivered a punishing blow to Patch and Tigg. He knocked them out of the game. However, as he reached to rake in his winnings, Patch grabbed his wrist, "I smell a cheatin' rat."

"You're crazy, gnomes don't cheat, I won fair and square. Though I did see someone take something at this table."

Patch released his grip, everyone eyed each other suspiciously. Trillius scooped his winnings into his pouch as he knew the finale was on its way.

"Which one, gnome?" Scurvy Joe asked.

How appropriate that it was him, he thought. Trillius responded, "Why don't *you* tell us."

"What? I don't know what ye be talkin about."

"You might want to check his pockets."

Scurvy Joe searched himself until he pulled forth the pearl. He stared at it in shock.

Big Jack jumped to his feet shoving his chair out into the crowd of onlookers. He pointed at Scurvy Joe and shouted, "Hey, that be me lucky pearl."

Scurvy Joe was flustered, he stammered, "No, Big Jack, I be hornswaggled."

Scurvy Joe's plea fell on deaf ears. Big Jack tossed the table aside; mugs of back-washed Grog flew into spectating pirates and cards flipped in all directions. He smashed his fist into Scurvy Joe's jaw, cracking the bone. Drunken pirates scrambled to sweep up the coins rolling around the floor from the upturned table, which caused more skirmishes to break out. Trillius slinked his small body through the jumbled mess of humans with his heavy, loot-filled sack in tow.

Young Lufra studied the long line of taverns lining the Alley, turned to El'Korr and asked, "What are we waiting for?"

"It's too risky to go poking around each of these joints looking for the pipsqueak."

Rozelle was concerned, "But what if he's in danger?"

"That gnome is a danger to himself. It's just a matter of time before he alerts us to his whereabouts."

Suddenly, from a tavern midway down the Alley, they heard hoots and hollers of the celebrants change abruptly to screams and grunts. Pirates and women clamored through windows and doors to escape the action inside the establishment, while other pirates fought their way inside to join the brawl.

"He's in there. I can feel it in my dwarven bones."

They rushed to the Fish Head tavern, where they heard glass being smashed inside. A chair flew out an open window and crashed into the street.

"You two stay out here while Rondee and I head in. Keep an eye open for Mister Guinea-sack."

The powerful fighters, El'Korr and Rondee, ran into the tavern slamming their fists into bloated guts and whiskered jaws; tossing pirates around like sacks of grain.

Trillius escaped through a side window of the tavern and hid in the shadows outside. He looked up and down the Alley and instantly spotted Lufra and Rozelle, focused on the bar, standing in the street. He easily snuck up behind them.

"You guys out for a leisurely stroll this fine evening?" asked Trillius.

Both of them jumped and turned around. Lufra turned pale.

Rozelle screeched, "Trillius! I'm gonna kill you."

"Wow, what seems to be the problem here?" he gazed at the huge brawl.

"As if you don't know," Rozelle mocked.

"Me? Why would I have anything to do with pirates fighting in a bar? It's not like this isn't normal for their kind. This probably happens nightly here. Boy, I would hate to be in there right now."

"El'Korr and Rondee are inside looking for you," Lufra exclaimed.

"Now why would they go and do a silly thing like that?"

"Cause maybe they care about you," Rozelle snapped.

"Me? I will tell you why they went in there. It is because dwarves and pirates have the same spirit—always looking for the next fight. It's certainly not my fault."

Rozelle turned and took a step toward the tavern. She closed her eyes and instantly transformed into a large black bear.

"Rozelle! No! Don't go in there!" Trillius yelled.

It was too late, the black bear charged inside the chaotic melee and roared. Shocked pirates and barmaids whirled in their tracks, facing the sound. Their eyes opened wide when the bear rose on its hind legs; the massive snarling beast clawed the air. Half-cocked fists froze and mouths dropped open at what loomed before them. Female screams were stifled in clasped throats. Concluding it was not a figment of their imagination, chairs and tables were pushed aside and overturned as terrified patrons scrambled out of the tavern.

El'Korr and Rondee emerged. They were battered and bruised. Blood trickled out of Rondee's nose and El'Korr's left eye was swollen shut.

"Nice one, Druid," El'Korr said while embracing Rondee with one arm around his neck.

They hobbled out into the street with Rozelle lumbering behind them. Trillius and Lufra stood outside waiting.

"Two things, Gnome. First, thank you," El'Korr stated with a grin.

"Really?" Trillius responded nervously.

"Yes, Rondee and I haven't had a bar-fight like that for quite some time. It reminded us of our younger years."

"Great, you're welcome, I guess."

"Second," El'Korr's tone became serious, "you will be giving all that money to Captain Elsbeth as your fee for stowing away on her ship."

"C'mon! That's not fair. I worked hard to get that money."

Everyone glared angrily at Trillius.

"Fine! I'll do it."

El'Korr nudged Trillius to start walking back to the ship.

Trillius turned toward them with his hands up, "Hey, it's still early guys," he pleaded.

"Not a chance Gnome, now move it before my fist uses your nose as a punching bag."

12

Bad Dreams

The heroes cautiously began to ascend the ancient stairway that led deeper and higher into the mountain. Abawken took the lead followed by Dulgin, then the ordakians. Suddenly, the roar of grinding stone echoed around them. They looked back down the stairs and saw the cliff wall come together, blocking the entrance and sealing out the light.

"No turning back now," Bridazak commented.

A soft glow permeated from the rock itself as they continued their climb deeper into the tunnel. The air was stale and the scent of wet granite increased the further they traversed.

"The tale of the frost dwarves says that they were the first of the dwarves to exist. Legends say that they are the creators of all the snow for the entire realm of Ruauck-El," Dulgin's voice spoke matter of fact and it echoed a calming effect on the heroes. "The ancient name for this place was actually Deegosh Sond, which simply means, 'white shield.' Now though, it's just Te Sond."

"Are frost dwarves friendly?" Spilf asked.

Dulgin turned and smiled, "Of course, just look at me, I'm friendly." His scowl then returned and he raised the right side of his upper lip.

In an attempt to keep his friend's courage up, Bridazak said, "Don't worry Spilf, I am sure they will greet us with open arms."

"Yeah, a festival in your honor awaits, little-ones," Dulgin teased as he continued his way up, "and dwarven ale, let's not forget."

"Yeah, how can we forget that gem, Dulgin?" Spilf turned and whispered to Bridazak, "How would my parents find their way, with what we just went through? It seems unlikely they would have made it this far."

"We must continue to have hope, my friend," Bridazak placed his hand onto Spilf's shoulder. "Have any of our steps led us to a dead end yet? Everywhere we've gone we've found another clue. Let's focus on where this path takes us."

Spilf nodded and grinned his appreciation of Bridazak's comforting words and then they continued.

They climbed what seemed to be an endless stairway, each step hand chiseled by the Dwarves. All breathed heavily as they increased in altitude; they gasped at the thin air as they slogged along, but finally Spilf wheezed and began to slow.

Dulgin turned and said, "Should I start calling you 'Wheezy' now?"

Spilf glared at his friend, but was unable to respond as he leaned his back against the rugged wall and bent over, breathing hard, steadying himself with his hands on his knees.

Bridazak said, "Let's rest to catch our breath."

Dulgin turned away and grumbled, clearly not wanting to stop, but knew he couldn't convince the daks otherwise.

Abawken shuffled down to Spilf's step, knelt, and offered, "Master Spilf, it would be wise to keep moving until we find a suitable place to rest. Climb onto my back."

Spilf looked to Bridazak, who nodded, and then he obliged the human and climbed aboard, wrapping his arms around his neck. Dulgin raised an eyebrow as Abawken passed by and then followed.

Suddenly, Dulgin turned to face Bridazak, "Don't even ask. No free rides on my back."

The halfling smiled and then reached for his coin pouch, "How much, then?"

Dulgin shook his head, "I'm not liking you right now." He then turned and stomped up the steps, climbing to catch up to Abawken.

Sweat dripped from their brows. Another hour elapsed of the hike into the mountain when they finally reached a flat chamber opening. The ceiling of the cavern scaled beyond sight, and on the opposite side was an entrance to another tunnel. A cold breeze rushed out from the new passageway. Blue icy tendrils wrapped themselves around the edges of the granite opening as if gripping the walls and trying to break out from within.

"There's a pile of wood over here and a burnt out campfire," Spilf pointed.

Abawken investigated the black soot of the long burned out fire, "It's old. No one has been here for quite some time."

"It's a frost dwarf sentry post, but they wouldn't need a fire. This wood came from someone else."

"Where are the sentries?" Bridazak asked.

"I don't know, why do you keep asking me?"

"Maybe cause you're a dwarf. Ever think of that?" Spilf quipped.

Dulgin pointed his finger, "Shut it, Stubby!"

"Let's rest for the night," Abawken suggested.

Spilf sighed in relief and plopped to the ground.

"Fine, I'll take first guard shift," Dulgin grunted. He threw his back-pack next to the wood. "Make yourself useful Stubby, and make a fire."

"Why me?"

"You found the wood, that's why. Unless you want to check out the tunnel with Abawken to make sure it is critterless."

Spilf looked at the imposing exit across from them, then said, "I'll make a fire."

Abawken wandered the dunes on the outskirts of his home in the east, under the relentless afternoon sun. The sand shifted under his steps. He knew better than to be distracted, but his mind was elsewhere. He didn't notice the tremors in the dunes behind him, or the slight hum of the desert monster Beltothi, the digging mouth filled with teeth and tentacles, moving slowly and methodically underground, sensing the vibrations of its next victim.

He took a deep breath. These daily solitary walks were not providing him the answers he needed to the problems waiting for him within the city walls. "Perhaps tomorrow," he sighed and turned, resigning himself to head back.

He noticed a moment before it surfaced; far too late to escape—his leg was quickly caught within the Beltothi's grasp. He already felt the strength of the squeezing arm, barely visible as it blended so perfectly. He looked frantically for his scimitar but it was not in sight. He bent toward the creature, trying to pry the arm away, but with no effect. It tightened its grip and slid further up his leg, sliding him closer to the gaping maw. He could see the sharp, criss-crossed teeth lining the wide opening in the sand. More tentacles slithered out and reached toward him.

Seconds remained before the human fighter would be consumed. Abawken looked around and noticed he was surrounded by large crested dunes. He knew in his mind that he would never travel to the basin of the hills knowing full well the Beltothi lurked in such places. *"This doesn't seem right,"* he thought.

Just then he spotted the silhouette of a desert nomad, cloak fluttering in the arid breeze, face wrapped, only revealing darkened eyes.

"Help me!" Abawken yelled, but the figure did not move.

He heard the sand cascading down inside the mouth of the creature as he was pulled to the edge. Abawken dug his heels into the hardened carapace lip, but felt sure his legs would snap from the tremendous strength of the Beltothi.

He looked back toward the figure, but the mysterious nomad was gone. His leg buckled and he felt the rising heat of his muscles tearing in his legs under the extreme pressure. The smell of death seeped into his skin as the mouth belched and gurgled.

Suddenly, the Beltothi was gone, and he lay safe atop the sand surface again. *"Sand Dragon must have scared it off,"* he thought, still dazed.

Abawken gripped his injured leg with his hands and then began to crawl away. As he turned toward his home, he bumped into the wrapped leather boots of the nomad he had seen earlier. He looked up, but the sun overhead caused him to squint and he could only see the halo of light around the cloaked figure.

"Who are you?"

A female voice responded, "I'm the hunter."

"There is a Sand Dragon nearby," Abawken warned, his mouth dry.

"No, there is not."

"You created the sound to scare the Beltothi?" he surmised.

"I'm the hunter."

"You hunt the Beltothi?"

"You assume much, my dear Abawken."

"How do you know my name?" he asked, struggling to stand. He was more terrified now than he had been in the jaws of the Beltothi a moment ago. Just then, the smell of Lilac infiltrated his nostrils and the sudden realization hit his face. "Devana."

"That never gets old," she said, "I like the way you say my name."

Abawken stood, "Devana, why do you torture me like this?"

"Oh, is that what I am doing?"

"You are a dream witch, nothing more."

"It is a shame that is all you think of me."

"You can't have it, Devana."

"You know it doesn't belong to you," she retaliated.

"It chose me."

She paused and smiled, "I would hate for any of your band of misfits to get hurt."

"Keep them out of this," he bit back.

"Where are you and these friends of yours going anyway?"

He reluctantly responded, "We are looking for Master Spilfer's parents."

"Oh, another noble quest for the famous Abawken," she mocked.

"Let me finish this journey, and then we can talk, Devana."

"I have my deadlines, but I have been quite entertained with you and your friends, plus I have missed our rendezvous of late. You do have some time remaining, but I cannot guarantee you will be able to finish, and you know I always catch my prey. It would make things a great deal easier if you simply relinquish what I'm hunting."

"Like I said, it chose me. I cannot give you what is not my right to give."

Devana's head tilted sideways and she grinned, "You have changed, Abawken. What happened to you?"

"Why have you chosen this life, Devana?" he countered.

"This life chose me and you know it."

"When we were kids, we talked about our future—"

"A future?" she cut him off. "With a former slave girl? What would that be? Come now, we were children with wild dreams."

"Devana, I still believe in you."

"So easy for you to say, but we've each made our choices."

"We saw things differently, and my father—"

She cut him off again, "Has paid me well to track you and retrieve his treasure."

"I could have never imagined what you have become, Devana."

"There is one thing certain in life, my dear Abawken, and that is death, nothing else. I have chosen to embrace it and work alongside of it. Relax, I *try* to make it as painless as possible for most."

Abawken looked away from her, but Devana compelled him to step closer to her. He tried to resist, but just like the world and creatures she had created, it felt outside his control. She unwrapped the linen around her face to reveal her smooth and perfect skin. Her bronze hair cascaded down below her shoulders and her chestnut colored eyes penetrated his very soul. He tried to look away but his will was overrun.

Without touching him, she abruptly pushed him away, "Remember what I said. Your time is running out."

Abawken awoke next to the dying embers of their fire. Dulgin poked at them, sending tiny sparks into the air. Bridazak and Spilf were asleep on the other side of the pit.

"Is it my turn to guard, Master Dulgin?" the human asked as he sat upright.

"Who is she?" the Dwarf asked while keeping his gaze fixed on the fire.

"I am not sure what you are speaking of."

"She broke your heart? Someone you left behind back home perhaps?"

"Just another bad dream, Master Dwarf."

"I understand. You miss this person." Dulgin continued to poke at the fire.

"She is not the one that I miss," the human whispered. His thoughts were no longer with the hopes of his past, but with the hopes of his future.

"Well, I'm quite aware of these so called *bad dreams* of yours, and won't make a second mistake of trying to wake you like before. Surprised you didn't wake Bridazak and Stubby over there."

"Past demons that haunt me still," Abawken responded.

"Oh, Dwarves call them ex-wives."

"You had a wife?"

"Don't be tryin to change the subject Huey, but no, I have not, just never was the settling down type, and never found the one with the right amount of facial hair."

Abawken chuckled, "Your females are bearded?"

"Of course. Most of our beard contests are won by the women. The pride they bring to our race warms my heart. Now why don't you tell me about what *chose* you," Dulgin's face turned serious and he glared at Abawken.

The human locked eyes with him and understood it was futile to dissuade the determined dwarf. "My sword. It chose me."

"Now you have my attention. Go on."

"The Sword of the Elements has an intelligent soul held within. It chooses its wielder."

"So where does this woman come into play?"

"Her name is Devana. We grew up together, but something changed along the way, and she chose a different path in life. She has been hired by my father to bring the sword back to Zoar. This sword has great meaning where I come from and has been only in the hands of Kings."

"Kings? Guess your sword had a change of heart then," Dulgin scoffed.

Abawken waited silently, holding his stare with his dwarven friend. Dulgin caught his look and saw the intensity in his eyes. "Wait, are you telling me you are of royal blood?"

"Yes, my father is the King of Zoar to the far east beyond the Horn Kings of your region. However, my call in life is not there, but here, with you."

"Yeah, I understand, but that makes you a Prince. Well, this changes things."

"How so, Master Dulgin? I am still the same man."

"Now, I need to be calling you Princey." They both chuckled softly so as not to wake the others.

Unbeknownst to them, Bridazak was awake, and had overheard the entire conversation. Their first adventure together had united the group of travelers to one another forever, though many still carried their hidden secrets. It was nice to hear Abawken open up, and especially with Dulgin. Bridazak would keep this information to himself and let the two of them bond a bit closer, but he would also be looking out for this Devana. Her name was not unknown to him, and those who lived and breathed the underground life, as he once had, all knew it well—the name of a hired assassin.

13

The Third Element

Veric was concerned. "The devling should have reported in by now." Daysho folded his arms across his chest, "I told you, you should have sent me instead."

"Then I would have been here telling my devling that Daysho should have reported in by now," Veric snapped.

"I can tell you're upset, Wizard, but you are in good company."

"How so, Assassin?" Veric emphasized Daysho's title mockingly.

The hooded killer smirked, "My contacts run deep, and I have word of your missing ship."

"Well done. Where is it?"

"The deeper I go with my contacts, the deeper you will have to go in your coffers."

"You people. You walk in delicate matters. I could destroy you where you stand, Daysho."

"If word went out of your hasty reaction, then my network would be a formidable enemy. It would not be wise to turn your back on the Guild."

Each man stared down the other. The wizard desperately needed the information his hired assassin had garnered.

Veric reluctantly said, "My apologies. You can understand my irritation."

Daysho smiled, his perfect set of white teeth glowing under the veil of darkness inside his cowl. "Of course," he mocked.

"Where is *A Pinch of Luck* located?"

"They left Pirate's Belly yesterday, and sailed into the Whispering Sea."

"Is that it? That's all you have?"

"That I give you for free, but what I have next will cost you dearly, rest assured."

"Fine, name your price, Thief," Veric snarled, "I'm not used to having my pockets cleaned out as I stand by and watch."

Daysho ignored the insult. "I was informed that they are retrieving an item."

"Yes, we know, the blue stone."

"Nay, not the blue stone. The Pearl of the Deep."

"A pearl? Why?"

"Supposedly, it is one of the elements required to destroy the Dragon Stones."

Veric cupped his hand around his chin, "Raina is craftier than I thought. Did they mention the blue stone?"

"Nay, there was no mention of it, only the pearl."

"Interesting. Yasooma's compass is leading them to his sunken ship, but they aren't aware that is the location of the fifth stone as well."

"That is my contact's understanding."

"If she doesn't retrieve the stone, then we have to. Are you able to—"

Daysho interrupted, "Already done, a ship sails in their wake as we speak."

Veric's eyes narrowed, "You are very good at what you do Daysho, and worth every coin." He grinned devilishly.

Whitecaps dotted the surface of the ocean as small waves broke. Howling wind filled the mighty sails of the four masted ship. Despite the heavy seas the two days since departing Pirate's Belly, the galleon pushed its way forward to its destination.

Captain Elsbeth shouted over the roaring wind, "We are close."

"Are you well, Elsbeth?" Raina asked.

"Yes. I remain apprehensive about going back."

"I understand, but this time it will be different."

Suddenly, the ship groaned to a stop; an unknown force below the surface of the water held the galleon frozen in place; all aboard stumbled about as the ship lurched and became stuck, in spite of the continued high winds whipping all around them.

Captain Elsbeth shouted, "Lower the sails." She peered over the side, "Raina, we are here."

The heroes were ready. They knew the mystery of Yasooma's ship, from all those centuries ago, was about to be revealed.

Skath and Myers gathered the crew. Captain Elsbeth stood on the upper section accompanied by the tortuous creaks and groans of her ship, and announced, "Men, we have travelled the Great Illustrya Ocean for many years together and we will continue to do so. It is not by chance we have come to this place. I have brought several passengers aboard, as you know. Remain vigilant during whatever may happen and follow the commands of your leaders. With my permission, Mistress Raina will address you."

Raina nodded and stepped forward, "I have brought you to this place not to fail, but to succeed on a great quest. There is a ship below us that holds items that will help us in destroying a great evil attempting to enter and overtake our realm. King Manasseh was the most powerful Horn King, and yet he has fallen by the grace of God, at our hands. With the same hands and the same grace, we will protect this ship."

At that moment, the swirling water spun forcefully around the galleon's hull, however, the vessel remained fixed.

"We're stuck in the middle of some kind of whirlpool," the captain cried. She shouted, "Men, weapons ready!" Elsbeth turned to Raina, "It's happening just like before!"

"I won't let anything happen to your ship," Raina responded.

"This had better work. I don't want a repeat."

Suddenly, the ship lurched and plopped lower in the water with a dull thump, causing all aboard to stumble, some grabbing on to each other to remain standing.

Many cried, "She's going down!"

Raina continued, "Everyone, I will protect the ship by keeping the sea at bay, but it won't keep anything else from coming in or leaving. Stay at the ready and kill anything that boards."

She turned back to her comrades. "Xan and Lufra will retrieve the items aboard *The Wave Rider*, El'Korr and Rondee will protect me from being disturbed. I will be in a casting trance, producing a large enough pocket of air to surround the ship. Once you have secured the items and returned, I will bring us back to the surface."

"What about us? We can help," Rozelle said.

"We can?" Trillius questioned.

Raina smiled, "Of course, you both may do what you can to help where needed," she said as she descended to the main deck, positioning herself with her back to the sterncastle for protection. El'Korr and Rondee took their places in front of her.

Xan weaved his arms in and out while quickly reciting a small incantation. The elf finished his spell and touched each of his comrades, including the gnomes, "This will grant you the power to breathe underwater." Concerned, several eyebrows rose. "Just in case," he shrugged.

Raina began her arcane invocation. Her voice carried a tone of power that came from deep within her soul. A shimmering force-field wall magically circled the perimeter of *A Pinch of Luck*. It gave off a hum and the crew backed away in fear.

Within minutes the mighty galley plunged below the surface. The water was held back by the power of Raina's protective shell, as she concentrated to keep the barrier in place.

The priest Anders produced a mystical blue light that hovered above like a flare as they immersed into the darkened sea. Swords were drawn from scabbards as the crew prepared for the unknown. Deeper and deeper the supernatural force dragged them. Periodically, crew would call out, alerting all to some movement in the dark-blue water.

The vessel finally came to rest, now hundreds of feet below. In an instant, several hideous creatures burst through the wall of water and boarded the ship, each wielding a trident. One struck a crew member with its weapon. The hapless man screamed and fell dead. Several sailors cried, "Kelpies!" Instantly, every man engaged the short, hairless, green-skinned intruders. Their bulbous white eyes turned in multiple directions, giving them a tactical advantage, but their webbed clawed hands and feet, designed for water, struggled on the deck of the ship, evening the odds.

Xan tugged on Lufra's shirt, "You ready?"

"What do you think is out there?"

"You can do this, Lufra. Your family's curse was lifted because of you, so whatever is out there is, I promise, no match for the fearless Lufra," Xan smiled.

Lufra nodded and followed his mentor into the wall of cold water that surrounded them.

Behind them, Rozelle directed her druidical spell at a group of kelpies, turning their tridents into harmless seaweed, which quickly entangled them.

Crewmen plunged cutlasses into the green skin of the entrapped creatures, and dark brown blood sloshed out onto the wooden beams.

Trillius patted Rozelle on the back and smiled at her magical prowess. "I love your style."

"I know," she winked and then prepared for another group of Kelpies flopping to the deck.

Suddenly, a mysterious voice clouded Trillius' mind, *"Trillius. Come to me."* The tone was haunting and hollow, like someone calling to him from a great distance. Two more kelpies came through and landed next to the gnomes, breaking him from his focus on the strange calling. Trillius hopped back behind Rozelle as she deftly responded with another incantation. Sharp quills were produced out of thin air and hovered before her face. She blew on them and they launched at the kelpies who were readying their tridents to attack. Each of them were impaled with the tiny spikes and shrieked in pain. More of the shipmates stabbed to finish them off.

"Trillius, I know you can hear me. I am trapped inside the kelpie treasure room. Rescue me and the riches are yours."

Trillius felt compelled by his own greed and the power of the mysterious voice to leave the ship. Because Rozelle was thoroughly engrossed in combat, he easily moved closer to the edge and dove through the barrier of water without being seen.

Meanwhile, El'Korr and Rondee, with their devastating magical hammers, protected Raina from the boarding kelpies. The Dwarven King's loyal bodyguard caught a glimpse of the shadow of a larger opponent and then watched it crash through the wall of water and send El'Korr to the deck. The sea monster was the size of a hill giant. Its bulbous head writhed with eight-foot long tentacles and its slimy ash colored skin gleamed from its webbed feet to the top. It raised a pike-like weapon high to bare down on the king.

"Me Malehk!" Rondee shouted with urgency, as the wild magic contained within his being burst forth. As he spun in circles, blades of various lengths sprouted all over his body. The tornado of steel launched at the hybrid giant before it could strike El'Korr. Blood canvassed the area as the creature was shredded at the knees down. The visceral blood sprayed Raina as well, but she continued to remain in her stasis of concentration. Rondee continued to spin out of control, hitting multiple targets of new kelpies who dared to come aboard, while shipmates dodged out of the way. El'Korr came to his feet, hammer in hand, ready for battle. Rondee slowed, and the distinct sound of blades sliding back into their sheaths resonated. The wild dwarf was dazed and tried to hold his head from spinning. El'Korr threw his hammer and crushed in the side of a kelpie's temple and then placed a reassuring hand on Rondee's shoulder.

"Thek tu, my friend," said El'Korr.

Rondee revealed his grotesque yellow teeth, and then smashed an incoming kelpie with his enlarged golden hammer, crushing its cartilage. Blood continued to drip off each of their weapons and armor. They both shouted battle cries of victory in unison.

Suddenly, swarms of the sea creatures arrived, and the deck became a frenzy. Captain Elsbeth and her commanders were valiantly fighting back while Anders made his way to the wounded, healing them with the magic of his clerical spells. Urlin Thoom, the ship's young wizard, blasted kelpies with his precision force missiles. Sounds of clashing steel and the screams of the wounded echoed all around them.

Meanwhile, after leaving the galleon, Xan and Lufra instantly spotted what had dragged the ship below the surface of the sea. An enormous, barnacle-covered cyclops, the size of three galleys, stood statue-like on the ocean's floor, holding *A Pinch of Luck* firmly in place between several huge claws. Xan knew the powerful sea cyclops were once numerous in the Illustrya Ocean, but he didn't realize any were left. This one had clearly been transformed into some kind of automaton in possession of the kelpies, and no longer truly alive. Massive chains held the legendary beast, but were rusted and nonfunctioning, clearly from a long-past era. Ranks of kelpies were commanding the natural magic occurring within the monstrosity in their unique underwater language. Other ships littered the seafloor, evidence that this location, considered cursed to those familiar with it, had been under the tyranny of the kelpies and their merciless ways for a very long time. Xan and Lufra dove deeper until they were below the hull of the vessel, free of any pursuit by the kelpies.

Glowing seaweed illuminated the bottom of the ocean floor where rock spires extended upward in varying heights. Overwhelming numbers of kelpies surged from the mouths of small caves. The enslaved leviathan's action of capturing the vessel had alerted the underwater hive, which massed in hopes of looting the galleon before it even hit the bottom. Lufra followed closely behind the elf, carefully avoiding another school of kelpies on their way to attack the ship they left behind.

Xan held Yasooma's compass, which pointed the way to *The Wave Rider*. The old sunken ship was rotted and broken in half, crusted with barnacles and sea creatures, and partially buried behind a thick crop of the gleaming seaweed. Xan and Lufra glided toward the ancient icon.

They swam past the tallest mast and the crow's nest high above the deck. Green vines of ocean plantain weaved and bobbed through the caging. Lufra recoiled when he saw a skull peeking through the ocean greenery, with scores of tiny white crabs filling the empty eye sockets.

The elf grabbed hold of the young boy's hand to calm him, and together they descended to the deck, making their way to the captain's quarters, bubbles of released air streaming behind them.

Before opening the door, Xan, still apprehensive, motioned for Lufra to wait where he was. He then pulled the cabin door open. Immediately, skeletal hands on bony arms lunged from the room and grabbed the elf, pulling him into the cabin.

Without pause, Lufra drew the magic sabre gifted to him from the Guardian, and swam quickly after his friend. Inside, the remains of many fallen crewmen grappled Xan; holding his legs and arms. A dozen others brandishing rusted, broken cutlasses were about to strike, but turned at Lufra's entrance, ready to attack him instead. Captain Yasooma's blade came to life as the glowing sword pulsated in the boy's hand. The waves of light encompassed the skeletons, and they abruptly stopped their hostile actions. Each stood at attention, facing the young boy. They released their hold on Xan and he swam to Lufra's side, showing a puzzled expression at the undead's apparent change of heart.

All of a sudden, Lufra became aware of a male voice speaking in his mind. *"Captain, we have waited for your return as instructed; we have kept your belongings safe."*

Lufra glanced at Xan and knew instantly that he had not heard the voice as he had. He tried to respond within his mind and thought, *"Thank you. May I have my items now?"*

There was no reply from the phantom voice within his mind, however, one skeleton nodded, giving a signal, which several of the undead responded to by bringing forth an old, locked trunk. It had not rusted and appeared new. They laid it at Lufra's feet.

"What are your orders, captain?"

"I want you to take your men and engage the kelpies who are attacking my other ship."

"Yes, sir."

"Yes, this way," it guided him. Trillius entered one of the numerous cave entrances, well hidden within thick seaweed. His gnomish vision meant he was able to see in gradients of black and white, even in the deep darkness, but color quickly returned as a strange glow cascaded toward him.

A voice beckoned him from the recesses of his mind, *"Just a little farther, Trillius."*

He followed his instincts and entered a large chamber supported by barnacle covered columns. Piles of treasure, sprinkled throughout, sparkled underneath string-like vines with colorful orange and yellow sea flowers sprouting out. This was definitely the treasure room of the kelpie's colony. In the center was the source of the brilliant light—a white pearl the size of his head rested on top of a pedestal formed from beige seashells. Trillius hastily swam to the fortune. He slowly reached for the item, his eyes wide in delight, his hair wafting in the water, and bubbles of air escaping from his mouth.

"Don't touch it, Trillius."

He stopped short, with his hand in grasping distance, *"You said I could have the treasure."* Suddenly, a thought struck him, *"Wait, are you the pearl?"*

The powerful voice, sounding stronger and much closer, answered, *"I am greater than the pearl. Rescue me, Trillius, and the pearl will be yours."*

Suddenly, several kelpies entered the room. Trillius darted behind a rock; the fishlike beings did not spot him as they dutifully set down treasure trinkets taken from *A Pinch of Luck* as the raid continued. The gnome spotted a distinct handbag being set down, *"Hey,"* he thought, *"that is my bag of goodies. Nobody steals what I have already stolen. That is just plain rude!"* They soon exited. Trillius approached his stolen satchel but became distracted, and instead rushed to an area bathed in a blue aura on the oppo-site wall. A patch of barnacles were the source of the mystical light. Trillius inspected it and soon realized that it wasn't the crustaceans glowing, but instead something underneath. He pulled out a knife and began to pry the shelled parasites away. The glow became brighter and a stone the size of a potato plopped into Trillius' tiny hands, and spoke in his mind.

"Very good, Trillius. You are now my master. I have great resources for you to uncover, and as a gift you shall be rewarded. Go back to the pearl and take it."

Trillius quickly hustled to the prize.

"Before you take this pearl, you must promise me that you will not tell anyone else about me. I'm your secret. If anyone finds out, then you will lose my power."

"I understand. You can count on me. I'm the king of secrets."

"I knew I chose the right gnome to find me. I've waited here for centuries for someone like you, Trillius. We will be good friends."

Trillius grinned happily and plucked the pearl from its perch and then swam out the way he came.

"So, you're a stone, huh? Do you have a name?"

"I am the Great Dal-Draydian."

14

Te Sond

The heroes' frosty breath became more pronounced as they slowly made their way deeper into the ice-crusted tunnel. Each deep intake of air chilled them to the bone. Frost particles began to gather in their hair. They took careful steps to prevent sliding and falling as they traversed. The blue-hued glaze cracked periodically as it expanded.

Spilf's voice echoed and his teeth chattered, "We are going to freeze to death before we reach this place."

Dulgin looked back and said, "You'll be fine, Stubby. Strike up another torch to regain your strength before we move on."

"Master Dulgin, what should we be expecting up ahead?"

"We are in the funneling zone. A common tactic of dwarves: funnel the enemies into smaller numbers. This is only one tunnel of many, so I suspect we will come out into a larger chamber that connects them all, and then the front gate of the Shield will soon be before us."

Spilf ignited the torch, and the flame fought to stay alive within the hostile environment devoid of much oxygen. "So, this is not the only way to the Shield then?"

Dulgin nodded, "It would be doubtful your family came this way without an escort."

Spilf and Bridazak sat on top of their backpacks and brought the much needed warmth to their hairy bare feet, the stabs of a hundred needles pricked through their tough, leathered soles as a small measure of defrosting started to take effect. A form of ecstasy engulfed them as the countering effect of the intense cold was soothed. Bridazak glanced down the cavern in the direction they were headed and spotted movement. He instantly stood and alerted the others.

"I saw something."

The ice tunnel was clear from what the others could see. "What kind of something?"

"I don't know. I don't see anything now."

Dulgin continued to stare in the underlit path ahead of them and then whispered, "This place feels strange; something is not quite right." Then he growled a command as he turned back to his friends, "Let's get a move on."

The light in the passage soon became brighter, and as the tunnel seemed to open a bit, the ceiling displayed frozen bubbles of captured air, and a strange static sound like a muffled rushing wind resounded in the distance. Several pillars of ice came into view ahead of them.

"This place is beautiful," Bridazak whispered. He marveled at the discernable change from the ice tunnel to the natural beauty of this frozen, light-blue ceiling, rippling beyond sight. This dazzling place reminded him of Heaven, which harbored glory itself. Bridazak thought to himself as he looked up in awe, *"I'm so grateful to be able to see this. Thank you for the chance to return to Ruauck-El and see more of its splendor."* Everything he now saw was a reminder of what awaited him, and what he left behind. He calmed his mind and pushed the feelings of regret away.

They passed several of the naturally formed columns, and then Spilf spotted something out of the ordinary. "What is that?" he pointed to a pillar to their left, moving closer to investigate the oddity. He suddenly noticed an outlined face frozen inside, eyes white and mouth agape. Spilf gasped, "There is someone inside!"

The group approached. Abawken wiped away the coating of frost around the encased face with his forearm. "Is it a dwarf?"

Dulgin responded as he stepped closer to inspect, "I can't quite make sense of this. There's no beard, so this is not a dwarf. Though its stature would indicate—"

Bridazak cut him off, "What happened to him, Dulgin?"

"I don't know," he responded as he glanced overhead, focusing on the smooth rolling ice pockets. Suddenly, a large shadow whisked by on the other side. His eyes widened in horror, "Move!"

110

An ear splitting crack echoed around them as a jet of water broke loose above Bridazak and splashed around him. The water instantly froze, entrapping him inside. Abawken withdrew his magical scimitar and touched it against the frozen block of ice as he uttered a command word to release the power held within, "Esh!" An intense countering heat rushed out, and the icicle column collapsed, freeing the dak. Bridazak, gasping, started to fall, but Abawken caught him and began to drag him away from the area. More splits of the ice ceiling were heard and more water tumbled to try to ensnare the group. Dulgin and Spilf reached the section of the tunnel where the dangerous water bubbles no longer lay waiting, and they turned to wave Abawken and Bridazak to safety. Another water spout crashed beside them in a near miss. Ice chips crackled and shattered around their feet as they hurried. Abawken was almost to them when another split occurred. He slung Bridazak ahead and the ordakian slid into Dulgin and Spilf. Abawken raised his sword up to counter the ice tentacle zooming toward him, "Esh!" Hot and cold water splashed over his body as he dodged out of danger and joined his friends.

"What was that?" Spilf asked frantically.

"Ice Pikes," Dulgin answered. "The frost dwarves raise the monstrous fish to help them combat, or in this case trap, intruders. We were under a river. I never thought my father's tales of them were so accurate."

Spilf shyly posed, "If that wasn't a dwarf trapped in the ice, then—" he hesitated.

Bridazak placed a hand on his friends shoulder and slightly nodded his acknowledgement of what Spilf proposed; the long-trapped soul had been an ordakian.

"What if that was one of my parents? If it wasn't, then how could they have made it inside such a treacherous place as this?"

Dulgin stepped forward, "We need to find out what has happened here. None of this is right, but I feel it in my dwarven bones that was not your family, and the truth of the matter is close at hand. You need, we all need, to keep the hope we have alive." Dulgin looked intently into Spilf's eyes, which were glassy, "You are more dwarven than you think, my friend. You have the heart of a warrior. You only lack the beard. We stand together, all of us, with you."

Spilf was shocked at Dulgin's words, and could not respond. He looked to the others, to Abawken and Bridazak nodding in agreement; they were with him all the way.

Tears slid down his cheek as he said, "Thank you, all of you. I'm ready."

Dulgin looked back at the Ice Pike chamber and said, "I always thought my dah's stories of this place were tall tales."

"Well, I suggest you start remembering everything your dah told you, so we don't run into any more surprises," Bridazak said.

"If his stories are true, then we have some mighty fine dwarven ale awaiting us," Dulgin smiled.

"Not sure how that information will help us any," Spilf said.

Dulgin smacked the dak on the shoulder, "It's called motivation, Stubby."

Dulgin's understanding of dwarven tactics proved dependable. The heroes emerged into a massive ice cave, as he had suspected would be the case. Dilapidated wooden war machines littered the outskirts. Piles of large boulders sat waiting to be hurled at invading enemies, but were now covered in layers of ice. Ballista contraptions, once used to impale intruders coming in from the tunnels, now lay in ruin. Beyond the grand ice arena was another cave with a brightness akin to the outside sky illuminating the entrance.

"What happened here?" Bridazak asked.

No one offered any response as they all took in the sight of the vacant strategic defense, now in shambles.

After the group had worked their way further into the mess, Dulgin observed, "There are no bodies, no melee weapons, no indication of a battle—nothing."

A howling, frigid wind and the sound of rushing water erupted from the broadly expanded opening before them. They approached with caution; the ground was layered in blue ice like frozen ripples of water. The roar intensified as they slowly made their way into the cavity that twisted back and forth in huge sweeping turns. The effect of Spilf's torchlight lessened as the bright outdoors came into view. They stopped to take in the incredible panorama.

The towering waterfall cascaded, roaring like a hundred dragons. The liquid was frozen on the inside, creating a spectacular crystalline effect of various sized icicles linked together. Fresh cold air whipped through, and blue, open sky was visible to the heroes. White-capped mountain tops were seen in the distance. Snow swept off the peaks as gusts of wind propelled the loose shavings into the air to form slow motion clouds.

The wide walkway arched around the breathtaking scene and there before the heroes stood the entrance to the Kingdom of the Frost Dwarves; the Shield.

Dulgin announced, "Welcome to Te Sond."

The Dwarven structure, as massive as the waterfall they had just walked behind, was formed from the mountain itself, coated in the same blue ice they travelled upon. An emblem of a round shield covered the center of the monstrous double-door. To open an entrance of this magnitude would take several giants, and to break it down would take just as many dragons.

Dulgin said, mesmerized, "The architecture is flawless."

"How does your kind make such things as this?" Spilf asked, clearly impressed.

"Legend says that the dwarves of old traded for the services of a great mystic to help create their kingdom."

"That must have made quite a dent in their pile of gold," Bridazak said.

"If we can't protect our gold then it is pointless to hoard it."

Standing at attention along the far wall were five statues depicting dwarven warriors. Each one stood eight-feet-tall, and had been chiseled from the rock cave. They stood proudly holding their weapons and shields by their side. Beards, frozen over with icicles, draped down to their chests. Helmets with spikes, horns, and nose-guards adorned their heads. The bland color of rock did not detract from the craftsmanship and detail of these battle-hardened frost dwarf heroes.

Spilf studied the monumental door with Lester and Ross while the rest of the party gawked over the inanimate objects of decoration, craning their necks to fully take in their features.

Bridazak called from his frozen position, "Did you find anything, Spilf?"

"It had some pretty elaborate traps but they are deactivated and according to Lester, it can only be opened from the inside."

"Don't worry, we will get in one way or another."

Abawken inspected and then pointed to the stone models, "I found something interesting at the base of four of the five statues." Each of them spotted the lettering and Dulgin announced they were Dwarven words and recited them aloud, "bact, estude, fen, neh."

"Are they the names of the warriors?" asked Abawken.

"No," Dulgin, puzzled, began, "it doesn't make sense. These words, in common, mean, one understand can no."

Abawken noticed, "All of them have a word except for the statue in the middle."

Spilf jumped to action, "I will check it out with Lester and Ross." After a minute, the Dak turned and shook his head, "Nothing."

"Master Bridazak, you seem to be contemplating something, what is it?"

"Perhaps this is a password of some kind. If you read the words in order from left to right, they do not make sense, and if you read them from right to left it still doesn't come together." Bridazak moved to the first statue on the left. "This says 'one' and if I skip the second statue then the next word is 'can'. Together it says 'one can'."

"One can what?" Dulgin was bewildered.

"The other two words are 'understand and no'.

Spilf lit up and shouted, "One can no understand!"

Silence fell over them as they tried to grasp what Spilf was so happy about when he thought he had figured out the riddle.

"That don't make a bit of sense, ya blundering fool!"

"It makes perfect sense to me, you talk like that all the time, I thought it sounded Dwarven."

"You are an edoti!"

"A what?"

"An idiot!"

"Wait," Bridazak stopped his comrades tirade of insults, "Spilf is on to something. It could be saying 'no one can understand'."

They mulled the new formulation of words inside their minds. Abawken asked, "What could it mean, Master Dulgin?"

Without answering, Dulgin walked closer to each of the statues to take a better look. He started on the left and moved right. He stopped at the middle statue and squinted in contemplation. The effigy had a slight difference from the others and he took a step backwards.

"There is something odd about this one," he pointed.

"Like what?" Bridazak asked.

Dulgin smiled as a sudden realization came to light, "Very clever."

"What is it?"

Dulgin walked to the statue, turned to the others, revealing his teeth, and said, "No one can understand 'wenthak'." He pushed and the statue suddenly jarred loose and slid on the ice beneath it. A secret entrance was uncovered. The statue locked into place after moving several feet back.

"Wenthak?" Spilf shrugged in confusion.

Dulgin turned, "Women."

Spilf laughed. "Oh, women! No one can understand women. I get it. Wait—that statue is a woman?"

"Yeah. Isn't she beautiful?" Dulgin beamed.

"I thought you were stretching the truth when you said dwarven females had beards, Master Dulgin."

The dwarf continued to smile, proud of himself on figuring out the dwarven riddle and nodded to each one of his friends as they entered the dark passage.

The heroes emerged from the secret tunnel to find themselves inside the Frost Dwarf castle. Dulgin slid the statue back in place and joined the others in gazing at the immense entryway. An intricate pulley system of wheels, ropes, and chain attached to thick rungs welded onto the massive double door revealed the incredible undertaking it would take to open the keep. The stone walls were formed of blocks of blue-hued quartz, which emulated ice. Huge pillars of the same material sprouted from floor to ceiling every twenty paces along the immensely wide corridor as far as the eye could see. The glorious and pristine beauty of craftsmanship overtook the heroes' senses. The smell was like fresh chipped ice, but at the same time the scene felt ominous, because not a soul could be seen or heard. A deathly silence greeted them and the chill of a foreboding danger pricked at the back of their necks.

"Where is everyone?" Bridazak said, his whisper echoing through the never ending hall.

"Yeah, thought we would be greeted by friendly dwarves, Dulgin," Spilf mocked.

"Me too," the Dwarf said solemnly to himself, gazing forward, as he walked down the monstrous hall.

Spilf looked at the others and shrugged. Each of them knew that Dulgin wasn't himself.

The ceiling arched high above and, unlike the ice-walls, it had a polished finish. A glow seeped through the exotic mountain rock and released a soft hue of twilight. A haunting breeze funneled out of several offshoot darkened passageways. They cautiously walked deeper and deeper into the ancient crag, searching to uncover what they felt—invisible eyes watching their every step. Abawken withdrew his scimitar and Dulgin's axe was at the ready. Bridazak gripped his magical bow, the Seeker, and then slid out an arrow from his quiver. Spilf held his dagger tightly. Their footsteps were precise, none of them tromped in haste. Each of them imagined at any moment that a flood of frost dwarves would charge from the darkened tunnels, but only cold air greeted them, which heightened their sense of danger. They had traversed only minutes when Abawken pointed out an amorphous form in the distance. The eerie hall now had an end in sight, and the heroes fought the crepuscular lighting to see the shapeless outline still hundreds of feet away. They crept closer and realized they had approached a throne on top of a raised platform, overlooking the entry hall. The dim light strangely lessened around the chair reserved for royalty.

Unintelligible whispering stopped Dulgin in his tracks. The others halted at his sudden frozen action.

"What is it?" Bridazak quietly asked.

"I hear something."

Each of them focused, but could hear nothing. The susurration continued, and amongst the perceived gibberish, Dulgin made out a single dwarven word.

"*Help.*"

Meanwhile, hundreds of millari away, the young boy of fifteen cycles, Jack, looked off into the distance. He searched within himself to understand his place in this world without his dad, who he left behind in search of his own destiny.

"Why did I leave you, Dad?" he whispered.

The sun was setting and a soft breeze shuffled the gold grass blades of the open plain. He glanced behind to see Geetock barking out orders to the dwarven army setting camp. They were heading to someplace called the Shield, a dwarven kingdom.

Jack looked back at the sun, closed his eyes, and deeply inhaled the earthy smell of the dried vegetation. He wished with all his might he was back in the Lost City. He opened his eyes and disappointment of his unfulfilled wish penetrated his heart. His face was solemn.

"Dad, I don't have any friends. I need you," he said out loud.

Jack thought of Bridazak. He often longed to be with the heroes of Ruauck-El, the ones that rescued him and his dad, the ones having amazing adventures. He desperately wanted to be a part of something epic, but he felt trapped amongst these ancient dwarves and elves. With the few humans in camp, he had found no attachment.

Jack pulled a diamond ring from his pocket. The large stone sparkled in the dimming sunlight as he fondled the bauble in his fingers. His dad had given it to him; it brought him comfort, but did not take the deep desire for something more. He looked up and said, "When I get my chance I will make a difference in this world. Dad, I will make you proud; I promise."

15

The Great Trillius

"El'Korr, Trillius is gone!" Rozelle shouted.

"He'll turn up eventually; he always does," El'Korr cried back over the din of the battle. The dwarves remained in place, protecting Raina from the attacking kelpies, as she focused her spell on the air pocket surrounding the ship.

Rozelle worried, "I hope he's not hurt, or worse." Unable to withhold her anxiety any longer, she dove through the dark blue wall of water. As she plunged into the liquid barrier, her tiny gnome body morphed once again, but this time she took on the form of a large, grey-skinned shark.

In her new body, Rozelle glided through the calm waters, sending surprised clusters of kelpies to vacate the area, until she finally spotted Trillius swimming toward her. Rozelle flashed a grin in delight and relief at the sight of him.

Trillius, however, saw the blurred grey mass approaching, and his secret worst nightmare came to reality as the shape of an enormous shark with razor sharp teeth seemed to be hunting him. Forgetting he was underwater, he let out a scream, but as the endless oxygen of Xan's breathing underwater spell continued to fill his lungs, he simply let out a long stream of bubbles. Turning quickly and beating the water with his short arms and legs, he made a hopeless effort to escape. *"I don't want to die. I don't want to die. I want the greatest of treasure with all of my limbs intact."* His thoughts were like a plea to an unknown god.

Dal-Draydian answered him, *"It is only a shark. Turn around and show it that you are the master."*

"I don't have that kind of power, you crazy rock."

She propelled to his kicking feet and then shape shifted back to her true self, grabbing his heel. Trillius expelled more bubbles with a muffled scream. He turned to see Rozelle shrugging with a grin and then he quickly swam to her side, relieved that he was not going to be eaten.

In his mind he heard the voice of Dal-Draydian, *"Is this someone you know?"*

"Yes, this is my girlfriend."

"She is weak and not worthy of the Great Trillius. You will see. She will betray you."

"No! She's not like that."

As Rozelle focused her attention to make their way toward the galleon, her eyes caught something. She tugged on Trillius and pointed.

He followed her leading and was shocked to see skeletons swimming to engage the kelpies. *"Where did they come from?"* he asked himself.

Dal-Draydian answered, *"They are mindless creatures doing a menial task as commanded them."*

Trillius was not used to having someone respond to his thoughts, *"Who commanded them?"*

There was no answer and then Rozelle pulled on Trillius to follow her back to the ship.

"Captain, the kelpies are retreating!" Skath yelled.

Elsbeth saw the same thing and couldn't understand why. She looked to the dwarves for some explanation. El'Korr threw his war hammer—it slammed into a nearby foe and then magically returned to his hand, ready to be thrown again. Crewmen slashed at the fleeing green creatures of the sea. The glistening kelpies webbed feet slapped against the wet deck before they dove back into their familiar ocean terrain, scattering.

Trillius and Rozelle burst through the wall of water and landed on the deck. The gnomes shouted in unison, "Undead!"

"Great, as if the kelpies were not enough," Elsbeth thought before calling out, "Prepare to be boarded!"

Skath and Myers regrouped the crew to prepare for the next challenge. Anders continued to heal the wounded, applying bandages loaded with ointments and casting minor cure spells. Urlin placed himself strategically in the middle of the sailors to assist with his spell power, ready to blast anything that boarded with his force missiles.

Minutes passed, and the only sound aboard was the heavy breathing of exhausted fighters and the sloshing of bloody water. Anticipation of the new threat heightened. Blurred images swam on the outside of the magical barrier, but none entered onto the deck of the ship.

Suddenly, Xan and Lufra came through the wall of water dragging a large dark metal trunk. The nervous sailors, expecting the walking dead to board any second, jumped in surprise, but were quickly relieved to see Xan and Lufra instead.

Lufra, exhausted, said, "The crew of *The Wave Rider* are attacking the kelpies."

"Undead crew," Xan clarified, "thanks to Captain Yasooma's sword and his kin who wields it." The blade continued to glow in the hands of the young boy.

Elsbeth said, "Even beyond the grave, Captain Yasooma is full of surprises. Excellent work, Lufra."

A Pinch of Luck suddenly lurched, and the ship swayed side to side under their feet. It felt as if the hold on the vessel had been released.

"We are rising," Urlin said.

A cheer erupted amongst the crew.

El'Korr slapped Rondee's shoulder and said, "You fought well, my friend."

"Fiethnok chariots gomeck flew," he responded.

El'Korr smiled, "Exactly." He then glanced at Raina. Her eyes were still closed and he noticed blood trickling from her nose. Her hands, palms up, moved slowly; rising with the movement of the vessel.

The dwarven king approached her and spoke quietly, "Hang on, Raina. Bring us home."

As *A Pinch of Luck* rose to the surface, the dark shadow of the ocean's depth slowly faded as the light from above strengthened. All eyes remained focused upward, waiting to burst out of their liquid grave and to breathe fresh air once again.

The beacon of the blue sky broke as the tallest mast speared through the surface. Hands covered eyes from the bright light as the misty salt water fell from above and they heard the open ocean once again. The thunderous crash of the water hitting the hull of the ship brought warranted cheers from the crewmen.

"Sails up!" Elsbeth called.

Her voice snapped the men to action and each member responded with a renewed spring in their step, grateful to have survived such an unnatural excursion.

Raina collapsed as her protection spell ended, but El'Korr quickly caught her, helped her to sit upright on the deck, and congratulated his friend, "Good work, lass."

As the injured crewmen were carried below to be tended to and the dead kelpies were being tossed overboard, the skeleton fighters from below, one by one, hoisted themselves up and over the railing. Their bones clacked and scratched against the hull. Crewmen yelled alerts and backed away as the bone-walkers gathered, and then waited.

Elsbeth called out, "Lufra!"

Xan and Lufra emerged from the cluster of weary shipmates, crowded together to see the remaining undead of Yasooma's fallen men. Lufra unsheathed his still-glowing sword and held it high in the air as he stepped forward.

Elsbeth approached and stood by Lufra's side. She leaned down and whispered into his ear, "You will need to release them. They have waited for you a very long time."

Lufra remained focused on the skeletal crew, "But how? What do I say?"

"You will know." She stepped back and looked at the gathered skeletons. These had been her shipmates, generations ago. *"Rest in peace, my friends,"* she thought to herself.

Lufra looked back at the heroes and then the former crew of Yasooma's, unsure what to say or do. One of the undead spoke within his mind, *"What are your orders, Captain?"*

Lufra took a deep breath, exhaled, and responded out loud for all to hear, "You have one last voyage to make for me."

"We are at your command."

Lufra could feel the power of the blade he held begin to activate. He looked up and was suddenly staring at the same angelic being he saw within the tomb of Captain Yasooma. It hovered above him and the angel nodded toward Lufra. The young boy brought his head down slowly, stared at the skeletons, and watched the original facial features, clothing, weapons, and all their equipment materialize in an incorporeal illusion. There was a glow around them all.

Lufra turned back to the heroes and said, "Do you see them? They are glorious."

They looked at one another, unsure of what Lufra was talking about. They only saw the bleached bones standing at attention, waiting for their final order.

A sudden surge of energy soared down the blade, through his arm, and nestled within his chest. Lufra shook his head slightly and then instantly he stood at attention, bringing the sword expertly down and then sheathing the weapon without looking.

"Men of *The Wave Rider*," Lufra began in a stern, yet slightly wavering voice, "I can say that I have never worked with a more stalwart, remarkable crew than you. I was blessed to be your Captain. It is time for a final journey into the kingdom of light. There you will find rest. I release you all from my service. It has been an honor. Thank you, all of you." Lufra pulled his sword out and one by one the skeletons approached, knelt down, and received their captain's release. As each one was touched by the sword, bone turned to ash. The ocean breeze carried their remains out to sea. Lufra ushered out his duty with growing pride, releasing sailor after sailor, until the last one fizzled away.

Deckhands retrieved water in buckets to clean off the bloody remnants; green pieces of flesh, limbs, and gutted kelpies. Riggers climbed to release the sails. Elsbeth walked the deck as her men worked. She stared out into the open sea, thankful and amazed to no longer be carrying the fear that this place once held over her.

El'Korr and Rondee dragged the metal chest closer to Raina, who had not yet awakened. Her brother moved to her side.

El'Korr said, "Xan, cast a healing spell for Raina."

"She is not injured, but instead drained of power. She needs rest."

Trillius ventured forth, crying out, "I love treasure chests! They are my specialty. May I?"

"Good luck. There is no lock to open, at least none that I can see," Lufra said.

"Oh dear child, your eyes are still innocent, and not able to see what the Great Trillius can see."

The voice of Dal-Draydian proclaimed in his mind, *"Well spoken. These fools need to understand your power. You know what to do now. Show them your greatness, my master."*

Trillius' ego swelled as he listened to Dal-Draydian's words. The spirit within the blue stone had shown him the magical glyph and translated the word of power to unlock it. He ran his stubby fingers around the edges playfully. The heroes, the captain, and her officers watched him closely. Trillius leaned in close and quietly recited in a tentative voice, "Serra. Tooma. Um, karta?"

A blaze of light burned around the lip of the container, revealing the seamed lid, and then it popped open with a loud hiss of pressurized air. Trillius sighed his relief and then swung back the cover to reveal the contents. Black felt lined the interior of the chest where three items rested on the lustrous fabric; a human fist sized, red gem with flames flickering inside was the most prominent object. Next, was a brown multi-faceted cut stone and the third was a rolled parchment emblazoned with Captain Yasooma's family crest.

Raina shifted everyone's attention toward her as she strained to speak, "The Fire Opal and the Earth Stone. Where is the pearl?"

"This was it, Raina. We hoped it was inside," Xan answered. "Are you alright?"

Raina's face contorted, still clearly exhausted from her spell, "We need to go back."

The Sheldeen Mystic struggled in her tired state. El'Korr and Xan held her back.

"You need to rest, Raina," Xan said.

"Give it to them, Master," Dal-Draydian directed.

Trillius answered in his mind to the entity within the blue stone, *"I have never given up treasure like this before. I am taking a big risk; are you sure about this?"*

"I have shown you glimpses of what is out there, hidden for centuries across all the realm. I will take you personally to them all, one by one, until they are yours," Dal-Draydian replied smoothly and confidently. *"We need these peasants to trust you, and carry us back to land. Now do it."*

Raina fought through El'Korr and Xan and stood, groaning, "Elsbeth, we have to go back!"

"No, we don't," Trillius chimed happily, as he pulled the magnificent Pearl of the Deep from his robes. Everyone's face lit up in a mixture of surprise and joy.

"Look at them, Trillius. They long to be like you. They are weak without you," Dal-Draydian continued, massaging Trillius' ego.

"How did you find it?" Raina inquired.

"Well, you see, I was forced to go off the ship due to the sheer numbers of those awful creatures storming the deck. I had no time to think."

"Makes sense," El'Korr interjected sarcastically.

"Very witty, I'm sure. As I was saying, I ended up hiding in a cave, and it turned out to be the place that the kelpies had the pearl. I swam out of there as fast as I could and Rozelle helped me find my way back."

"We are very fortunate for your accidental discovery," Raina said.

The gnome beamed, but inside, the thought of releasing his promised treasure burdened him. He asked in his thoughts, *"Dal-Draydian, are you sure you will show me even greater wealth than this?"*

His thought pattern was shattered when Rozelle asked, "How did you know what to say to open the chest?"

Dal-Draydian scoffed, *"I told you she wouldn't understand. She can't accept who you are. She wants to change you."*

Trillius answered Rozelle, "It's the dragon language, and it means 'X marks the spot'."

"Since when did you start speaking draconian?" she pressed further.

He sighed heavily before answering, "I'm the Great Trillius, remember?"

"I thought you were 'Silly Samuel'?"

"There, you see?" The Dal-Draydian voice snapped, *"She questions your every move. She wants to keep you from becoming even greater."*

"Can't you appreciate what I've done here, Rozelle, for once? I mean, it was no small feat to go and fetch this pearl, and then come back and open this magically sealed chest."

"Hey, why don't you settle down," El'Korr interjected.

"You are not my king, so don't start telling me what to do!" Trillius barked.

El'Korr erupted into a hearty roarous laughter, but stopped abruptly when he saw in the corner of his eye, Rondee the Wild, clenching his fists as he stepped toward the disrespectful Trillius. El'Korr caught his arm and said, "Now, now, Protector, I don't think that is necessary." Rondee looked at his king with pleading eyes to let him carry out his desire, but relented when the gnome stormed off. Rozelle stood there in shock.

Trillius could feel the power of Dal-Draydian welling up inside of him. His mind continued to link with the entity, *"Very good, Trillius. My power is growing in you and soon everyone will see how great you truly are."*

The night approached and the fighters had begun to settle. The crewmen rehashed the battle, mourned the twenty who had lost their lives, and tended to the many wounded. At sunset, Captain Elsbeth delivered a sermon for each of the deceased as their bodies slid from a tilted plank into the ocean with a splash.

Later that evening, Captain Elsbeth called for a meeting in her quarters with her officers and the adventurers. Trillius leaned his chair back against the wall, seeming uninterested in the conversation. Rozelle stared at Trillius across the room, growing in concern at his distance to her and the others.

Raina addressed the group, "Before we reach Pirate's Belly, Captain, I will be teleporting our group to our next destination just as soon as my power returns."

"What is the next destination?"

"A place called the Shield—it is a dwarven kingdom."

"I've not heard of it before. King El'Korr, is this where you come from?" Elsbeth asked.

"Nay, the Shield harbors frost dwarves. We are not sure how they have fared over the centuries, but most likely they have buried themselves in the mountain, with the Horn Kings in control of the lands."

"Raina, you have but three elements, the fourth is still unknown. How do you plan to move forward with destroying the Dragon Stones?" Elsbeth asked.

Raina replied, "There was a parchment inside the chest. I opened it and have studied it already, and found a sketch of some importance. It notes a place called the Kouzfhan within the Shield."

El'Korr jumped in, "That is an ancient dwarven word, which translates to the Cleansing."

Raina nodded and then continued, "Captain Yasooma listed the elements, and the proper locations to deposit them. The fourth is listed as—" Raina was interrupted by a smooth, hypnotic voice.

"The Sky Diamond."

Everyone, startled, turned and saw Romann de Beaux in their midst. His red velvet jacket with gold buttons draped to his calves and covered most of his black leather pants. White frills sprouted from the long sleeves and he wore the same swashbuckler hat as before, the yellow plume prominently displayed. Elsbeth quickly stood.

"Your grace," she said and bowed slightly.

"You may be seated, Captain. My ship was in the area. I hope I'm not intruding."

"No, please. You are always welcome."

"You know of the Sky Diamond?" Raina inquired.

"Yes, and I know of its location."

El'Korr asked excitedly, "Where is it?"

"My dear dwarf, you should know this."

"He is clueless, like always," Trillius quipped from the rear of the room.

Romann de Beaux clasped his hands behind his back and slowly walked toward the gnome. Trillius remained leaning in his chair with no evident concern on his face.

"How is my little snack doing these days?"

"My name is Trillius," he snapped with confidence.

"My apologies. Your voyage has changed you it appears. Interesting. I sense…" Romann interrupted his own sentence, narrowed his eyes and then turned back to address his remarks to the group, "The Sky Diamond is what gives the Shield its power. The frost dwarves use it to protect their kingdom. I trust this information is useful to your quest."

"Very," Raina responded, noting the vampire's sudden shift away from Trillius, "and thank you."

"My pleasure. I am very glad I could assist. Well, I must be on my way. Captain, I hope to see you soon, and Raina and Xan, you are always welcome at Pirate's Belly." Romann pulled his broad brimmed hat from his head, its yellow plume swaying as he swept it across his chest and bowed low to the gathered party. He then faded into a blurred mist, dispersing until completely vanished.

Conversations began with everyone, except Trillius, whose thoughts were focused on the inner voice of Dal-Draydian, which was filling his mind.

"The Vampire knew who I was, and it recognized my dominant strength. That is why it fled, and that is just a small taste of my power, Trillius. Our time of greatness is approaching."

Romann de Beaux was settled in the cabin of *The Rose*, surrounded in total darkness.

"Daysho, can you hear me?" Romann said from inside his mind.

An echoed hollow response answered, *"Yes."*

"The gnome, called Trillius, has the fifth stone."

"I understand. Once I have what you want, then we can finish our dealings, as you have promised."

"Just get me my prize, Daysho. I have never failed at my word, and I have lived a very long time. Tell that mage, Veric, they will be arriving at the Chamber of Cleansing tomorrow."

"It will be done."

Romann smiled and his fangs glowed in the darkness.

16

A King's Errand

A shadowy figure sat upon the blue-ice throne, overlooking the vast hall of the Shield. At first, Dulgin could only understand the word *heefa*, or 'help,' in the common tongue, but now a flood of emotional telepathic sentences endlessly rang inside his mind.

"Stop all your blabbing, dammit!" the dwarf snapped.

The others understood by his outburst that the entity must have contacted Dulgin alone, and they were not surprised at their gruff friend's reaction. He was not accustomed to others' thoughts in his mind.

They waited at the foot of the long-fanning, smooth marbled steps, which formed a wide semi-circle leading to the ice carved throne. The backrest towered several feet high, and Dwarvish runes lavished the sides of the armrests, which resembled mighty war hammers. Behind the throne there hung a tapestry from floor to ceiling, depicting the image of the frost dwarf king. He had blue skin, matching the color of the ice, a white icicle beard, and wore brilliant full-plate armor. The image of the King's eyes had been purposely burnt out, the only apparent damage to the stitched masterpiece.

Dulgin, not taking his eyes off of the entity on the royal seat, stepped toward the figure. His friends followed, and soon they looked upon a dwarf encapsulated by a layer of clear ice, his burly arms with bracers of gold pinned to the chair. His eyes were a mottled white, locked into an endless stare straight ahead.

The deep voice resonated, this time in the common language, within each of their minds, *"You must help my kingdom."*

"You are—" Bridazak gasped.

"I am Morthkin, King of the frost dwarves, Ruler of Te Sond, Protector of Guul-Fen, and harborer of all those who take refuge in my domain."

Dulgin asked, "What happened here?"

"The demon, Shiell-Zonn, entombed me and opened the doors of the goblin under-dwellers to sack Te Sond. I have been trapped here for over a century, calling in the dark, waiting for someone to hear my cry. In order for this curse to be broken, you must retrieve the Sky Diamond, which must be in the possession of a worthy dwarf."

Dulgin, accepting this mission without question, lowered his voice, narrowed his eyes, and asked, "Where is this Sky Diamond?"

"Below us, in the tunnels of Gock-Turnin."

"Gock-Turnin?" He reeled back in surprise. "That scum!" Dulgin spit on the ground in disgust.

The others did not understand the name or the meaning behind it. Bridazak asked, "Who is this Gock?"

Dulgin replied, "He is the Goblin King, nemesis to all dwarves."

"Yes, and he beseeched the demon, Shiell-Zonn, to infiltrate my kingdom, ensnare my physical body, and enslave my people."

Spilf asked with trepidation, "Did you, sir, have any ordakians under your care?"

"All races of peace are allowed in my domain."

"I'm looking for my family. They might have come here for refuge. A small village east of here was taken over by humans and a group of daks fled this way."

"We had a small community of Ordakiankind within Te Sond. They came from several locations, perhaps the one you speak of, but I do not have intimate knowledge of their names."

Spilf exhaled in relief, again feeling his hopes and doubts seem to battle within his heart. Even though he felt closer now than ever before, he was not certain if they were still alive. *"Wait,"* he thought to himself. *"God told me they were still alive."* Spilf turned to his friends and said aloud, "They are here. I know it."

"There is a secret door behind the tapestry. Only dwarfkin can open it. Head through my private chamber and take the stairway down. It will take you to the lower levels, where you will find the evil goblins of Gock-Turnin. They are using

the Sky Diamond to enslave the people, forcing them to make their tunnels. The curse will end once it is in your hands."

"Well met, King Morthkin. We will free you," Bridazak said.

"My name is Dulgin Hammergold, and my brother is El'Korr, King of the Remnant. He will be coming with a small army in the near future."

"Free me, Dulgin of the Hammergold clan, so I can prepare for his arrival as a true King. He will see the hospitality he so deserves."

Abawken called, "Let us go."

The heroes began to follow until King Morthkin stopped them, *"You are being tracked."*

Bridazak stepped back, "By whom?"

Abawken and Dulgin exchanged glances. The human could no longer keep the truth about his assassin hidden from his companions, "Her name is Devana."

Spilf coughed, "Devana? The assassin, Devana? That Devana?"

"Yes, it is her."

The mind-link of the frost dwarf ruler deepened, *"No. It is King Manasseh."*

Bridazak snapped, "What did you say? King Manasseh? That is impossible, he was killed over two moon cycles ago."

"Then he has returned from the grave. I can hear his caustic mind relentlessly spewing his hatred."

"You must be mistaken."

"He comes for vengeance; he comes for someone named Bridazak."

The heroes were not prepared for King Morthkin's words. This pivotal information verified that it was, in fact, the fallen Manasseh, back from the dead.

"It is me he is looking for. Where is he now?" Bridazak asked.

"He entered the lower chambers of my domain. Lift the curse and I will help you."

Abawken called from the tapestry, "C'mon, Master Bridazak!"

He held the drapery away from the wall as his friends, one by one, entered behind it to the secret door. Spilf, with the help of Lester and Ross, discovered the elusive entrance and pointed it out to the others. The dak studied a small stone nestled in the wall. He slowly moved it aside and found it covered an imprint of a hand. Dulgin didn't wait for instructions, and slapped his palm in place. With a loud grinding sound, the mighty ice wall cracked into the formation of an entrance and the foot depth of wall pushed in and then shuffled to the left.

A magical chandelier dangled from the ceiling by one immense iced stalactite, giving off a dusky orange aura from the hundreds of perfectly shaped icicles of various lengths hanging from the circular frame. Decorative shields of all sizes and shapes adorned the walls like trophies. A frosty glass case held an array of drinking mugs, chalices, and horns.

The heroes slowed their pace as they entered in awe. Mammoth sized furs of numerous species littered the floor of the fifty-foot chamber.

Dulgin gasped and let out two distinct, high pitched yelps. His comrades' eyes looked the direction he was staring, and locked on the brilliant Dwarven full-plate armor set on display upon a wood mannequin. Its adamantine metal gleamed like a beacon for any lost dwarf looking for protection. Like an entranced dwarf gazing upon a mound of gold, he took his fateful steps closer and closer.

"Finally, Dulgin. Now you can replace that ugly armor of yours," Spilf called out.

The Dwarf's plate mail had been an eye-sore for years, and with each combat encounter, it became worse. It was more of a liability for those in the vicinity with its sharp rusty protrusions of peeled metal from the open gashes, slashes and holes punctured into it. Bridazak, Spilf, and Abawken watched together as their burly friend was almost upon the much needed new suit of armor. They looked forward to the forthcoming improved Dulgin Hammergold.

Dulgin began to stretch out his arms and clopped along faster with each step as his stiffened legs mechanically moved toward the item. The faces of his adventuring comrades suddenly shifted, however, when he stumbled right past the magical armor and locked his muscled arms around the keg just beyond. He positioned himself to take a mouthful of the mythical substance that had diminished over the centuries within the human communities that flourished across Ruauck-El—his beloved dwarven ale. He released the corked bottom and was rewarded with the high alcohol content filling his mouth, sloshing over the sides, dribbling through his red-beard, and cascading down the front of his dented armor.

"Unbelievable," said Spilf.

"Yep," Bridazak groaned.

Abawken stepped forward. "Come on, we will need Master Dulgin's senses about him for what lies ahead of us."

They hurried to Dulgin's side and pushed the cork back into the keg, cutting off the dwarf's freely streaming ale. Dulgin stood and pulled forth his waterskin, where he proceeded to squeeze the fresh water from the container, emptying it completely. The others folded their arms across their chests and waited as Dulgin filled his waterskin with the alcohol. When he finished, he smiled and lifted his red bushy eyebrows in victory.

"Are you ready?" Bridazak spryly asked.

"Do any of you want your waterskin filled?"

"We prefer our water," Spilf retorted.

"Fine, suit yer self. Let's go," Dulgin turned to the cask of ale, gave it a hearty pat and said, "I will be back for you later."

"What about the armor, Master Dulgin?"

"What about it? It's ugly. Something my brother would wear, not me. C'mon, we have your family to rescue and King Manasseh to deal with, *again*."

The band of heroes made their way down the circular stairway, noticing the ambient temperature becoming warmer the lower they descended. The chrysalis-like finish lessened and the smoothly worked stone turned rough, raw, and jagged. The pure, cold air gradually shifted to a grimy and humid draft, with the dust of chipped stone and a sulfurous odor assailing their nostrils.

"Well, at least we are going down this time," Spilf gripped Abawken's backpack to keep from falling with dizziness, not used to the excessive elevations rise and falls they had recently travelled.

"Yer heavy breathing will alert anyone we're coming, that's for sure," Dulgin retorted.

Bridazak suddenly stopped. Spilf said, "Oh good, a break."

"No, listen."

They all did as instructed. Spilf focused his labored breaths and cocked his head slightly to make out what the sound was, but deep down he was thankful for the rest as he leaned against the wall. Distant clanking of metal into rock echoed up the stairway.

"Someone is doing a bit of mining," Dulgin said. "C'mon, lets have a looksee."

Once they reached the bottom, Dulgin, using his natural ability to see through the darkness, led the way. The passages, although not completely dark, were difficult enough that the others could not navigate effectively without bumping into a corner of a wall or possibly stepping into an open chasm in the floor.

The dwarven tunnels, engineered long ago, were well structured and interconnected, lacing the lower levels to harbor and convey the many dwarven brethren, though all the passageways were now creepily empty. Strong, reinforced wooden doors with metal banding were held open by pitons. They cautiously walked further through the halls until finally finding a strange opening that did not match the dwarven engineering. The sound of hammers striking rock echoed strongly. An abhorrent odor assaulted them from the visible break in the wall along with a strange red aura casting an eerie glow.

"That is rank," Spilf said.

"Goblin. A smell every dwarf is warned about at an early age."

"We have encountered this race above ground, but never smelled anything like this before," Bridazak stated.

"Gock-Turnin and his foul breed are the underdwellers of the goblins. They give off a fine mixture of feces, sweat, and death, something us dwarves like to call *fengle*."

"Is there anything we should be aware of when we encounter them, Master Dulgin?"

"Yeah, don't let them breathe on you. I have seen them put down the mightiest of dwarves with that alone. Other than that, they bleed, and they die. We will find small groupings patrolling their tunnels, and one is required to escape to alert the horde while the others keep us occupied. Their strength is in their numbers and we cannot afford to alert the horde. Bridazak and Spilf will focus on the *goffen*, the runner, while Abawken and I will take the others. Don't worry about the noise as they don't hear well, but their sight is uncanny."

"What about their sense of smell?" Bridazak asked.

"Bah, with that bad breath of theirs they ain't be smellin nothin but their arses."

They looked down the crumbly-edged passage. Floor pedestaled braziers contained heated stones that rested inside the cast iron, giving a crimson glow. A magical source of lighting produced eerie shadows, and gave the sense of lava flowing nearby. The smell intensified, and the orda-kians and human had to cover their noses with their hands at times. A maze of chaotic mining tunnels engulfed them as they slinked beyond the frost dwarf lair. Precision was not a necessity for the goblins. These pas-sages had been developed in haste and with poor care. In some cases rudi-mentary beams appeared to be more decoration rather than structurally sound. There seemed to be no rhyme or reason to the passageways—more like aimless carvings in the earth, resembling the paths made by worms in search of food. When they came to another intersection of the woven tunnel, the sharp sounds of metal on hardened rock pierced more predomi-nantly. Dulgin peered around the corner first, and then quickly retreated with his back against the wall, and the others, hastily following his lead, did the same.

He whispered, "Mining slaves and a group of rovers passing by. Get ready."

The heroes could barely make out the trodding footsteps of the gobli-noid party, except to note that the barefoot creatures of the underground realm marched right by them, apparently not concerned with their passage-way in the slightest. The range of rusty red to dull green skin was the only difference to discern one from the next. Their eyes were a milky-white, loose skin sagged on their cheeks, no discernible outer ears, but instead sunken clefts where ears would have been, and misshaped bald heads rounded out the four-foot-tall foul race. A slender goblin, surrounded by his sword and spear-wielding kin, appeared jittery and held no weapon.

The heroes exhaled, relieved their first encounter would not be a fight. Dulgin waved them to follow. They turned the corner and walked only a few paces before discovering the source of the mining noises. A few frost dwarves slogged away at the tunnel wall with archaic picks, along with two humans, and an ordakian. Each miner focused on their task and mechani-cally swung away, as if in a trance. Spilf rushed to the dak and spun him around face to face. The frail male's face was blackened with the soot of mining, hair greasy and matted, and his eyes were a reflective purple.

"We are here to save you," Spilf said, but the expressionless face wanted to continue on with the meaningless job set before him. Spilf let him go and the ordakian carried on as if no interruption had occurred. Abawken and Dulgin approached the other slaves, who also had the same eye coloration.

"They are spellbound," Abawken announced.

"It must be the power of this Shiell-Zonn demon and the Sky Diamond," Bridazak surmised.

Suddenly, a different squad of goblins shuffled into the corridor further ahead of them, and instantly spotted the adventurers. A loud screech echoed from the reddish-green band as they charged. The weaker member of the clan sprinted back the way it came.

Dulgin shouted, "Get the goffen!"

Bridazak cried, "The what?"

"The runner, get the runner!"

17

The Sky Diamond

Bridazak, his bow at the ready, quickly drew an arrow from his quiver, notched it, and let it fly. The cold steel point pierced through the left calf of the fleeing goffen. Immediately, the runner's protectors charged the heroes, as the wounded goblin hobbled from sight to alert another group, working to create a chain reaction that would rally the entire horde. The clank of steel on steel echoed in the tunnels as Abawken and Dulgin, weapons in hand, engaged the six foul creatures. The dark dwellers swung recklessly, with the ferocity of madmen, while the fighter from Zoar had an elegance and skill unmatched by any in this region. The dwarf angrily met the group head on with overpowering strength behind every swing, shattering the first goblin's spear and then disemboweling the next, spilling its guts on the ground.

To bypass the melee, Spilf and Bridazak scooted along the wall, making it to the other side and entered a new tunnel. They followed a trail of blood that guided them through the twisting passage and soon came upon the wounded goblin, crawling and clawing away. His labored breathing created a reverberating whine. Bridazak readied another arrow, but Spilf unsheathed his dagger, and turned the goffen over to face him, straddling him to keep him pinned.

The goblin, in its scratchy voice and broken common language, threatened, "Horde come. Horde kill."

THE DRAGON GOD

"What are you doing with all of these slaves?" Spilf demanded, grabbing the leather strap across its chest and shoulder, and lifting him up to his face to intimidate him. Spilf was suddenly overcome by the smell and stumbled away. The creature pulled out a hidden knife, and shakily aimed it at Spilf, but an arrow slammed into its abdomen and the creature gurgled its final breath.

Dulgin and Abawken finished off the remaining goblins and then trotted down the tunnelway to find Bridazak and Spilf.
Dulgin chuckled, "Looks like you found Fengle Breath."
Spilf looked at him as he gagged. He leaned against the rock wall.
Dulgin said, "Just smell your pit. It will settle your stomach."
Spilf didn't argue and did as instructed, taking big whiffs of his sweaty armpit, then he relaxed and breathed a sigh of relief. Bridazak was by his side.
"I wasn't kidding about that smell."
They dragged the goffen corpse back to the group where Abawken and Dulgin had easily finished off the small band. Spilf used powdered rock dust to cover the blood trail and caught the dwarf eyeing him. Spilf said, "Learned this trick in my early days as a thief covering up a killing in Baron's Hall."
Dulgin nodded, "Nice trick."
The others carried the dead enemies back into the dwarven keep and piled them inside one of the many barren rooms. They had their first encounter of roving goblins and the goffen and felt ready to move deeper into Gock-Turnin's lair.
Bridazak and Spilf made their way ahead of Dulgin and Abawken, hiding in shadows cast by the glowing braziers stationed throughout, and then informing the others to follow once it was clear. The maze of tunnels continued without end. They came upon hundreds of mindless slaves hacking away at the walls. They stopped several times, but discovered it was nearly impossible to discern if Spilf's parents were amongst the many ordakians, because of the heavy layers of dirt covering their faces. Some of the entranced souls had died and lay along the passage; the smell of death intermingled with the goblin stench.
Spilf announced, "We are not going to find anything out until we free these people. Let's focus on retrieving the diamond and breaking this spell-trance they are in."

They nodded in agreement. The heroes eventually discovered metal tracks in the center of the red-hued walkway. Dulgin informed them that this was dwarven design; originally these depths had been mined for raw materials for building up into the mountain, including these rails to cart away debris. They followed the tracks and further down, they came upon a group of slaves throwing larger pieces of rock into a wheeled wooden box, reinforced with metal strapping.

"I have an idea," Bridazak said. "Spilf and I will hide inside a cart while you both cover yourself in the soot and pretend to be one of the Shiell-Zonn drones. Dulgin, you will have to remove your armor and also hide your weapons in the cart with us."

"Not really liking this idea much," the dwarf scoffed.

"We will be fine, Master Dulgin."

"If there is any action then Spilf can quickly hand you your weapons while I slow them down with arrows."

Dulgin reluctantly accepted, "Fine."

All weapons and Dulgin's armor were placed inside the wooden box. The daks climbed in after helping the others with their dirt smudged disguise. Bridazak and Spilf smirked after seeing the vibrant glow of their eyes under the blackened soot. Even Dulgin's red beard was darkened, completely transforming him into another dwarf.

The cart wobbled along the barely functional track system, accompanied by a persistent squeak, which echoed through the tunnel. Their wary eyes glanced down side channels, where more slaves hammered and chiseled away. The further on the track they went, the more slaves they encountered. Soon throngs of them combined, forming a cacophony of ear-splitting mining. Dulgin and Abawken spotted several goblin patrols in the vicinity, but none close enough to be a threat, but then they turned a bend and saw a band approaching.

"This is it; time to test out your plan," Dulgin whispered.

The dwarf and human kept their heads down as they slowly pushed the heavy load. The ordakians sunk lower and readied for any failure in the ruse.

The smelly goblin patrol, surrounding their goffen, came closer. The heroes' senses heightened as they held their breath in anticipation. There were hundreds of goblinoids in the area. One miscalculation would end their lives here in Ruauck-El. Dulgin and Abawken could feel the Goblin's eyes scanning them as they watched their sludge-covered feet pass by.

The human staggered as the overwhelming toxic fumes assaulted him. Thankfully, he was able to support himself on the wooden carriage. They had made it. The trick had worked, but before they could let out a sigh of relief, Dulgin stiffened as a trailing goblin decided to take a whiff of the dwarf. Short bursts of inhaling, like a dog sniffing after a scent, encompassed Dulgin's ears. Then it faded and the goblin returned to its duties.

The dwarf let out his held breath, "That was close."

"Too close," Abawken responded.

Dulgin squinted and pointed up ahead, "The tunnels are becoming more numerous, and I see more tracks. We might be approaching the sifting chamber where they will screen the rock. At least that is a dwarf thinkin, not one of these goblins. Who knows what the hell they are up to?"

After another hundred yards, they emerged into an immense cavern. Slaves, too numerous to count, littered the depot as they mingled amongst roaming guards. Carts came and went from tunnels in all directions, dumping their payload into rock piles where a collection of trance-induced races would sort and sift through the debris. Others broke the larger rocks brought to them into the quarry.

A diamond, the size of a Dwarven fist, was nestled twenty feet overhead. Its dazzling brightness stood out atop of the stalagmite structure in the center of the chamber. Beams of light spread out with a magical power resonating from inside the gemstone.

"How are we going to get that?" Spilf gasped as they slowly continued on the worn track system.

"We will have Huey fly up and grab it," Dulgin suggested.

"Master Dulgin, King Morthkin stated that only a good dwarf can obtain the Sky Diamond."

"Well, I can't climb up there."

"I can, for lack of a better term, float you up to it. Once you retrieve it, then the curse will be broken."

Bridazak added, "We can't have the horde come down and destroy everyone. All the slaves will be wiped out, including us. We have to create a distraction that won't bring the masses to investigate."

"What exactly are these goblins doing down here?" Spilf asked.

"Who knows, Stubby? These are mindless beasts, but if they continue digging all these tunnels without any rhyme or reason then they will be having some cave-ins for sure."

The group slowed their walk into the cavern, continuing to ascertain the situation and come up with a plan. They were running out of track as they approached a waiting group of slaves going through the piles. The heroes spotted a back section where the drones were pitching the debris into a mine-shaft, but instead of piling up, it vanished into the endless darkness below. Bridazak noticed several tunnels with a strange wooden marker above their entrances. They saw no patrols, nor slaves enter or exit these openings.

"Dulgin, what do the signs say above the darker tunnels?"

"What signs, ya blundering fool?"

He pointed in the direction and the dwarf squinted, "It says in goblin, 'Crash', but that don't make a bit of sense."

"Maybe, it is a tunnel ready to collapse," Spilf suggested.

"Let's make our way to one of them so we can hide and strategize. Those tunnels don't have any movement," said Bridazak.

The ordakians crept from the cart just before reaching the end of track. They distributed Abawken's and Dulgin's weapons and huddled around the dwarven armor, carrying it together, as they kept their heads low and weaved between the endless slaves, avoiding the guard patrols. Within a minute they reached one of the 'Crash' titled openings, hurried in, and hid within the shadows, peering back out into the lighted work camp.

"Now what?" Dulgin asked while donning his dented armor.

"Let's find out what 'crash' means," Bridazak suggested and then took a step into the passage.

Dulgin led the party until they were out of sight of the main chamber. Once there, Abawken caused his sword to glow.

Spilf frowned, "I have been lighting torches and this entire time you could have had your sword do that?"

"My apologies, Master Spilf, but it only gives off low light, and you needed the warmth."

The dwarf snapped, "Shut your traps. I see something up ahead."

They crept closer to the strange stalagmite Dulgin had seen and pointed out to the others.

"What is that?" Bridazak asked.

"Not sure, but it is no *fichin*." The dwarf answered their questioning looks before they could speak, "Dwarven word for stalagmite."

"How can you tell?"

"Cause it's moving."

They approached the strange silhouetted object, slowly. When they were thirty-feet from it, Dulgin raised his closed fist sharply, halting them. He nodded, indicating they were to turn back. They did as instructed. When they were far enough away, Dulgin said, "That is known as a screamer. Any loud enough sound will cause it to shriek uncontrollably as a defensive measure. I've seen their shrieking bring down the toughest of dwarves. The goblins use them in their warfare tactics."

"Why is it down here?" Spilf asked.

"Because they want the tunnels to fall," Bridazak answered. "They plan on bringing down the Shield once and for all. That is why they are digging all the tunnels and they have the slaves to sacrifice. It will kill them all."

"They still have several months of work to do before that will happen," Dulgin surmised.

"Somewhere amongst all these people, are my parents. How are we going to find them?"

They looked long and hard at one another as the complexity of the situation continued to layer itself. Bridazak placed his hand into the middle of their gathering. The others understood and each placed theirs on top.

Bridazak prayed aloud, "Lord, we need your help. We are not sure what we need to do and ask for your guidance amongst our enemy." He ended and everyone nodded in agreement.

"Well, did you get the answer?" Dulgin blurted.

Bridazak chuckled, "No my friend, not yet."

"Why isn't he answering us?"

Bridazak smirked, "C'mon, it will unfold itself in due time."

Staying hidden in the shadows, they made their way back to the opening.

"Why don't you just call on him like you did at the village and smite all the goblins?" Dulgin asked.

"That time, I felt a sort of instinct, almost like an invisible nudging to do that, but I'm not feeling anything like that right now."

Dulgin suddenly pushed Bridazak, "Did you feel a nudge now?"

Bridazak smiled, "It doesn't work like that my friend."

"Well, he gave you the box, the Orb of Truth, a magical bow and arrows, ability to see angels, oh, and don't forget about challenging other gods and winning. I'm sure a nudging is forthcoming."

Spilf pointed to the chamber, "Guys, something is going on out there."

The goblins throughout the massive enclosed space fell to their knees and lowered their faces into the dirt. A golden statue of a huge, muscled goblin adorned with a gem encrusted crown was slowly being carried through the room on the shoulders of several robed members of the foul race, on display before the bulk of the goblin army. A metallic voice echoed from the image, "Roth kemtock viemont koth-vutoth!"

In unison, the goblin followers yelled, "Gock-Turnin!"

As the effigy passed, the clan rose one by one, and followed the procession back into the largest tunnel entrance in the area.

"What is happening?" Spilf asked.

"This is their time of worship to their king. The prideful bastard Gock-Turnin needs his followers to revere him."

"I believe God has given us our answer. This is the moment to get the Sky Diamond, and get our people out of here."

Dulgin grinned, gripped his axe, and said, "Nudging time."

Several minutes passed as the throngs of goblins exited the area, but a handful of guards stayed behind.

"Dulgin, are Stone Elementals common for goblins to encounter in the mines?" Bridazak asked.

"Not common, but I'm sure it has happened. Why?"

"Time for our distraction."

"I'm not following you."

"Let's see what happens when you combine a rock monster, some goblins, and a screamer."

18

King of Secrets

Rozelle found Trillius below deck, sitting on a wooden crate in the same storage room they had hidden in when they first stowed away aboard *A Pinch of Luck*.

"What are you doing, Trillius?" she demanded.

He casually turned, rolled his eyes, and sarcastically answered, "Um, it appears that I am sitting on my favorite crate within my favorite room."

"No, I mean, what is wrong with you? You have been distant, irrational, irritated, and—"

He snapped, "And what, Rozelle?"

"I don't know, you are just different."

"I am finally being me. If you don't like it, then leave," Trillius scoffed.

Rozelle's brow furrowed, "How can you say that? You are nothing but a *phelping, sootkin...*" she stuttered, searching for more gnomish insults, shoulders tense, until she let it all out with a shout, "I am leaving you!"

Trillius smirked, hopped down from his crate, took Rozelle's arm, and ushered her out the door, "Give my best to the trees."

As she stormed off, Trillius playfully swayed back and forth as if he were waltzing with an imaginary partner and danced back to the wooden crate.

The soothing, powerful voice of Dal-Draydian, continued to coach him, speaking inside his mind, *"You have done well, Trillius. Beyond my expectations. You will have unfathomable wealth. Each day I grow stronger because of you."*

"Thank you," Trillius replied and chuckled, *"Care to dance? I am feeling a whole lot better now that I am rid of that heavy sack of grain."* He tilted his head back, spread his arms, twirled in his dance and laughed, *"As usual, Dal-Draydian, you were right."*

The day of their departure arrived. A cloudless sky and beaming sun lifted the spirits of everyone aboard, many still adjusting from the underwater encounter and the loss of crew members. The heroes gathered before Captain Elsbeth and her commanders. It was time to bid a final farewell as Raina prepared her magic that would transport them to the Shield.

"Captain Elsbeth, thank you for your trust, and for having the courage to go back to a place of sorrow," Raina said.

"It is I who should be thanking you. My faith has been restored, and I am sure it is not solely because I conquered my fear of going back to *The Wave Rider's* resting place."

Raina smiled knowingly, "The God of all gods has opened his arms to all, including you."

Elsbeth returned her smile and nodded.

Xan locked arms with Lufra in a warrior embrace, "Lufra, you will do well, young lad."

"So you aren't mad at me?"

"It warms my heart that you have decided to become part of the crew of *A Pinch of Luck*. Just promise me something."

"Anything, what is it?"

"Lead with your heart and keep practicing your skill with the blade."

"You can count on it. Thank you for all you have done for me and my family. I will never forget you."

"Nor will I, Lufra Yasooma."

"Maybe someday we will meet again."

"I'm sure of it."

El'Korr approached Anders the Priest at the back of the crowd. He extended his arm, "Well met, Anders."

Anders grasped the dwarf's forearm, "Blessings upon you—" Anders felt another coughing frenzy upon him. He tried to let go but El'Korr held on.

The Dwarven King said, intensity in his eyes, "Priest of the Most High, you are a father to many aboard this ship and not one of them would you give sickness to prove or test your point. The true God releases you of this burden but only if you acknowledge what I have said unto you."

Anders stared back at him, while trying to keep the cough at bay.

El'Korr brought him in close, "Let it go, my friend, and be free of this."

With glassy eyes, the human lunged at El'Korr and latched onto his full plate armor. Ander's throat was dry as he gasped, "I heard Him. He spoke to me through you."

Instantly, Anders spasms ceased. He rubbed his throat in shock, but also a sense of joy on his face. Anders began to walk away, without another word, but then turned and said, "Thank you."

Knowing Anders had an encounter with the God of all gods, El'Korr smiled and returned to his friends.

Rondee the Wild was bear-hugging every crew member, thanking them for showing him the ropes. Every time he hoisted a man in his burly arms, a cheer erupted from their shipmates. Rondee's broad smile prominently displayed his yellow teeth through his grizzled beard.

As he approached Skath and Myers, both quickly held their hands up in front of them indicating they were beyond hugging a dwarf, but Rondee would not be put off, he pushed their arms aside and bull rushed them to the deck.

"Kay meosh like te!" he said in his unique gibberish.

In spite of being thrown to the deck, Skath and Myers couldn't help but laugh and then slapped Rondee's back to acknowledge his love for them.

El'Korr responded, "Not many people of Ruauck-El can say they hugged a wild dwarf and lived to tell about it."

Raina bowed her head slightly to Urlin Thoom. "Well met, Urlin. Your knowledge of the arts is well founded and I hope you will continue to utilize your power for good."

"I will, Mistress Raina. It has been an honor to serve you and I hope our paths cross again."

Rozelle sullenly gathered with the group. Trillius was not with her.

"Where is Long-nose?" El'Korr asked.

"Don't know and don't care," she retorted.

His bushy orange eyebrows raised, "Oh, are we having a gnomer's quarrel," he laughed. Rozelle did not share in his humor.

Raina announced their departure, "It is time for us to leave. Are we ready?" She looked around, "Where is Trillius?"

El'Korr answered, "Apparently, not go—"

"I'm right here!" Trillius emerged between the legs of one of the sailors who jumped back in shock when the gnome emerged from under him. He walked to Rozelle, "I apologize for my actions," he mumbled.

Her brow crinkled in thought, not believing his words, and waiting for him to turn on her again. Trillius grabbed her hand and placed an item into it, "This is for you." It was a shiny seashell. Rozelle glared at him, holding back a smile.

Trillius playfully said, "Something I picked up along the way."

She hugged him and kissed him on the cheek.

As he thought, *"Well that was easy"*, Dal-Draydian's voice flooded into his mind, *"Well done, you are following my instructions perfectly; keep your enemies close."*

Raina approached Trillius and Rozelle, "You both are free to leave on your own. Your services and debts are paid. There is no need for you to accompany us."

Trillius looked to Rozelle, she smiled lovingly, and he enthusiastically replied, "We wouldn't want to be any other place. We are looking forward to getting off this ship. No offense, Captain."

Elsbeth grinned, answering, "None taken, we share the same goal." Skath and Myers chuckled.

Trillius locked arms with Rozelle, turned to Raina, and said, "We are ready."

"I never noticed your eyes before," Raina announced, studying a trace of glowing blue in Trillius' irises.

Trillius tapped his nose, "Most notice the nose first. I get my eyes from my mother."

In this special moment, Trillius's brain rang with Dal-Draydian's spirit voice, *"Excellent. Well played, Master Trillius. This elf wizard will take us directly to the place of power, where we will both be free, and you Trillius, will become the Dragon God."*

19

Crash!

Bridazak, with his bow and arrows hidden inside a mine cart, once again mingled with Spilf amongst the slaves. They crossed to the other side of the cavern, mentally marking out the remaining goblins; twenty spread throughout the cavernous area, plus one goffen, who took position by the large opening leading back to their massive army. When Bridazak and Spilf were in place for their plan to unfold, Bridazak nodded to Abawken, who waited, hiding in a dark passage with the dwarf.

"Are you ready, Master Dulgin?"

"C'mon Huey, let's get Bridazak's plan in motion before I change my mind."

Abawken pointed his sword and softly spoke the word to release its magic. A growl echoed from the cave that held the screamer. The surprised goblin troops tentatively approached the tunnel, weapons at the ready. Abawken's summoned rock elemental emerged out into the lighted area, causing green humanoids to freeze in astonishment. Several goblins threw their spears, which ricocheted off the massive rock beast. It slunk back into the dark tunnel. The goblin band followed, leaving two to guard the opening.

As Bridazak watched, Abawken soared out of an adjacent tunnel. Dulgin was draped over his back, holding on for dear life around the human's neck. They flew toward the Sky Diamond. The goffen spotted the intruders and turned to run, but Bridazak had fired his first arrow, in anticipation, which slammed into its back, sending the goffen sprawling face first into the dirt floor of the cave.

Spilf alerted his friend, "Bridazak, here come the two guards."

The goblins charged from the far side. Bridazak aimed his bow in their direction, but suddenly spotted the distinct glowing yellow eyes of a hovering shadow next to the stalagmite that cradled the Sky Diamond.

"Reeg!" he yelled to alert his partners in the heist of the new threat, and just as quickly fired his arrow at the specter-like menace. The whistling shaft flew through the bodiless image with no effect. Bridazak knew the Reeg would report back to the Dark Lord of the underworld—something far worse than the horde of Goblins. Bridazak no longer had any special arrows, so, remembering their last encounter with the reegs at the temple within the great Everwood forest, he realized Abawken's sword was the only thing that could damage it. He was about to run toward Abawken, but Spilf, dagger in hand, stepped up to intercept the pair of goblins that were almost upon them. Bridazak glanced to where the goffen had fallen, but quickly noticed it was gone—a trail of blood led into the large tunnel. The goffen had lived, and the plan was unraveling before their eyes. The reeg had backed away, ready to vanish into the shadows and teleport back to Kerrith Ravine with its findings. Bridazak refocused his attention on the brazen goblins who were about to impale his friend. Ignoring the reeg, he fired an arrow. It slammed into the thug's chest, propelling it several feet backward with a force that swept the creature's legs up into the air. Bridazak was unable to get the last attacker as Spilf held his dagger ready to fight it.

"Slow down, Huey!"

"Are you ready, Master Dulgin?"

"I'm not flying with you for fun, Princey. Yeah, I'm ready!"

The brilliance of the Sky Diamond intensified, it rested at the top, and waited to be in the hand of a good dwarf. They were a body's length away when Abawken suddenly slammed into an invisible wall, sending Dulgin flying through the air, arms flailing, and then impacting the rock column. The human fighter slid down to the ground, dazed by the force. Dulgin, unaffected by the magical barrier, clung to the stalagmite in a desperate hug, his battle-axe strapped to his back. Glancing up, Dulgin realized he needed to climb a few more feet before grabbing the precious stone.

Abawken, shaking off the effects of his crash, called, "Master Dulgin, can you make it?"

"Not if you are going to be blabbing the entire time. Help the others."

With nothing more that Abawken could do to help Dulgin, the human ran off to assist Bridazak and Spilf. The dwarf had made it through the invisible wall, and was on his way to touching the gem.

Spilf was surprised when a lizardman fighter miraculously blurred into view as it parried the goblin's sword that came down to strike the ordakian. The new visitor, wearing nothing but a leather loin cloth, blended into the environment like a ghost, but when steel met steel, the defender material-ized. Its slithery tongue hissed and its scaled tail swished back and forth as it brought up its longsword and shield.

Bridazak cried out, "It's okay Spilf, it belongs to Abawken!"

Spilf backed away as the goblin and lizard creature battled it out. Bridazak looked for the reeg once more, but the shadowy wisp had van-ished. A chill ran through his body in remembrance of his encounter with the evil lord, ruler of Kerrith Ravine, within King Manasseh's cell.

"C'mon, let's get to the tunnel and make sure none of the other goblins escape."

They met up with Abawken who had arrived at the tunnel the same moment they did.

"Where is Dulgin?" Bridazak asked.

"He is getting the Sky Diamond, something he must do on his own."

At this point, the lizardman, with mucus blood dripping off of its blade, sleekly walked up behind them and waited for his next orders. Abawken held up his hand, indicating it was to hold for the time being.

"Thanks for the help," Spilf said to Abawken, who nodded.

The sound of muffled echoes of distant fighting further down the tunnel, informed them that the goblins and the rock elemental were close to the screamer.

Bridazak sighed, "I hate to say it, but the goffen got away. He is injured, but there is no telling how long we have."

"Let's go after it, then," Spilf suggested.

"Too dangerous, Master Spilf. Our best option is to retrieve the Sky Diamond and get these people back into the castle to set up defenses."

Just then, a high-pitched, ear-splitting screech reverberated around them. They quickly clamped their hands over their ears as they winced in pain and backed away from the entrance to the tunnel. Stones along the edging vibrated and then the walls cracked. In seconds, the entire structure collapsed into a debris-showered pile of rubble, sealing it off. Clouds of dust poured from the tunnel and enveloped the heroes. A wooden sign fell at their feet, the single goblin word carved into its surface proclaimed what had happened, and exactly as they'd hoped: *crash*.

Coughing, Bridazak said, "It's up to Dulgin, now. C'mon."

Beads of sweat trickled down Dulgin's brow, dripping through his red bushy eyebrows as he climbed another foot closer. A determination to free the people still mindlessly slaving below brought him an inner strength. With weathered hands, he navigated the rough stalagmite, feeling the uneven indentions with uncertainty, and using his leg muscles to clamp and help push himself higher and higher. It was slow going, but he was getting a feel for the rock tower as he approached the tapered pinnacle, where the Sky Diamond shined brightly.

Dulgin's heart stopped in shock when Abawken, hovering just outside the protective invisible shield, said softly, "Master Dulgin, we know you can do it."

Dulgin gasped, "Damn you, Huey! Don't be sneakin up on me like that."

Suddenly, the reeg that Bridazak had spotted earlier materialized between Abawken and the rock climbing dwarf. Its yellow eyes glowed within its shadowy blurred outline, glaring at Abawken.

"Master Dulgin, reeg."

"What? Where?"

"Move with haste, Dulgin!"

The reeg, still too far out of reach to attack, continued to stare at Abawken behind the shield, which would not hinder the creature from launching itself at him. However, it did not. He noticed that this reeg was different than the others he had encountered. Its features were similar to the shadowy beings, but this one had a stronger pull of evil. Abawken felt despair rising inside and his heart quickened with heightened thumps. The eyes of the assailant burned a bright yellow with a tinge of red and the black smokey substance that formed its body appeared thicker and more tangible. Abawken thought, *"This isn't me."* He resisted the sudden bout of fear and he felt the burden on his shoulders and chest lift away. Abawken realized this reeg was the demon, Shiell-Zonn, the dwarven king spoke of.

Dulgin glanced quickly over his shoulder and then hollered, "Holy orc-shit!" He shuffled around the cone shaped rock, where he found a larger palm sized opening to grip firmly. Only a foot's distance now separated him from the prize—the Sky Diamond.

Suddenly, the reeg, moving in and out of the dimensional plane of shadows at will, a creature unhindered by material objects, faded away before Abawken's eyes. "It's gone," the human announced. Bridazak and Spilf searched desperately for an opening in the shielding below him.

Dulgin had no time to keep track of the reeg, and kept his focus on holding tightly. A bitter cold gripped him as the spectre from Kerrith Ravine slowly materialized within the stalagmite. Its glowing eyes, showing through, stared directly into Dulgin's face. His hands began to shake and lose strength as he tried to back away. The infernal beast was draining the life from Dulgin's body. It pulled on his energy. He could not hold on much longer. His friends could do no more than watch in horror. The dwarf bellowed as one hand lost its grip and fell away from the rock. He dangled from his last good grip. The shadow crept over the remaining hold. Anger swelled within the dwarf. He pulled out his father's axe with his free hand and hooked the edge at the top of the naturally formed column. The reeg edged out further, making contact with the dwarf's chest and arms. Dulgin roared and fought through the draining effect, pulling himself higher until he was close enough to reach the diamond. The shadow immersed itself inside Dulgin, who barely held on. With one hand on his axe, he quickly reached up and snagged the valued treasure. The reeg screeched an unworldly cry as the light of the Sky Diamond, now in a worthy dwarf's possession, incinerated its murky outline. Dulgin crashed to the ground, and tumbled into a roll, adding another dent to his armor. The invisible shield crackled away, and his friends were quickly by his side, rolling him over to face them.

"Are you okay?"

"I hate climbing."

His friends chuckled with a sigh of relief.

"Can you stand?"

"Yeah, help me up." As they assisted him, Dulgin winced in pain. "My lucky rib is broken again."

"Lucky?" Abawken questioned.

"Lucky it was just one," Dulgin responded, bringing more laughter.

"Hey guys, look! Everyone has stopped working," Spilf alerted them.

They gazed about and saw that the mining had ceased and the simple tools had fallen to the ground. The denizens slowly returned to their natural state. Bewildered faces, followed by a sea of murmurs of, "Where are we? What happened?" echoed as clusters of former slaves formed.

Dulgin held up the Sky Diamond, the beacon of light. Enslaved frost dwarves' strength returned, icicles formed on their soot covered beards and hair, and a blue hue crept out from under the layers of dirt on their faces and bodies.

Bridazak stepped up and yelled out, "We need to head back to the castle. The horde of Gock-Turnin will be coming."

Not a soul flinched from his announcement. Dulgin blared, "Get movin!"

A few raspy, dry voices sounded in several directions, "This way!" The throngs began their march through the endless tunnels and back into the fortress. Frost dwarves took over commanding the masses more and more as their senses returned.

"Master Dulgin, your axe," Abawken said as he handed him his inherited weapon after retrieving it atop of the stalagmite.

"Many thanks, Huey."

After trudging through the tunnels for the better part of an hour, Spilf, out of breath as he still adjusted to the elevation sickness, said, "My parents are amongst these people. How are we supposed to find them?"

Bridazak, smiling, clasped Spilf's shoulder, "You will see them soon, my friend. We did it. They have to be here. Once we return the Diamond, then we can find them."

They had reached the castle wall that led to the many barracks of King Morthkin's keep, but smiles turned to concern when heightened voices sounded in front of the heroes; gurgled screams, muffled yelling, and clashing of steel echoed off the tunnel walls. A crowd surged toward them as they fought to see what was causing the commotion. They finally broke through and saw a black armored knight, wielding a two-handed sword. He was surrounded by frost dwarves.

Manasseh pointed his blade's tip toward the heroes and his booming voice resounded, "It is time for my revenge, Bridazak."

20

Dragon's Lair

El'Korr, Rondee, and Xan were joined by Trillius and Rozelle as they surrounded Raina the Sheldeen mystic, who stood with her arms tightly at her sides as she bowed her head in preparation. The powerful ritual she was about to begin would transport the entire group to a new location within the realm. A hush fell over the crewmembers of *A Pinch of Luck* as they watched the magical feat with great anticipation.

Raina, with her eyes closed, took a deep breath and then exhaled slowly, raised her arms to the bright blue sky and chanted, "Alu thornec fehu trechts gaar." Eerie whispers echoed her words as she continued, "Urus fe, gewareda haal noths." Crackling energy manifested and encircled the gathered band. The soft glow shifted to a deeper yellow and blurred the outlines of the individuals inside. "Ezec eis quairtra daz!" A perfect sphere of topaz encapsulated them and then instantly imploded. The distant sound of thunder rumbled and faded. Light ocean spray and calm winds remained as the crew stared wide-eyed in wonder as the adventurers teleported to their next destination.

The Guul-Fenn Mountain range, an isolated section within the fallen North Horn King's territory, extended for hundreds of miles to the northwest. The largest peak, known only as the Shield, contained the legendary fortress of the frost dwarves.

Raina and the group found themselves before an opening in the mountain. Frigid air encircled them. Icicles formed at the cave entrance like jagged teeth. They had been transported to an icy ledge thousands of feet above the ground, high in the clouds, where they saw the peaks of mountains poking through the billowy blanket.

Raina said, "My spell has only brought us close to our destination. We must travel by foot the rest of the way. This cave must lead to the Chamber of Cleansing."

El'Korr shivered, "Let's get movin before we freeze to death."

"I will take the chill off our travels." Raina waved her arms about and whispered incantations until lanterns materialized and hovered over each of them, producing light and the warmth they yearned for.

Trillius snapped, "I prefer not to have a beacon over my head alerting every creature, 'here I am'."

"As you wish," Raina said and then dispelled his lantern.

Trillius stomped ahead of everyone, snow crunching under foot, as if bothered to be in the presence of the group that followed. Raina edged close to King El'Korr. "Be mindful of the gnome. I have noticed a shift in his attitude since he discovered the Pearl."

"Aye, so have I. Do your magical senses tell you more?"

"There is a cloud around him that obscures my detections. I didn't notice it before."

Xan and Rondee were also discreetly warned of the change in Trillius. Rozelle noticed close whispers from the back of the pack and her gnomish instinct immediately sensed it was about Trillius.

The six of them wended their way slowly on the slippery blue ice floor of the tunnel a few miles into the mountain. The massive tube snaked through until bursting into a gigantic cave. Icicles clung to the ceiling, some of which were the size of large tree bases. Frozen stalagmites and boulders dotted the surface and a distinct odor of frozen meat greeted them at the entrance.

"Is this the chamber you were talking about, Raina?" El'Korr asked.

"No, according to Yasooma's journal, it is much smaller. He also mentioned being greeted by frost dwarves at some point—the militia of the Shield."

"It is deathly quiet," Xan said in a low voice.

Rondee sniffed the air with short intakes, and snarled, "Draco piete."

"What did he say?" Rozelle asked.

"Dragon shit," El'Korr translated.

"Where is Trillius?" Raina asked.

Everyone turned and scanned the area. They spotted him on top of a large ice encrusted boulder twenty-yards ahead. The three-foot gnome raised his hands and smiled.

"C'mon! It is only dragons, nothing to fear."

As he called to them, a majestic, white, horned dragon with scales that glistened like mirrors, rose behind him and flapped its leathery, translucent wings. Its streamlined head had a high crest at the back of the skull and a frothy frost built at the edges of its jaw line. The cottage sized wyrmling roared forth an ear splitting screech. It reeked of a vague chemical odor.

Raina, fearful to cast a spell as Trillius was in the way, yelled to him, "Duck!"

Trillius grinned and said, "You have your own friends to deal with, don't worry about me little-Elf."

Suddenly, two more white flying beasts, sleek like the other, dropped from the ceiling behind them, camouflaged amongst the stalactites.

The heroes spun and Raina shouted, "Get behind me!"

The group did as instructed. The two white dragons swooped in and released their breath weapon—cones of freezing air intended to engulf everyone, but Raina had quickly cast a spell and their blasts were blocked by a fiery shield that she leaned into as the two energy forces collided. The hiss of steam combined with the howling frozen wind assailed their ears while huddled tightly behind Raina.

Thanks to the broken curse of the Burning Forest, El'Korr and Rondee were granted the innate ability to summon fire. They broke away with their weapons ignited. El'Korr hurled his magical warhammer and it toppled end over end until finding its mark. It slammed into the right leg of the pearlescent creature who had just zoomed past them. Glistening scales shattered and fell. The beast craned its neck while in flight to see who had damaged it. Rondee did not have a missile weapon, but instead waited for it to come back around for another attack.

Xan made his way toward Trillius, longsword drawn, "Take cover, Trillius!"

The gnome crossed his arms, confidently smiling, "My dear Xan, the time has come for you to witness the true power of the Great Trillius."

The elf watched as the dragon that stood behind the gnome ignored Trillius and flew toward the other two serpents, crashing into one and engaging it with a claw-raking frenzy until it fell to the ground. The third shot passed the jumbled mess of its kin and narrowed in on the dwarves instead.

Raina quickly launched another invocation. Rays of scorching heat sprouted from her fingertips and bore into the beast, melting its scales. With its flesh sizzling, it screeched in pain, but continued its attack with alabaster eyes focused on Rondee, who frantically waved his arms around to grab the attention of the beast.

The wild dwarf stood his ground, pointed his tiny golden hammer toward it and felt the surge of his wild magic bursting from inside him. His arms vibrated and then his entire body transformed. Skin, clothes, armor, and weapon, all morphed into a gigantic steel-tipped spear anchored into the ground.

The dragon flew into the suddenly changed dwarf, impaled itself, and toppled to the floor of the cave, crashing through iced stalagmites, lifeless. Raina, El'Korr, and Xan ran to the carnage and watched the pointed tip of the spear sticking through the neck of the dragon, convert back to Rondee the Wild. He smiled, his yellow teeth prominently glowing amongst the gore, as blood dripped down his face. His head was all they could see as the rest of his body was stuck inside the fallen creature.

Echoed claps resounded behind them. They turned to see Trillius applauding the outcome. "Very entertaining."

Rozelle had moved closer to her partner while the fighting had gone on, thinking she would protect him, "What are you doing, Trillius?"

He smiled down at her. His eyes glowed a bright blue. She backed away, fearful. The other two dragons continued their internal fighting in the background. Each had deadlocked jaws into the other's body in an all-out death grapple.

El'Korr and Xan cut open the dead dragon to release Rondee, who shook the guts and blood from himself and scraped off larger chunks from his arms and chest. Raina kept her wary eyes on Trillius. The heroes gathered next to Rozelle.

Raina addressed the male gnome, "Trillius, are you okay?"

He scoffed, "Of course I'm okay. I feel great!"

Rozelle said, "What's going on Trillius? You are different."

Trillius took a proud stance, "I am no longer weak, and all those who stand against me will feel the wrath of my power." Electrical snaps sparkled in his eyes.

"You have to fight, Trillius; don't let it overcome you," Raina commanded.

"My dear little-Elf, you have no more say over me. You are indeed powerful, but the time is coming when you will bow before me. All of you will bow before me." Trillius laughed as he raised his arms, and a bolt of lightning materialized. The heroes quickly turned away from the intense light. With a booming crack of thunder, Trillius instantly disappeared.

21

Who Was That?

E l'Korr, reacting to Trillius' disappearance, approached Raina, "Who was that? It sure wasn't Trillius."

"Trillius has succumbed to the power of an ancient soul of a blue-wyrm. He has the fifth dragon stone."

"What do you mean succumb to the power?" Rozelle asked.

"The dragons held captive within these stones are the most powerful of the entire realm. They look for the weak minded so they can dominate them. Only those with the strongest will can compete with the warring spirit, but even then it is a constant battle."

Xan joined the group, "Where did he acquire it?"

"I suspect it was at the time he found the Pearl. We all noticed how his attitude shifted after the kelpie encounter. Even Captain Romann saw a change in him."

"We have to save him! Stupid Trillius. He has a sickness, Raina."

"What ailment do you speak of, Rozelle?"

"He can't stop stealing things. He is always in search of the next big thing."

"But where did he go? How are we supposed to find him?" asked El'Korr.

"In order for the dragon to come back, which is its ultimate goal, it would have gone to the Chamber of Cleansing."

"But why?" Xan asked, puzzled.

"From what I have gathered, the chamber was used as a conduit in conjunction with the elements to summon, entrap, and then banish the dragon god."

"But we can use the elements to destroy the blue rock, right?"

Raina paused, "Yes, but," she turned to Rozelle before continuing, "I am uncertain as to what will happen to Trillius."

Rozelle began to walk away. Glancing over her shoulder she cried, "C'mon, we need to get him back before it is too late. He is a thief on the run, nothing else. I know that his mind is still in there fighting this dragon entity."

"You understand, now that he has the fifth stone, the other dragon spirits will be coming. It will be difficult to get to Trillius and destroy it before it destroys him."

"Then why are we still here talking about it? Come on, let's go," Rozelle snapped.

They marched on across the immense chamber to find a marked tunnel. Four symbols, indicating the four elements, surrounded a star in the middle.

El'Korr lingered at the back of the group with Rondee. He spoke to his guardian in Dwarvish so the others could not understand, "Rondee, do what you have to do in order to stop Trillius. This Dragon God cannot come back."

Rondee the Wild nodded his understanding.

Unbeknownst to the dwarves, Rozelle understood most of the languages in the realms, including the dwarven tongue. *"They don't understand you Trillius. You do have good in you. I won't let them hurt you,"* she thought to herself. The entire situation caused anger to boil inside of her, but regardless, her anger was focused on Trillius and this blue stone that had corrupted his mind.

Trillius appeared inside the doorway to the Chamber of Cleansing. Blue electrical discharges snapped around his body and his eyes were brighter than ever. He surveyed the room. It was circular: four stone pedestals surrounded a gaping hole in the earth almost as large as the room itself, where it plunged into an unknown depth. A catwalk archway, inscribed with ancient runes, ran across the middle of the opening. At the apex of the curved walkway was another pedestal with five colored markers that looked like clawed hands to hold the dragon stones. Trillius stepped forward and peered down, seeing a swirling black and grey cloud, like a whirlpool, moving slowly.

Dal Draydian's voice vibrated excitedly in Trillius' mind, *"I can sense the other spirits coming. Now place me in my position in the center of the room, bondservant, where I will be set free."*

"Bondservant?" Trillius felt groggy, trying to comprehend why something didn't quite feel right. "Oh yeah, I guess I am a bondservant," the queasy feeling passing as he relaxed into the idea. "I wish Rozelle were here; she always takes care of me when I feel sick. Hey- where is Rozelle anyway?" His mind and body began to ache in the swirl of confusion. The gnome felt as if he was losing control of himself. "Where are all my friends?"

"Friends? I'm your only friend now. You have been picked on by every race, you have been unloved by your own family, no one knows you like I do, and no one will give you what I can give you. Riches!"

Fighting against the power in his brain, touching his temples and scrunching his face, Trillius cried, "No, it can't be true. They like me, I'm different than the others, but they still like me. I can't see them get hurt."

Suddenly, a forgotten memory flooded into the forefront of his mind as Dal-Draydian manipulated the gnomes deepest and darkest secrets. Trillius was huddled in the corner of a dark room, arms wrapped around his knees, and his head buried between them. Muffled yelling slowly transformed into his father's voice. Trillius was young and fear gripped him in his solitude. Then the blocked words hurdled toward his heart from his father, "I wish it was he that was dead and not my oldest boy! He is a waste of the air we breathe and is no son of mine!"

Dal-Draydian's voice slipped in, soothing and confident, *"I know your pains, Trillius. It is time for you to make your father proud of you as I am proud of you. We are now family, something you have always wanted. Take your destiny back and be free from the bondage of your past."*

Trillius lifted his tear streaked face, slowly smiled and took his first step onto the arch.

The black robed mystic stood with the assassin, Daysho Gunsen, and two other hired bodyguards on a ledge overlooking the Guul-Fenn Mountains. Before them, waited an icicle covered cave entrance.

"Raina was here. I can smell her lingering magic," Veric's words bit like the cold wind.

"I will retrieve the last of the stones from the gnome," Daysho responded.

Veric pointed toward the opening, like a commander giving orders. The two leather-armored humans nodded and entered, followed by the assassin and the wizard.

Daysho approached the hour that would change his life forever. It had taken him years to gain Veric's trust. The wizard was careful and calculating with those he worked with, as he should be. Daysho heard of Romann de Beaux's hatred toward the West Horn King's daughter, Ravana, and set his determined plan into action by contacting the vampire. The deal was to bring him Veric's head in exchange for Romann to usher Daysho into the blood-sucking family. As to why Romann wanted his head was no concern of his, perhaps to send the King a message. His chance to have the mystic distracted was forthcoming. He would only have one chance, one moment, but he needed to be patient and wait for the spell-slinger to drain his power enough that he could strike without his intent being detected. Veric was extremely powerful and Daysho had no desire of losing his life this day. The human assassin brought his black cowl to drape his face and to hide his smirk. The group traversed the icy terrain a few miles until reaching the breathtaking chamber where Raina and the others had recently been.

"I smell death," Daysho whispered.

Veric turned to respond, but stopped short when the assassin was gone. The evil mage quickly spotted a blurred, near-invisible form moving deeper into the chamber. Veric nodded for the other men to move out.

At the center of the subterranean area, they found the body of a white dragon. Its red blood, now frozen amongst the rocky terrain, contrasted with the bluish ice in the cavern. The back of its head was completely blown out. Its beige tongue hung out of the jaw and pearlescent eyes were foggy and lifeless. Scorched blast marks peppered the rest of its body.

Daysho, now visible, spoke as he approached Veric, who surveyed the fallen beast, "There are two more, further on, both dead. They apparently fought each other to the death."

"This one was killed by magic, combined with a strange weapon of some kind," Veric determined.

"Could it have been this elven mystic, Raina?"

"She is powerful. Be mindful of her before you strike."

Daysho intently stared at Veric, "Of course," he answered, but it was Veric's power he would be mindful of instead.

"The dragon entities can sense each other; the Dal-Draydian awaits us at the Chamber. Come, this way."

22

Revenge

A small unit of frost dwarves ushered others along the tunnel walls out of striking distance of the risen Manasseh. Abawken, preparing for the coming battle, gripped his scimitar and moved into a protective position in front of his friends, saying, "Since his return from the dead, we can't be certain of how much of his former power he has retained. Be mindful, Master Bridazak."

There were still hundreds of dwarves mingled within the other races. All were trying to escape the goblin tunnels; the horde would be coming.

Bridazak stepped forward, "Manasseh, what do you want?"

"Your head on a spit!"

"His head is perfect where it is," Spilf jumped in.

Dulgin raised an eyebrow, "Good one, Stubby."

"You thought you destroyed the Orb, Manasseh, but you, in fact, set it free. I had nothing to do with your fall. It was by your own hands."

"No!" Manasseh countered, "It all started with you and now it will end with you."

"There is nothing to gain by my death. Your reign is over."

"None of that matters, only your—."

Suddenly, a steel-tipped spear pierced through Manasseh's chest, interrupting his threat. Stunned, Manasseh looked down at his black blood covering the weapon and fell to his knees. The restored Morthkin stood triumphantly behind him, gleaming in his full plate armor, white hair as bright as snow, and icicles dripping off of his beard.

Manasseh, dropping his sword, grabbed the shaft of the spear with both hands and slowly began pulling the lance from his body. An evil laugh bellowed from under his dark helmet.

King Morthkin spoke, his voice was deep, "You must hurry. This man before you is cursed, and can only die by the hands of the one from whom he seeks revenge." Everyone turned to look at Bridazak, but Morthkin continued, "Take the Sky Diamond to the Kouzfhan. It must be set into its place in order to return its power to my people, and for us to deal with the coming horde."

"Where is this place?" Spilf questioned, still shocked by what was taking place. Seeing Manasseh face to face again, and recalling all those days of torture he had endured inside his dungeon, unnerved him.

"Not far, but you need to leave now!" He commanded. "I will only be able to hold him back for a short while. Manasseh will follow you to the Chamber. It is there you will defeat him by sending him into the Pit of Darkness. You will know when you see it. Now go!"

Abawken led the way as King Morthkin and other frost dwarves pointed the direction. Dulgin paused beside the noble dwarf leader, holding the Sky Diamond, and said proudly, "I know what needs to be done."

The frost king nodded.

Just then, Manasseh pulled the last part of the spear out of his body and tossed it away. The black blood that had gushed from the wound, slowly receded as the gaping hole magically sealed. He grabbed his two-handed sword and rose to his feet once again. Dulgin moved quickly out of the area, but turned to see Morthkin launching hammers of ice supernaturally from his hands. Manasseh's roar echoed down the halls.

Spilf and Bridazak reached the massive double-door first. The iron portal, with layers of gold melded into it, formed intricate designs and images of dwarves holding shields. White gold emblazoning the trim of the pictures brought an aura of power to the depictions.

Spilf withdrew his trusty thieves tools, Lester and Ross. *"Okay boys, time to work your magic."*

The dak heard the magical picks voices cheering within his mind.

The telepathic voice of Lester spoke first, *"This is quite a find, Master."*

"Why is that?"

"Tell him, Lester. Boy, what a find."

"I'm going to, Ross. Stop repeating what I say. You know if you would just listen more and—"

Spilf cut him off, *"We are in a bit of a hurry, what is it?"*

"Oh, yeah, sorry about that. This door has twelve distinct traps for those coming and going through it."

"You can disarm them, right?"

"Lester, did he just ask us that?"

"Ross, quiet. Yes, of course we can disarm them, but it will take us a good amount of time."

Spilf responded, *"Then get going. Which one first?"*

"Let's start with the worst one, the Death Blast."

"C'mon Lester, let's put another notch on our belt."

Spilf mentally understood their direction as the picks and his mind linked to the desired location. Lester responded, *"Ross, we don't wear belts."*

"I know, but I heard one of our masters say it before."

"Ross, he was skinny, that is why he said it. He literally needed to make another notch in his belt to keep his pants on."

"But why did he say it each time we helped him?"

"He was cursed Ross, remember? The witch he partnered with put a spell on him; he didn't know he would lose weight each time he performed any kind of thieving after he stole her necklace."

"Oh, I had no idea. I liked that necklace, what did it call itself again?"

"She called herself Veera. She was kind of creepy."

"That's right, Veera. Yeah, she had some nice craftsmanship."

"Wow Ross, I never knew you took notice of her design like that."

"I'm only a pick, Lester. Even I recognize beauty when I see it. The facets of her jewels were so perfect."

"Yeah, she did have nice jewels, that is for sure."

Spilf interjected, *"Guys, can you rehash your love interests another time. We seriously need to get through this door."*

"Okay, one death trap now dissolved. Onto the Disintegration."

"Uh-oh, Lester. Here comes Grumpy."

Dulgin entered, holding the Sky Diamond in his cupped hands. Abawken walked backward, making sure his friends were protected in case Manasseh showed up. He recalled his weeks of practicing his mind link with Raina, but he struggled to access it with the stress of the situation, *"I wish you were here, Raina,"* he thought. The burly red-bearded dwarf walked to the door. Spilf lurched backwards when several clicks inside the iron beast resounded as mechanisms of multiple locks tumbled. The gateway opened, revealing an ice covered cavern.

"C'mon, the Chamber of Cleansing is this way," Dulgin said, walking through the doorway.

Spilf rolled Lester and Ross back into his leather pouch, hearing them protest the dwarf's disrespect of their profession. *"Grumpy stole our work."*

Bridazak scrunched his face and complained, "It smells weird in here," and followed his friend.

Abawken, trailing the others into the cold cave, kept a wary eye behind them. As the door magically began to close, he saw Manasseh charging with the frost dwarf king in pursuit. It clanked shut with a loud metallic thud and locked itself once again, just before Manasseh reached the closed entrance. Bridazak heard the rage-filled, muffled scream of Manasseh on the other side of the great door. The dark magic released into the evil human was powerful, and he knew that even the Dwarven door would not hold him back.

The source of the strange aroma revealed itself when the group encountered two carcasses of white dragons. The powerful mandibles of the beasts were clamped into each others' necks.

"What happened?" Spilf asked.

"I think they didn't like each other," quipped Dulgin, as he passed by.

Abawken surmised, "Dragons are territorial, but not usually against themselves. This happened recently."

"How do you know?" said Bridazak.

"I can see traces of steam from the wounds," he pointed.

Dulgin's voice echoed, "I found it. Hurry up, ya blundering fools!"

The others quickly followed and saw the tunnel the dwarf had discovered. Four symbols were etched into the wall. Bridazak delicately traced them with his hand. One was of encircled flames, the next depicted the shape of an open clam with a pearl resting inside. The third resembled a generic faceted outline, perhaps a gem, and the last was clearly the Sky Diamond. Each carving surrounded the symbol of a star in the middle, but none of it made sense.

"What exactly is this Chamber of Cleansing?" he whispered.

"Master Bridazak, let us keep moving. I am afraid the dwarven door will not stop Manasseh for long."

Manasseh turned around to face the twenty frost dwarves and their King. He scoffed, "You cannot stop me."

"Aye, but we can slow you down a bit." King Morthkin projected his hand and a flurry of ice hammers shot out from his open palm. Each weapon slammed and shattered into the chest of the armored human, knocking him back into the sealed door. His brethren took a step forward, brandishing weaponry and shields, but he halted them. "No, I will deal with him alone. Join the others to keep the goblins out of our home."

Manasseh regained his stance. He pulled his closed-faced helmet off, allowing his jet black hair to cascade to his shoulders. His once steel blue eyes were now glowing gray. Manasseh's sunken face and pasty white skin revealed the darkness that embodied him.

King Morthkin materialized a two-handed, blue hued hammer within his grasp. "Time to test your power, Manasseh."

"I look forward to cutting off your head and spiking it for all to see, Dwarf."

23

The Chamber of Cleansing

Raina and Xan entered the shadow filled room at the end of the iced tunnel, followed by King El'Korr and his trusted bodyguard. They had arrived at the Chamber of Cleansing, the location to destroy the Dragon Stones by utilizing the four required elements. An arid breeze swirled within the confines of the circular obsidian walls and the domed ceiling went beyond sight. Cautiously, Rozelle peeked inside and felt an overwhelming sense of dread emanating from the gaping pit in the center of the room.

"Where is Trillius?" Rozelle asked, her voice echoing.

"I'm right here." The three-foot gnome flipped into the air and proudly landed on the center pedestal, his hands were placed on his hips, and he wore a confident smirk. Trillius sat at the edge of the pedestal, dangling his feet over the black and grey smokey whirlpool below. He leaned his chin against one hand and with the other, pulled out the blue stone that harbored the spirit of the mighty ancient dragon, Dal-Draydian.

"Trillius, you can still fight. You must not let it take you over." Raina said.

"I am afraid Trillius is unavailable right now."

"Who are we speaking with, then?"

The gnome scoffed, "I know about you mystic-types, always wanting a name so you can do your spell casting afar in your towers and from your tomes. My name will be known shortly, but for now you can call me D."

Raina turned to the others and whispered, "Take the elements and start placing them into the marked spots." She addressed Trillius, now controlled by the entity. "You want to be released back into the realm, but for what purpose?"

Dal-Draydian growled, "For domination. For power! You of all people should know about such things and understand an insatiable thirst for more."

Xan distributed the Stone of Earth to Rondee, the Fire Opal to El'Korr, and he held the Pearl of the Deep. The small group began to slowly skirt the walkway outlining the room.

Raina continued, trying to keep "D" occupied, "And after you take over the realm, what then?"

"You are boring me. Do you take me to be a fool? I am two-thousand years old and yet you treat me like I'm a child. The time of the dragons has returned and those who do not bow to me will be destroyed."

"I see. You are clearly much more intelligent than I had thought; my apologies. An elder dragon of your status requires worthy social protocol."

"Don't mock me, Raina. I do respect your magical prowess, but it is inferior to my own."

Rozelle scooted past the female elf wizard and surefooted the arched pathway leading to Trillius. The stone footway was no wider than twelve inches and below was the deceptively peaceful-looking swirling smoke.

"Trillius, I know you are in there and I know you care about us, about me. Don't let this thing take over your mind."

"You dare call me a 'thing'," Dal-Draydian roared. "Trillius willingly let me in and he watched as you betrayed him. I opened his mind to the truth and your controlling ways are now over."

Rozelle pleaded, "Trillius, I love you."

There was a sudden lurch in Trillius' body, now held captive by the creature, and he arched backwards, draping over the pedestal. He flailed about in convulsions and uttered ever so slightly, "Help me, Rozelle."

She rushed toward him, balancing herself on the narrow path. Her pudgy frame leaned against him and she wiped the sweat from his forehead trying to comfort him. His continued spasms caused Rozelle to gasp with concern.

"I'm right here. I won't leave you."

Trillius relaxed, his eyes closed, but suddenly with his free hand he grabbed her throat. "Oh, boo-hoo, I love you," Dal-Draydian teased. "You are so easy to convince. Raina, this world is full of creatures like this one, weak and useless in their magic compared to us. They will be purged, eradicated, and remembered only to give thanks that they no longer exist."

He lifted her off her feet and dangled her over the swirling void, then roared with laughter and released his grip. As Rozelle tumbled into the unknown, she flailed her arms. Almost immediately her body polymorphed into a hawk and soared away from the darkness to the far edge and landed.

"Ah, a pathetic druid, you will beg me for mercy soon enough."

Rozelle screeched in response.

Raina walked quickly to her side, stroked her silky feathers, and whispered, "You will need to be ready to grab Trillius when the time is right."

Rozelle emitted a few high pitched chirps, beat her wings, and flew to a higher perch.

"Raina, your quaint fondness for animals is refreshing, and might I—"

The elf cut Dal-Draydian off and snapped, "And some animals need to be put down!"

"I like this side of you more, Raina."

"Enough! You will be defeated by my hand or the next if I should fail."

"Really? I see one, two, only three elements, but you need a fourth in order to make that happen."

"And I see you have only supplied a blue rock, at the hands of a stolen gnome lost in your charades. Still, you are unable to be released without all five stones."

"Well, it appears we are at a crossroads then."

The three items were placed into the marked locations equally dispersed around the room. Each of the heroes stood by them, waiting for something to happen, looking at one another to see if there was any indication of a change, but there was nothing.

Raina settled herself and asked, "If you know of the elements then why allow Trillius to give us the Pearl?"

"Ah, good question, Trillius has been very insightful and has informed me on the status of the realm. I am not concerned about your elements, but I needed you to bring me to the Chamber. The Pearl was the key to unlock the door I needed open."

"You say you are not concerned about the elements, but what if I told you the Sky Diamond was here?"

Dal-Draydian laughed, "What if it was? But what if I could help you with your Horn Kings and swiftly dethrone them?"

"We would only be replacing one evil with another, besides, one King has already fallen."

"Impressive, but as thousands of innocent people suffer at the remaining three, I could be their salvation."

"You have already expressed your intent to kill and destroy."

Trillius' eyes flared brightly. "Yes, I have, haven't I? You are right, I am not in the business of saving people. As I said, we are at an impasse, but only for now. I can sense the others growing nearer; it will only be a matter of time." Dal-Draydian sighed, smirked, and slowly curled himself as he laid down within the bowl of the pedestal, "You all bore me. I might as well get some rest for my upcoming rebirth."

Raina stood by El'Korr, where the Stone of Earth was positioned. She inspected the pedestal, but found nothing that could help the situation. They needed the final element. She whispered to El'Korr, "Romann de Beaux said the Sky Diamond was here at the Shield."

He responded, "Perhaps the frost dwarves keep it hidden somewhere else."

"They were supposed to be guarding this area according to Yasooma's journal. Something is not right and I am afraid to leave in this predicament."

"I will go with Rondee and fetch the Diamond. You and Xan can dragon-sit Trouble over there."

She paused before nodding. El'Korr quickly whistled to alert Rondee and then waved him over. "C'mon, we have a mission."

Dal-Draydian lazily peeked one eye open and watched from his makeshift podium, "And where do you all think you are going? Off to search for your diamond?"

"None of your business, dragon-brain!" El'Korr countered.

"I don't think you will get too far, Dwarf."

El'Korr ignored the dragon spirit and headed out the exit with his trusted sidekick. Seconds later the two dwarves were walking in reverse, backtracking into the Chamber. Raina noticed they were looking at something further down the tunnel.

"What is it?" she asked.

"They smell and look like bad guys to me."

Veric and two men entered the perimeter of the room. There was a long pause as everyone looked around sizing each other up. Daysho remained hidden using his magical ring of invisibility.

"Let me introduce myself. I am Veric, personal mystic of the West Horn King."

24

Convergence

Veric's black robes melded into the shadows as he strode into the Chamber of Cleansing. Each step was punctuated with the sharp tap of his jade, ruby-topped, staff. His men, with long swords in hand, maintained positions on either side of the outer walkway. Veric glanced at Trillius and quickly saw the blue and final stone he needed. The power of the other dragons imprisoned inside his magical belt pouch called to him. They were tucked within the confines of an extra-dimensional space, which allowed Veric to distance his mind from the intelligent and calculating entities.

"You must be Dal-Draydian," Veric scowled.

"Soon to be a god, slave," the dragon in the gnome countered.

Veric smirked and then switched his focus to the female elf, "Raina, I have heard so much about you. Your reputation lingers even after all these centuries of your absence."

"I wish I could say the same about you."

"My reputation?"

"No, your absence."

He chuckled, "How witty you are."

El'Korr added, "My hammer is also witty. I can show you if you like."

"Ah, self-proclaimed, King El'Korr. I guess it is easier to become a king when there are so few of you left. Cuts down on the opposition, don't you think?"

El'Korr said, "One human kingdom has already fallen. I foresee more."

"If you are referring to King Manasseh, I assure you he has not fallen, his spirit is quite alive."

"You are another delusional wizard, just like Manasseh's mage."

Veric half-smiled, "That mage was my brother."

"That explains the familiar stench when you came in," El'Korr quipped.

"My brother, Vevrin, did not die in vain, however."

"I am thinking a family reunion is in order on this day, spell-caster."

Veric stared at each of the heroes. When his eyes rested on the smiling gnome, he smirked.

Dal-Draydian said, "I am quite enjoying this verbal sparring. Please continue."

Veric asked, "What are your plans once you are released, Dragon?"

"After I feed on your soul, I will then strike the Horn Kings and drive the realm to their knees to bow to me. Yes, that would be a good start."

Veric raised his eyebrows, "Indeed, a grand start." The human turned toward Raina, "If we work together, Elf, we can destroy the gnome host body."

"This gnome is our friend. We will not be harming him."

"How touching, but he is already dead."

At that moment, Rozelle, in her hawk form, screeched from above, alerting Veric.

"Ah, there you are, Druid. How sad, your boyfriend is no more. I hope you have said your goodbyes." Turning sharply toward the elf mystic, he raised his voice, "Raina, if we cannot combine forces, then the Dragon God will be released."

Raina replied, "I have my own plans to combat that. We are quite aware of your intentions, Veric. If not the gnome host, then you would most certainly choose yourself."

"Oh, dear, not me. That is why I have brought others," he pointed at his adjacent guards who stood ready to implement Veric's commands. "I plan to rule alongside the new deity, not be the deity."

Dal-Draydian responded, "Really? You think I would need someone as weak as you?"

"I could assist you in your world domination. Be a voice to announce your arrival. You would surely outlive me, so why not grant me favor by allowing me to be your advisor?" Veric bowed, "Every ruler has their minions."

Dal-Draydian beamed at the thought and sat proudly on his make-shift throne. He could feel the power swelling, and sensed that the other entrapped dragons were eager to be released. The human mystic was a fool, but Dal-Draydian looked forward to manipulating him. The dwarves and elves watched in anticipation while bordering the ringed walkway, and standing next to their precious elements designed to thwart his reign. He couldn't have brought about a better situation than what stood before him.

"Come to me human, and kiss my hand," Dal-Draydian beckoned.

Veric, tapped his staff quickly on the floor and in an instant he appeared next to the gnome in the center of the room. Dal-Draydian extended an arm. Veric bent to plant his lips on the back of Trillius' hand in deference for the dragon deity within, and at the same time took hold of the Blue Dragon Stone. He felt a tingly sensation when he grasped the smooth blue rock.

Veric said, "Thank you, Gnome, for fetching me the fifth and final stone."

Dal-Draydian retorted, "It is I who is giving thanks today."

"Oh, and what thanks is that?" The mage touched the tip of the gemmed staff to Trillius' chest. Veric's cocksure grin faded when it went completely through the gnome's wispy body. He lurched back in surprise as the shimmering illusion subsided. There was no Trillius, nor the blue stone he thought he held. The wizard, unsure of his safety, transported away from his unsatisfactory attempt, and was now back where he started.

"Thank you for bringing my friends to me," Dal-Draydian said as Trillius' body materialized suddenly at the center podium once again. He held up Veric's satchel and the human, motivated by reflexes, reached for the missing item. The gnome now possessed all five. "We have waited far too long for this, my brethren," Dal-Draydian whispered as he withdrew one colored stone at a time and placed them into the required location. The swirling vortex below increased its speed.

The invisible assassin, Daysho, watched from the opening leading into the Chamber of Cleansing. He studied the body language of all inside, their mannerisms, and their personalities. Three distinct camps resided within the room: Raina's team, the gnome, now controlled by an egocentric dragon, and Veric with his guards.

Daysho, hidden from them all, made a fourth camp lying in wait for his opportunity to strike. Veric's back was to him, but it was still too soon. The mage's powers were strong, and his magical protections were still in place.

Daysho saw through the ruse. Trillius' true body, manipulated by the dragon, stepped into the same stream of invisibility he walked in now. The dragon-possessed gnome implemented its illusion spell the moment Veric teleported to his platform. The cunning Dal-Draydian spotted the well-hidden Daysho and cockily gave him a wink, then turned his attention back to the idiotic mage, falling for the illusion. Trillius' thieving finesse came in handy as Dal-Draydian stole the Bag of Holding from Veric, then returned to his place, causing the alarmed mage to transport back to his original location. *"Veric, you are draining your power more and more. Keep depleting your magic abilities, and bring me closer to my destiny,"* he thought.

A bright light emanating from the tunnel caused Daysho to spin around and look back down the passageway. He squinted to see more clearly, and heard the echoes of several individuals approaching. Through the brilliance, he saw a red-bearded dwarf lumbering toward them, holding what he suspected was the Sky Diamond. Following the dwarf were two ordakians, and a human. *"What group is this?"* he thought. Daysho remained hidden and kept the approach of the mysterious fifth camp to himself. He thought, *"An assassin always needs information before he strikes."*

25

Reunion

Pointing his staff at Dal-Draydian, Veric launched a black ray beam that struck the gnome squarely in the chest, causing him to stagger backward with a loud grunt and then disappear in a wispy cloud. The center of the chamber filled with smoke and the sound of crackling fire.

Veric scoffed "You see, the mighty have fallen." He turned to Raina, "Now we will discuss your surrender, Elf."

El'Korr growled, "Dwarves don't surrender."

"This one lacks her staff and your meager weapons will not affect me."

Raina proclaimed, "I have ascended and have access to the highest power, I no longer require a staff."

"We shall see about your so called highest power." He turned to one of his men, "You know what to do." Veric smirked.

The human henchman nodded with a grin, sheathed his weapon, and taking one careful step at a time, approached the narrow, arched walkway.

Turning quickly, Raina pointed at the approaching guard. Bolts of electrical energy shot forth from her hand and streaked toward him. However, the charged light impacted and dissipated against a magical unseen shield made momentarily visible by the blue glow of a fleeting power.

Veric laughed, "Your spells will not touch him."

El'Korr threw his hammer, which struck the human, shattering his ribs; forcing him off the narrow walkway. His scream faded to silence as he plummeted through the churning grey vortex below.

El'Korr's hammer returned to his hands. He gloated, "My weapon seems to affect your men just fine."

Veric growled as he touched his hand to the shoulder of his remaining guard and then tapped the end of his staff on the ground, teleporting himself and his man to the center pedestal where the Dragon Stones rested. He then commanded his follower to stand in the middle of the colored rocks.

Suddenly, as the guard took his position, the gnome appeared out of thin air and hovered before them. "I grow tired of you all."

Dal-Draydian opened Trillius' mouth wide, releasing the breath weapon of the ancient dragon. A thunderclap erupted and a brilliant blue-white electrical bolt sizzled through the human warrior and pierced Veric's body. Both were sent flying across the room. Veric slammed into the wall and fell hard against the floor while the human's body shattered into dust upon impact. The echoing thunder clap faded and the smell of burnt flesh filled the area.

Dal-Draydian floated and rested softly upon the Dragon Stone altar. With that, a mystical mist materialized and each of the colored rocks began to glow, matching their distinct hue. Sharp beams of radiance suddenly shot into the gnome's body. Trillius' chest heaved forward and his arms spread wide.

Bridazak and the others reflexively ducked as a bright light emanated from deep in the tunnel followed by a crack of thunder.

Spilf exclaimed, "What the heck was that?"

"Shut it, Stubby," Dulgin whispered harshly, "Looks like we are not the only ones in the Chamber of Cleansing."

Bridazak said, "Manasseh will be coming and we need to get the Sky Diamond inside."

"Abawken, take point," Dulgin commanded. "Whatever is in there, I need you to handle it while I place this gem into its rightful place."

Abawken nodded, and moved forward, scimitar in hand. The others followed.

A hum of energy echoed off the walls and a diffused light beamed out of the chamber in front of them; they were unable to determine its source until a childlike creature came into view. The mysterious light pierced its body and a blue-white glow spewed forth from its gaping mouth and wide staring eyes.

Abawken emerged cautiously from the tunnel, sword at the ready to act against the spectacle in the center of the room. However, when he heard an all too familiar voice call, "Abawken!" he turned quickly in shock and saw Raina, King El'Korr, Rondee, and Xan. A groan coming from his left alerted him to a groggy mystic in black robes, smoke wafting up from his clothes. Dulgin entered with the diamond in hand.

"Quickly, Dulgin!" Raina shouted, "Set the Sky Diamond in place directly in front of you, there is no time to waste!"

The dwarf hurriedly set the Sky Diamond into its designated location. It set perfectly, nestled into its designed home. Instantly, a single ray of light sprung forth, striking the possessed gnome. Then a luminous beam ushered forth from Xan's Pearl of the Deep. However, the Fire Opal and the Stone of Earth remained in their places with nothing happening.

The popping sounds of bone being wrenched from their sockets and the tearing of flesh reverberated in the room. A skeletal framework of dragon wings sprouted on Trillius' back. Translucent leather began to form and the gnomes tiny hands elongated into sharp claws.

Trillius' mouth moved, but a different, booming voice reverberated from his body, echoing throughout the chamber, "I am the Dragon God!"

Raina couldn't understand why Dulgin's and Xan's elements had activated and the others had not. There was a sudden flash of realization, *"Raina,"* she said to herself, *"how could you have missed that?"* She knew what had to be done and called out, "Abawken, join Rondee, and Spilf, make your way to El'Korr!"

Spilf peeked out wide-eyed from the tunnel and saw the elf mystic waving him over. He looked to Bridazak who nodded, giving him the confidence to proceed. He scampered past the human mage who was still struggling to his feet. Abawken activated his blade, flying across the room. Avoiding the morphing dragon, he landed next to Rondee. The dwarf backed away and Abawken stepped in front of the Fire Opal. A sudden blast of light hit the center. There was a noticeable lurch of pain from Trillius as it struck.

Raina shouted, "Spilf, hurry!" The ordakian was the final ingredient to destroy the stones and was steps away from completing the process.

Electrical arcs spat forth from Trillius' body, hitting all around the room. Buzzing charges of energy sizzled in front of Spilf. He halted, fearful of contacting the discharge, then the bluish light snapped closer to him, forcing him back where another electrical arc flashed behind him. The randomly arching zaps were almost on top of him when Raina suddenly appeared from a dimensional door next to him. She quickly grabbed Spilf, yanked him inside, and the portal sealed behind them.

In an instant, Raina and Spilf materialized at the final station. Raina pushed the dak in place and the final beam of light ignited. Dal-Draydian bellowed out in pain—the sound of five dragons in unison blared in agony. As the heroes watched, an outlined shape of a multi-headed mythical entity flashed before their eyes. The immense spirit-hydra encompassing the transforming Trillius, reeled in horror and began to shrink.

Veric now stood, assessed the situation, and started an incantation. His words alerted Raina, who waited to counter his forthcoming spell. She saw that Dulgin was his closest target. Veric pointed his jade staff at the unsuspecting dwarf and a searing jet of flame shot forth, but Raina shielded Dulgin with her own spell; a wall of ice appeared just before the fire ignited him. The heat and cold clashed and sent a blast of steam into the area. Veric snarled at Raina. The two powerful mystics locked eyes, ready to go spell to spell.

Bridazak, uncertain as to how to help his friends, stood at the ready at the tunnel entrance to the room, his bow, the Seeker, in hand. He couldn't make sense of what was happening, or how or why Raina and the others were here. *What is the Dragon God?* This sole question must have been what brought the others, but why here, of all places? Spilf, Abawken, Xan, and Dulgin were busy manning the required stations in order to activate these mysterious items. Raina and this other mystic paired off, leaving El'Korr, Rondee, and himself at the ready, but ready to do what? This was not the reunion he had hoped for.

Then he heard the voice of Manasseh, "I see you, Halfling. Time for you to be reunited with your maker."

Bridazak turned and saw the damaged Manasseh approaching. Pieces of his armor were missing revealing his injured flesh, but the wounds were regenerating. Melting ice dripped from his face and he walked with a noticeable limp. Bridazak pushed away the thought of a defeated King Morthkin, and what would happen to the people, fighting the horde bubbling up like a volcano, without their leader.

Bridazak backed into the chamber and moved toward the right, away from the spell-slingers. He saw Xan's eyes widen in horror as Manasseh stood at the threshold. "He only wants me, Xan," Bridazak assured him before he could say anything.

"Bridazak, he is under a curse of the dead. He will not rest until you breathe no more. You are the only one who can destroy him."

"Yeah, heard that one already. I will figure something out."

Daysho watched the events unraveling before him from his concealed location, which unnerved even his steely confidence. A fallen Horn King strode past him, but took no notice, as he was intent on killing the famous Bridazak of the North Kingdom. The same one whose wanted posters could still be found plastered all over the region, placed by Manasseh's order, but left up in celebration of his demise—a demise that was apparently faulty. Regardless of these unsettling sights, Daysho's mission remained the same: collect the head of Veric and return it to the vampire. Daysho inched his way closer to the mage as his powers were being depleted by each spell he cast and each injury he sustained, but he needed to be mindful of Raina's potent incantations being released in his direction, and not get caught in any area affected by the invocations of either mystic. Timing was crucial and his escape just as important. Daysho had never lusted after power, like what was on display before him, but the prize of everlasting, immortal life, waited for him at the hands of Romann de Beaux. He could not afford to make a mistake.

26

Tides of Change

Manasseh no longer possessed the power of the fallen Tree, and his mind bore the loss like a deep scar. He sought only to quiet his tormented soul by reaping the command of vengeance he had retained after death. The legendary curse that was placed upon him as part of his resurrection coursed its dark magic through his whole being, and could be ended not with spell or entrapment, or even bodily harm. Only the hand of the one he sought revenge from could destroy him, and he had named Bridazak, upon whom Manasseh was now focused. His altered soul despised Bridazak with so much contempt that he could think of nothing but his destruction.

The ordakian, bow in hand and backing away, shouted, "Manasseh, look around you. The tides of change have come to Ruauck-El."

Manasseh growled, "You ruined everything."

"We were all part of something much bigger than ourselves. I had no idea what I carried at the time."

"Oh, you were innocent? I think not, you brought your army with that cursed orb."

"The Orb of Truth delivered the voice of God. He is restoring his once-great realm and the people he created. He can restore you, Manasseh, it's not too late."

Manasseh's face contorted in disgust as he bellowed, "I don't care about your god or this once-great realm," and swung his two-handed sword.

Bridazak adeptly ducked out of the way as he continued backing up. He was almost to Abawken's station when he loosed one of his arrows which penetrated the dark knight's armor, covering his left leg.

Manessah, dismissing his pain, continued relentlessly fighting.

The wound from the arrow had slowed him, and the dak noticed that whatever harm he brought directly to Manasseh, the infliction remained.

Bridazak notched another arrow, pulled the Seeker bowstring back, aimed for the Manesseh's head and let it fly.

Manasseh parried the steel-tipped shaft with his sword and charged Bridazak who dodged the lunge and tumbled into the narrow walkway leading to the center pedestal where Trillius hovered in the air as multiple beams of energy pelted him.

Abawken, nearby at his station, pointed his sword at Manasseh, preparing to release an elemental beast.

Bridazak shouted, "No Abawken, this is my fight!"

The fighter stopped short, and then noticed Veric across the room, preparing an incantation intended for Raina. Abawken hastily stepped forward and summoned a rock elemental next to Veric, successfully distracting the wizard from his attack on Raina, but the focused light from the Fire Opal dissolved, and broke the chain of the four elements. A sudden surge of energy from the Dragon Stones rebounded and Trillius' head contorted, elongated, and formed the snout of a scaly beast. At the same time, his shoulders burst open and two more heads sprouted. Abawken refocused his attention on his gem and the aura returned, halting the gnome's hideous transformation.

"It's gaining power!" Abawken called.

The three-headed, disfigured dragon roared in pain, struggling with the tug-of-war between the spirit realm and the flesh.

At the moment the giant rock elemental emerged from the ground behind Veric, the shambling monster raised its arms to pummel the puny human. It towered over him with its earthen clubs, but Veric calmly brought his hand up toward the creature. A platinum ring on his index finger pulsed with magical energy. He turned to face the stone beast, which was frozen in place, and ordered, "Kill the dwarves." Another flare shot from his electrically charged ring, causing the monster to triplicate itself. The row of three monsters, standing side-by-side, turned in unison toward their new targets.

Rondee's magical, tiny hammer morphed into a great maul, and El'Korr and his faithful protector met their foes head on, swinging their mighty war hammers. Dulgin, however, manning his element station, had to tumble out of the way to avoid being pulverized. The Sky Diamond's light dwindled and Trillius again began to morph.

Dulgin withdrew his axe, "Come over here, Rocky. I got somethin for ya."

Veric tried to divert Raina's attention with a scorching ray of fire, but with her immunity to flame she was unharmed. She took the opportunity to unleash her invocation, not at the wizard, but at the elemental attacking Dulgin.

"Ver atu me hosht." She shouted and extended her arm, and pointed a finger encompassed with a ray of light. The sound of cracking stone, like a building shaken by an earthquake, resounded, and the rock formation turned to flesh. Dulgin, was facing a meaty beast, and knew his axe could do great damage. The dwarf did not hesitate. He lopped off a leg at the knee. Sand poured out of the wound. He chopped at the other leg and laughed, "Coming down to my size, hey Sandy?"

Veric responded, "Nicely done, Elf, but my resource of spells goes deep. How far can you go protecting everyone?"

"As far as it takes," she said.

"You can't protect them all, Raina. Even now, your Bridazak is fighting against death itself."

Dulgin yelled, "Hey, melon-head, once I am done with this dragon deity, then my axe has your name on it."

"You dwarves are all the same. Your axe will never get close enough."

"Funny, that is exactly what your brother said. You're just a little uglier than him."

"Focus on returning to your station, Dulgin," Raina ordered.

The human mage's eyes flared a bright pearlescent orange. Raina recognized the intent and countered with her voice, "Sheloc!" She successfully blocked another attack.

The spellcasters were entranced, pitted against one another. Veric loosened the tightness in his neck by moving his head in a circular motion, but never took his eyes off of her.

"Tehloc!" he shouted.

"Vuasec!" she countered the unseen magical force.

"You are good, Raina. I'm impressed at your skill, but even now, the Dragon God strengthens."

At that moment, Raina shouted, "Dulgin! The Sky Diamond! Hurry!"

By the time the dwarf finished with the creature and started toward his post, Trillius' body was no more. Instead, floating in the center of the room was a massive, writhing, five-headed dragon. Its wings unfurled, revealing each scaled skull a match to one of the colored stones.

A low, guttural laugh rose, and the beast roared, "Your existence has come to the end."

The Sky Diamond flared back to life as Dulgin took his place, and impacted the Dragon God. The blue head, in the middle, stretched toward the dwarf.

The voice of Dal-Draydian, through clenched teeth, fighting the pain of the four elements' effect, bellowed, "Veric, kill this dwarf, and I will accept your offer."

Dulgin shouted, "You will be the only thing dying today, Bluey." Dulgin suddenly felt a shift within his body, his spirit aligning with the element, as the Sky Diamond pulled on his inner strength and determination. His focus on the Dragon God caused his beam of light to intensify.

Dal-Draydian screeched, retracting from the blast. The white dragon stone suddenly shattered apart, a strange sound of hissing rain permeated the airwaves, and the white head phased from the main body. The Chamber of Cleansing shifted abruptly from the explosion and then settled.

Raina instantly took notice of what had just transpired and yelled earnestly to the others, "Focus your intent on destroying the stones, hurry, before it is too late!"

Manasseh crept toward Bridazak on the narrow walkway, but the orda-kian kept out of reach of his sword and fired an arrow. It slammed into Manasseh's left shoulder. He quickly let loose another, but this one was swept aside by the former king.

The Dragon God loomed above them, its massive, multi-colored, scaled underbelly hovering ten feet in the air. A whirlpool of grey shadows swirled rapidly below in the dark void forming an eye, that stared at him, sending a cold chill through his body.

Bridazak's back pushed up against the central pedestal, entrapping him and halting his escape. Manasseh laughed as he loomed over him and raised his sword, "Time to die, Halfling."

Bridazak drew another arrow from his quiver, quickly notched it, and let it fly. It struck Manasseh in the chest, causing the human to stagger backwards. He quickly regained his stance and brought his blade down toward the now helpless dak. The roar of the dragon above, coupled with the walkway swaying suddenly, forced Manasseh to shift his attack to main-tain his steady position. His arms swung out to maintain his balance.

Bridazak seized the opportunity, and grappled the human's legs, caus-ing him to topple off the edge, but the former king, through reflex action, grabbed Bridazak's bow and held on. Bridazak wrapped his legs and arms around the one-foot walkway, still holding his bow, and Manasseh. He was about to let go of the Seeker and end the human's life, when the voice of God penetrated his mind, *"Do not kill him, Bridazak. Show him mercy. Reveal the truth."*

27

The Decision

Raina had been in several wizard duels in her lifetime, and this was not one to take lightly. Keeping her keen senses on the alert, she waited for Veric to cast his next spell. Her next move was risky, but would be worth it if she could execute it perfectly.

The evil mage glared at her and snarled, "Where were we, my dear Raina?"

She taunted, "I am still not impressed, Veric. Your skill in the art is lacking."

Growling, through gritted teeth, he pointed his staff at her. Immediately, a yellowish cloud reeking with the stench of sulfuric acid engulfed the elf.

In a flash, Raina transported herself and stood right next to Veric, thusly avoiding his spell.

Surprised, Veric attempted to recoil, but Raina magically formed her hands into elvish daggers and slashed his face with supernatural speed that manifested into several clones of herself weaving in and out of her body.

Her razor-sharp grafted weapons split his skin across his right cheek like a plowed field, splaying blood against the wall, sliced his lips, and gouged out an eye. Another slash lopped off an ear and opened crimson rows down the left side of his face, now drenched in blood.

Veric howled in agony, but Raina did not let up. She continued her quick swipes; shredding his robe and digging the flesh from his body.

Fighting through the pain, Veric shouted toward the rock creatures and commanded, "Kill the Halfling!"

Raina stopped her attack on Veric, turned and saw that the two remaining earth beasts, battling against the dwarves, had suddenly focused their attention on Spilf.

One of the elementals blocked the dwarves as the other swiftly moved to the fragile ordakian, who focused on the Stone of Earth post. El'Korr smashed the leg of the one in front of him, toppling the creature, while Rondee followed with a head crushing blow with his massive maul, but they could not get to Spilf in time. The second monster swatted the dak, launching Spilf through the air hard against the back wall where he fell to the ground and lay motionless. The dwarves quickly intercepted the last one before it moved to finish off Spilf, when an ear-splitting roar from the multi-headed dragon stopped them in their tracks and they turned to face the creature.

The Dragon God expanded in size once again, even without the white dragon present, it now took up the entire central opening of the chamber. The blue head zipped in quickly, like a snake, before Raina and Veric. "I will have you watch me destroy this entire realm, Elf," it hissed.

Veric laughed.

Dal-Draydian spun around to face him.

Veric stopped, with lip quivering slightly, his one good-eye looked away.

A mental link was established and the dragon spoke, *"I need you to kill the other element carriers so I can be completely free. They are chains around me still."*

Veric nodded, and then swung his staff at the distracted Raina. It connected and the elf twirled in the air and fell to the ground, with a grunt.

Focusing on a new spell, Veric raised his arms high holding his jade staff tightly and shouted, "Thekno-tu-kethnok- vee-tu-themoku!" Immediately, a forceful wind filled the room building in ferocity with each passing second.

Meanwhile, El'Korr and Rondee dodged the earthen club attacks, tumbled and rolled past the creature, and then went to work counter striking it with their bludgeoned weaponry.

While the dwarves fought the last stone monster, Raina stood, ran to Spilf, and turned him over. The ordakian's breathing was labored, but he was alive. His eyes fluttered open and he asked in a gravelly voice, "Did we win?"

"Not yet," Raina responded. "I need to get you back to the element." She lifted him to his feet and guided him to the vacant pedestal, fighting against the building wind. Spilf groaned and held his side as an intense sharp pain hit him with each step. He sensed a wetness around his torso and discovered a rib poking through the blood-soaked clothing.

The Dragon God hovered before them in the center of the wind tunnel created by Veric, which continued to increase in intensity.

Six muscle-laden legs with razor sharp claws formed. Its scintillating scales glistened as its power increased. An immense tree sized tail with spikes along the spine trailed to the tapered end of the barbed spear-like appendage. It writhed about menacingly, like an angry snake prepared to strike.

The red dragon head pointed upwards as it bellowed to the ceiling and released a torrent of fiery red and yellow flames from its maw, which swirled and spread along the contour of the rounded apex and was picked up by the cyclonic winds. The cool air quickly superheated, became a whipping blaze, and small sparks jumped onto every flammable thing it touched.

Raina, El'Korr, and Rondee were unaffected by the fire, but Dulgin, Xan, Abawken, and Spilf, were vulnerable to the burning inferno that scorched their skin as it spun through the room. Xan cast a fire resistance spell upon himself to help shield the brunt of the energy and Abawken summoned a fire elemental to block and repel the torrential storm around him. They fought against the hellish heat, all the while bolstering their resolve by yelling in anger. Raina, in the meantime, had almost gotten Spilf back to the Earth Stone. The ordakian needed protection from the flames more than any of the others, and she helped shield him as they moved.

Veric continued to call forth his summoned wind, which voraciously built in speed. The wild air and licking flames danced around him and Daysho.

The invisible assassin, his blade now in hand, stealthily positioned himself directly behind the bloodied wizard, ready to sever Veric's head. Everything was perfectly timed to take out the mage and make his exit. Daysho thought, *"The mystery of Veric's death will be considered a small matter within the scope of this situation."*

Bridazak tried to understand why God did not want him to kill Manasseh. His mind formed the words, *"How am I supposed to show him mercy, Lord?"* No answer came forth. He focused his concern on Manasseh whose grip was weakening, "Hold on Manasseh, hold on."

Manasseh's evil glint changed to defeat, "You, the lowliest of the races in the realm, have bested me twice. Release me and be done with it."

"No, hold on."

"My destiny awaits me in the underworld."

Bridazak grimaced as he strained to lift the heavy human, but he could not budge him. He yelled to the Lord, "If you want me to save him, give me the strength!" His face turned red as he tried again, but to no avail. Breathing heavily, he looked at Manasseh, who seemed to be studying the Halfling.

The human said, "You are pathetic and weak. Even now you try to save me. Why?"

"I don't know," Bridazak strained, "but God wants you alive."

The human snarled, "Your god wants to torture me. He will need to get in line."

"God wants to forgive you."

Manasseh, hanging on the nub of the bow, slipped slightly more. He looked down into the pitch-darkness of the vortex's eye and then back at the Halfling. "Forgiveness will accomplish nothing. Clearly it is too late."

Bridazak was without words, unsure of things happening around him and confused about the doubt that crept into his heart and mind.

Manasseh responded, "Your hesitation is my answer."

With that, the once mighty Horn King let go his grip of the bow and plummeted through the black veil. Bridazak's stomach instantly lurched in nausea as he extended his hand out, even though he knew the fallen King was gone. His dirt smudged cheek rested against the edge of the walkway, confused about what had transpired in mere seconds. Then the grey swirling mist below him suddenly formed into the face of the Dark Lord; the ruler of the realm of Kerrith Ravine. The massive image advanced toward him; its jagged smokey teeth extended out as it opened its jaw. Empty eye sockets, a boney-nose, and horns had brought Bridazak the chill he had felt while encountering the fiend within Manasseh's dungeon weeks earlier. A hollow and sinister voice penetrated his mind, *"Your soul escaped me, but Manasseh's is mine."*

Bridazak clutched tightly to the rock walkway and cried, "I will trade you my soul for his."

"Impossible, Halfling. Your name is written in the Book of Life. No one, not even your God, can change that. I will show Manasseh pain and suffering he rightfully deserves as does all mankind."

Bridazak looked at Abawken. The human was focusing his attention on the stone and battling the firestorm. He then turned toward to his longtime friend, Spilf, who Raina was helping to the pedestal while shielding him from the flames. He could not see Dulgin, who was behind him on the other side. The last person he gazed on was the elf, Xan. Xandahar, gripping his podium with scorched arms and face, had carefully watched Bridazak's struggle with the vile Manasseh. He had already made up his mind to ready a healing spell to help his friend, even if it meant risking his own life or the further progression of the Dragon God's summoning.

Bridazak locked eyes with Xan, nodded at him, and mouthed the words he could only hope the elf understood. He rolled off the edge of the walkway and plummeted into the formed mouth of darkness, vanishing into the realm beyond.

The image of the Dark One screamed in contempt of the ordakian's actions. The face fizzled, and the swirling whirlpool returned. Xan's eyes flared wide in shock, but since there was nothing he could do, he did not leave his position. For reasons known only to Bridazak, the ordakian was now gone. Xan surely believed he would be seen again when they all went back to Heaven to reunite.

28

Where, O Death, Is Your Victory?

Spilf placed his shaky hands upon the pedestal. The Stone of Earth ignited once again. Raina blocked what she could of the whipping, heated wind. Spilf yelled as the pain wracked his body from the protruding broken rib. The beam of light intensified as it shot out into the Dragon Stones, and the green rock exploded, causing the emerald headed beast to fade from existence.

Holding up their arms to shield themselves from the dust and debris, El'Korr and Rondee, leaning into the cyclone, stood their ground and finished off the final rock elemental. The shattered fragments instantly caught in the wind.

It was time to deal with the evil mystic and stop the chaos. El'Korr alerted Rondee with a tap on his shoulder and then trudged closer toward Veric.

Raina closed her eyes and cast a spell. Her voice echoed in the ears of the heroes, "Dal-Draydian's power grows when you lose focus. All four elements are required to be in unison. Concentrate on the power of the element and your inner strength to destroy the stones."

One by one, the adventurers turned from the defensive into a resolute determination to end the pandemonium. Strong pulses of energy surged into the remaining Dragon Stones. The black rock split apart and crumbled, and the ebony headed beast writhed and roared in pain as it faded away, being overtaken by the power of the elements. The red dragon, still spewing its fiery breath into the ceiling, suddenly ended its torrential flames. It reeled back in distress. Shards of red rock flew in all directions. The distinct sound of shattered glass could be heard faintly through the maelstrom as the spirit held captive within was silenced forever.

The final dragon head remained—Dal-Draydian.

Daysho saw that Veric's back and his target, the nape of the mage's neck, was to him. The time had come. With the end of his mission in sight, to the point where he could almost taste his reward, he took precise deliberate steps toward Veric.

The violent gale continued to increase, but the air around Veric remained calm and soundless as he held his staff high above his head, causing the vortex beyond his safe zone to appear, from a distance, like looking through blurred glass.

Daysho had come to the moment that would mark his greatest kill. His honed body zeroed in on the distracted mystic with his blade, positioned perfectly, and ready to strike. Standing behind the mage, he quickly flicked his wrist, swiping his weapon at Veric's neck, but his sword struck the wizard's staff, which Veric held at a precise position to intercept his attack. On impact, Veric turned sharply to face Daysho, who had stepped out of his invisibility stream in order to take his long-awaited action, relinquishing the magic of his cloak.

The bloody-faced one-eyed wizard smirked, "It saddens me Daysho, that you think me so weak. Did you imagine that I would not be able to defend myself against a lowly assassin like you? Mistress Ravana of the West informed me that you might betray us. She was right, as always."

Daysho backed away, stunned at the counter knowledge revealed by Veric. His house of cards now tumbled before him, he needed to escape the situation before the mystic incinerated him.

Veric continued taunting him, "What, no words of wisdom from the fool that walks in shadows? I am surprised at your silence. You spoke to me as an equal before and now where is your resolve? It seems, it has suddenly vanished, but don't be frightened, Assassin." He snarled, "Death is inevitable," and pointed his staff at Daysho. Suddenly, Veric was struck from behind and sent sprawling on the ground. He quickly rolled over and saw the dwarves hulking over him.

"Death is certainly inevitable," El'Korr exclaimed as his hammer boomeranged back to his hand.

Rondee jumped in the air and brought his mighty maul down to strike Veric, but the mage deftly turned sideways and the weapon struck the rock, blasting fragments in all direction.

Daysho backed toward the tunnel exit as the dwarves fought within the shielded globe of space Veric had around himself.

El'Korr stopped him, "I am not sure of your motives, but if you want to finish what you started, then don't be leaving just yet. We can be using another sword, right about now."

Suddenly Veric magically jumped to his feet and chimed, "Yes, Daysho, leaving so soon? After I take care of these minor specks then I will deal with you." He launched a lightning bolt from the rod in hand. It sizzled through King El'Korr and sent him flying into the wall.

Rondee swung his giant hammer, which slammed into Veric's right leg, flipping the human in the air and slamming him on his stomach.

Veric looked up, growled at the wild dwarf, and pointed his staff. A black serpent-like pillar of smoke sprung toward Rondee and wrapped around his neck. He dropped his weapon, attempted to pull the summoned creature from his body, and gasped for air. The wild dwarf could do nothing on his own but the wild magic inside finally burst forth. He phased into a ghostlike image of himself. The phantom snake had nothing to grab hold of and dissipated. Rondee reached for his weapon but could not pick it up as he remained in his spectre form and could do nothing until his unpredictable wild magic wore off. Veric popped to his feet and turned toward Daysho at the tunnel opening.

"Where were we? Oh, yes, I was about to destroy your soul." He bore his staff at him, but before he could utter the command word and release the power held within, the area suddenly was silenced. His lips moved but no sound came forth. Veric twisted backwards as El'Korr's hammer slammed into his chest and he soared through the air, landing next to Daysho.

Raina had magically silenced this section of the room with her spell just before Veric could do anymore damage.

Veric saw her from his crumpled position, barely able to breathe from the hammer's impact. He desperately needed his voice in order to cast his invocations.

Daysho watched Veric struggle to breathe; the dwarf's powerful weapon had partially caved in his sternum. Daysho palmed Veric's bald head with his left hand, bringing the mage to a sitting position, and then lopped his head cleanly off with his longsword. No blood came from the stump because a pulse of magical energy, a potent enchantment upon Daysho's blade, cauterized the wound. He retrieved the hairless, tattooed head, and placed the trophy inside the empty sack dangling from his belt.

El'Korr and Rondee watched the assassin as he nodded in thanks, pulled his hooded cloak over his face, and disappeared from their sight.

The sounds of the chamber returned when Raina ended her spell of silence. At that point, the cyclonic wind dissipated and everyone refocused their attention back to the remaining dragon, who was writhing in pain and anger at the elements that held him at bay.

Rondee, still within his phased state of being, saw the blue beast stretch its spirit from its body toward Raina and El'Korr, who could not see the ethereal form. It prepared to attack as they unsuspectingly watched the dragon's body struggle against the beams of light shooting at it from the positioned heroes. Rondee stepped in front of the beast and it recognized that the wild dwarf could see his true nature. Dal-Draydian knew he was losing. His eyes flared wide in anger, and in a sudden moment of desperation, the blue dragon head lunged for Dulgin, who was still focused on the Sky Diamond before him.

"No!" Rondee yelled, stepping in the path of the attack. The magic contained inside him folded within itself, expanding his ghostlike body into a gigantic shield of energy. Dal-Draydian rammed it and Rondee materialized, bringing the dragon spectre along with him back to the plane of reality. The wild dwarf flew backward, slammed into the chamber wall and slunk to the floor, blood gushing from the horn wounds caused by the dragon. The specter of the beast violently reeled back into the writhing body. El'Korr ran to his bodyguard. Raina waved her hands, uttered a command word, and teleported across the chamber next to her brother, Xan. She touched his shoulder, combining their force. The white beam emanating from the Pearl of the Deep intensified and surged.

Raina said to Dal-Draydian, "I want you to look into the eyes of the one that brought you your demise, Dragon." The blue headed behemoth swung its scaly face in front of her. It's silvery glistening eyes sparked with electrical charges. The elf continued, "I am Raina Sheldeen, the great mystic of the Elves."

Dal-Draydian snarled at her. "My hate for you, Elf, is beyond measure. If there is a way, I will find you, even under the veil of the underworld." The dragon then reeled back in pain, lurching, contorting, and diminishing in size as the final blue stone cracked and it crumbled into dust.

El'Korr sat, back against the wall, embracing his longtime friend. Rondee's blood soaked both of the warriors, gushing from the wild dwarf's chest and waist, where the horns of the beast had punctured his body. His wounds partially closed, and opened up again, as his body phased in cycles between the material plane and the ghostly one. The healing El'Korr had summoned again and again could not overcome the wild magic within Rondee, as it burst out in fits about them. The loss of blood was very great. King El'Korr whispered, holding back tears, "I can't heal you this time, my friend." The faithful Rondee phased fully into his physical being for the last time, coming to rest in his king's arms. El'Korr said quietly to God, "Take good care of him. I expect him in tip-top shape upon my arrival."

Dragon flesh folded into itself, wings snapped off and fell away, sizzling out of existence. The tail ignited like a fuse and disintegrated along with appendages. Popping of bone curling back within itself echoed in unison with its gurgled cry. Within seconds, a brilliant flash of light caused everyone to look away and then faded, casting the chamber into a low resonating glow from the four elements at their stations.

A high-pitched birdlike screech alerted the group, and Rozelle, in her new hawk form, swooped down and grabbed hold of the unconscious Trillius falling downward into the slow moving portal to the underworld. Rozelle snatched hold of the gnome with her claws and flapped her giant wings, bringing them both to safety on the outer walkway. She instantly morphed back to her true self and held Trillius close to her bosom. Trillius' eyes were closed, but he was breathing. She looked up with tear-filled eyes and pleaded, "Somebody help him."

The battered and scorched heroes gathered around as Xan kneeled, whispered his incantation, and then laid hands on the gnome's chest. The healing was administered, however, Trillius still did not awaken. Xan stood and waited. Rozelle looked around frantically as the heroes watched.

"There is nothing more I can do," said Xan.

Rozelle, crying, kissed Trillius. She reeled back, suddenly startled when Trillius opened his eyes and stared back at her.

Trillius chimed, "Well, if that is how a gnome needs to garner a kiss these days then I will have to play dead more often."

Xan and Rozelle couldn't help but chuckle; Trillius was back to himself once again. The gnome said, "I had an amazing dream of riding a five-headed dragon all over Ruauck-El and then I found myself inside a huge room filled with mounds of treasure as far as my eyes could see and chests laden with gems strewn about. It was truly heaven."

Again, they laughed and then Xan said, "Nice to have you back."

Trillius looked around at all the unfamiliar faces, "Where are we, and who are all the new people?"

Spilf approached with panic in his voice, "Where is Bridazak?"

Each of them scanned the room. Xan stepped forward and replied, "He is gone."

"What do you mean gone? Gone where?"

"I'm sorry, Spilf. He sacrificed himself to kill Manasseh. He has returned to the Lost City. He is now with God and our loved ones. We will reunite with him in the future, when we are called home."

Spilf was confused, but the others bowed their heads in acknowledgment of the tremendous loss. Abawken pulled Raina close to him in a grieving embrace. Bridazak, who had been the carrier of the Orb of Truth, was held dear in everyone's hearts; none more than Dulgin and Spilf, who had fallen to his knees at the edge of the chasm, shoulders bobbing as the grief of his friends loss was unbearable. Dulgin laid his hand on Spilf's head and said in Dwarven, "Kawnesh di lengo mi diember faustuuk."

Xan saw El'Korr holding Rondee and was about to rush over when El'Korr raised his hand and nodded silently, indicating it was too late. The weight of these losses increased upon Xandahar's mind. He kept to himself the private exchange he had had with the ordakian. Surely he was in the hands of God, Rondee now by his side, and not with the wicked in the underworld.

What Bridazak had mouthed to him would be sure to cause an extreme, ill-advised reaction, and Xan knew he would be foolish to share it now. In time he would reveal what was truly said, though even he couldn't fight the doubt of Bridazak's statement, "I will be back."

As Bridazak plunged into the darkness it was like a deep ocean. He sank into the depths feeling the heaviness of the essence he now travelled; the underworld, a destination reserved for those separated from God. He could see nothing in the murky blackness as doubts of his decision raced to the forefront of his mind. He was isolated, no longer with his friends. He slowly fell through the realm into the world of the Dark Lord's domain.

Bridazak's speed increased as if he was attached to an anchor driving him deeper and deeper to the ocean's floor.

He was in total darkness; nothing for his eyes to latch onto to give him any bearing of his final destination. He wondered how he would find Manasseh in such a place.

Other eyes watched as Bridazak plunged, like a beacon of light into the darkness; resembling a meteor entering the atmosphere on a moonless night.

They watched in disbelief for they had never seen light before. Dazed, they came out of their somber holes to investigate the strange phenomena.

29

The Past Reconciled

A squad of frost dwarves marched down the corridor, forcing Spilf to cling to the wall to allow them to pass. The dwarves' vitality had returned since the Sky Diamond was returned to its place. Their blue-tinted skin glowed and the light of the torches revealed that they shimmered, covered with thousands of tiny ice crystals. Spilf felt the chilled air as they passed.

Continuing into the hall alone, Spilf replayed the previous day's events in the Chamber of Cleansing. *"This must have been what Bridazak felt after he thought I died,"* he pondered to himself. He still couldn't believe his best friend was gone, knowing that his dearest friend was in Heaven with God brought him some comfort—some. He always imagined being with Bridazak till the end and learning more from him. Spilf thought, *"God, this hurts. Why did he have to go?"*

He stopped at a wooden door and stared at it. He thought to himself, *"Bridazak, you were supposed to be with me for this."* Spilf rested his forehead against the cold metal strapping next to the release lever. He took in a deep breath and then exhaled. He whispered, "Help me, God."

The panel suddenly opened, gravity pushed Spilf inward, burying his face into the chest of an ordakian who was in the middle of a sentence while opening the door, "I am going to find out what the—" He stopped, surprised, and then asked, "Who are you and why have we been locked away from our people?"

Spilf heard a surly voice, deep for an ordakian, but a voice he recalled from the vision God had given him in the Lost City. Without a doubt, it was the voice of his bapah. He slowly lifted his head and looked into rich, wheat colored eyes, wrinkles on his brow, brown hair, like his, but with a touch of grey on the sides. His bapah stood a foot taller, arm muscles bulged from his beige robe.

"Well?" his father demanded.

"I-I..." Spilf stuttered softly, as he was hit with many emotions all at once.

"I demand to know what is going on. My wife and I were shuttled off to this room, isolated from the others. Supposedly, we are to talk with some-one, and we would like to know who that someone may be."

Spilf looked quickly toward the back of the sparse chamber. His momah stood next to the fireplace. The orange flames cast her in a beautiful light; her fair skin glowed. She held her hands in worry, close to her chest. Her soft brown hair, naturally curled, draped over her shoulders and her deep mocha colored eyes narrowed when she saw him. A look of recognition spread across her face.

"Spilfer?" she asked, guardedly.

He nodded. Tears flowed. They ran into each other's arms. As Spilf buried his face into her chest, he immediately remembered her scent—the smell of berries. His father stood there, uncertain as to what was happen-ing. "What is going on, Lyla?"

She looked into her husband's eyes, still clutching Spilf, and said, "Your son has come home."

His breath caught in his throat, "My son?" He took hold of Spilf's shoulder and turned him. They were face to face. As their eyes locked, he realized his anger had blinded him from the truth. He quickly wrapped his arms around his wife and son and the reunited family cried together.

Spilf, in a voice cracking with emotion, murmured "I found you."

In the lower tunnels and castle complex, the bloody battle between Goblinkind and Frost Dwarves raged on.

One after the other, the injured arrived at the makeshift infirmary where Xandahar and Rozelle extended their expertise to help. Xan utilized his clerical powers to heal the wounded. Rozelle helped Xan where needed and concocted druidical ointments for minor injuries. The mixed aroma of blood, sweat and natural spices permeated the room. The floor of the tunnel was littered with hundreds of cots holding patients whose painful cries assailed their ears.

Xan and Rozelle shifted their attention from their current patient when King Morthkin and King El'Korr entered, bleeding and battered, with several other fighters coming in behind them. The two leaders shrugged off the helping hands that instantly lurched toward them, commanding the healers to tend to the others instead. Xan and Rozelle approached.

"We are just getting our second wind and will be leaving shortly," El'Korr said as he leaned his head back against the wall and closed his eyes.

The faces of the kings were covered with heavy grime and their armor and weapons bore the dried gore of battle. El'Korr's magical full-plate still shined bright as new, with the bloody remnants sliding to the ground.

"Your brother, Dulgin, fights well," Morthkin said.

"He has lost a good friend, as have I, and is upset about it, so what better way than to kill some goblins?" he chuckled.

"We will all have lost good friends before this is over," Morthkin responded.

Xan asked, "Are we gaining ground?"

"Nay, but we are not losing any either. We managed to keep them in the lower levels, but they are persistent little insects. It will take weeks for our outer walls to heal themselves."

Rozelle asked, "Your walls can heal?"

"Indeed, due to the Sky Diamond."

El'Korr said, "Have we heard from Raina yet?"

Xan started to shake his head in the negative, but suddenly he spotted Raina standing in the doorway. She was wearing white fur draped over her neck and shoulders.

Raina said, "I have news."

"We were just talking about you," El'Korr said. "Let's hear it."

"Your army is a day away. I made contact with Geetock."

"That is good news. We can use the few hundred extra hands right now."

"No longer a few hundred hands, King El'Korr."

"I understand. What are our losses?"

"You mean what is our gain?"

"Spit it out, Raina. What happened?"

"Initial numbers from Geetock are estimated at eight-thousand and continue to grow. Apparently, all the races in the North have heard of our massing and came to join."

"Dwarves?"

"All races, some dwarves, some elves, but mostly humans."

A broad smile spread across El'Korr's face. He called to King Morthkin, "Time to send this goblin horde back into its hole."

"Come, we will prepare for your army's arrival."

Raina held up her hands, halting them, her face more serious, "There is more." She lowered her hands and continued, "Another army approaches from the mountains in the North."

"What army, Raina?"

"A large contingent of dwarves."

"Dwarves? That is great news." El'Korr's face beamed and he grasped King Morthkin's shoulder to rejoice.

Raina said, "These dwarves are not led by your general Geetock, but by Bailo."

El'Korr dropped his hand and his face turned sour. "He is still alive?"

"Apparently so."

"How many follow him?"

"Estimations at this point say it is tens-of-thousands."

El'Korr's bushy orange eyebrows raised, "So much has changed over the years. It is time that I speak with him."

King Morthkin spoke, "Who is this Bailo?"

"He is my Uncle. He was a Hammergold, who was banished by my father. He split our clan and fled to the mountains when the humans surged for power. Bailo wanted no part of the human's societies, and my father blamed Bailo for separating our people. We had heard rumors that he died in the crags we call Glandi—the Forgotten Mountains. How far away are the dwarves?"

Raina said, "Bailo waits at the front gate."

Morthkin addressed the two flanking guards standing at attention behind Raina, "Show him in."

The ice encapsulated kingdom chilled Bailo to the bone as he was escorted through the Great Hall to the chamber of the throne. Hundreds of armed warriors marched in unison on both sides of his small contingent. Their heavy boots reverberated loudly and then faded as they passed by.

When the escorts stopped at the base of the stairs leading up to the throne, Bailo recognized the gleaming full-plate armor of El'Korr, standing near the throne where King Morthkin sat. El'Korr looked to the frost dwarf monarch, and received the nod of his approval to proceed.

El'Korr's deep resonant voice echoed as he turned toward Bailo, an outcast of his own family of the Hammergold clan, and spoke, "I heard you were dead."

"Likewise," Bailo snapped.

El'Korr noticed that Bailo didn't actually seemed surprised. Bailo's quick response alerted his instincts that this old dwarf had come out of the Forgotten Mountains on purpose. "What brings you out from hiding?" El'Korr asked.

Bailo took a step forward, but was quickly halted by the guards. The dwarf looked up at El'Korr and said, "I have seen with my own eyes the fall of King Manasseh at your hands and I have come to pay homage."

"Homage? You have come to pay homage? I cannot wait to see what sort of homage you have in mind!" El'Korr incredulously replied.

"May we talk in private, El'Korr?"

"Nay, you will speak for all to hear."

Bailo took a deep breath and exhaled. "Very well. Centuries have passed and memories of the former times have become distant, though they haunt me to this day."

"As they should," a voice called from outside the room.

Bailo turned quickly and saw Dulgin entering from an opening on the right of the Great Hall.

Bailo was stunned, he exclaimed, "Dulgin, is that you?"

"Yeah, it's me, Baily. I'm one of your haunting memories you were talking about and this ghost is going to kick yer arse."

King Morthkin waved his guards to intercept the hasty red-head. Dulgin stretched forward trying to break through the defense.

Bailo lowered his head and said in a low hoarse voice, "I never wanted any of this to happen. I have caused grief beyond comprehension."

He fell to his knees in remorse. El'Korr approached, his every step echoing in the hall, "Bailo, the time has come for your judgement."

The dwarf king spoke in a hushed tone, "Tooneck-di-vigosh."

Bailo quickly looked up. El'Korr grabbed him by the arms and hoisted him to his feet.

Dulgin broke through the guards, smiling, and said, "I forgive you also, except for the scar you gave me. I still owe you for that one."

Bailo, dumbfounded, uttered, "I don't understand."

Dulgin smacked him on his armored shoulder, "You have always been dense, which makes you a Hammergold for sure."

"We forgive you," El'Korr stated plainly.

"But—"

"But nothing. Our father told me to prepare for the past," Dulgin said.

"The past?"

"Yeah, at the time I didn't understand until my brother told me you were here at the front gate."

"Your father is alive?" Bailo asked, in confusion.

"Alive and well, in a manner of speaking. Come, we will explain everything."

30

The Funeral

I t was the seventh sunrise since Bailo and El'Korr's armies had arrived and helped to fortify Te Sond from the evil horde of goblins. Things had finally settled down enough to survey the damage, and the emotions held at bay were breaking free. The dead were mourned and many private services were held. Two official funerals were planned as well, amidst the chaos of recruitments, and early training exercises already beginning. In small measures, preparation for future military action in hopes of defending from any attack was bringing hope back to many, even those with the heaviest of tasks still before them.

The solemn drums beat in unison. The wild dwarves marched, taking one step with every resounding tap of the cadence beat. El'Korr and Dulgin, along with two other dwarves, carried the wooden bed, fashioned of smooth calboar wood, sourced from the high peaks of Guul-Fen at great cost. Resting on top was the body of Rondee the Wild, a fallen hero of the realm, but more importantly a fallen friend to those who surrounded him now.

El'Korr took each step with pride, his face resolute, eyes focused on the chamber they approached. Dulgin glanced at his brother and could feel the emotion he was holding back or was it his own emotion he was holding back? So much loss they had all experienced with the fall of Bridazak and Rondee and more loss was inevitable with war against the remaining Horn Kings on the horizon.

The light of the torches lining the walls lit the pathway, and the smell of burning oil filled the tunnel. The crisp chilly air filled their lungs as they marched one step at a time, following the staggered drum beat. The cold brought numbness to the depth of their bones like the sorrow they carried in the depth of their hearts.

Geetock led the eighteen remaining wild dwarves, who unwaveringly held the tradition that only dwarves would be permitted to partake in the funeral of one of their own. The drums were also a deep part of the little-known tradition; they signified the announcement of a great warrior into the afterlife, calling for those in God's realm to prepare to receive Rondee. King Morthkin marched just behind the funeral bed, feeling the weight of having lost so many of his own to the goblins, but thankful for another chance to redeem them. Scores of frost dwarves followed the brigade to show their respect, and to partake in something none of them had ever experienced, as the clan of wild dwarves were even more isolated than themselves.

An ice-rock altar, flat topped and custom built for the dwarf, stood barren in the middle of the circular room. The wild dwarves marched around one to each side, alternating, continuing to beat the drums that were strapped across their shoulders. El'Korr and Dulgin brought Rondee to the center and laid him down on top. The drum beat increased.

The frost dwarves stood in resolute military ranks and files outside the chamber, offering honor worthy of a fallen king.

The drum strikes became faster and faster, still in unison, until finally coming to an abrupt halt, and the echo faded to silence. Each dwarf could still hear the beating inside their minds, but it soon quieted. No one made a sound.

The wild dwarf brigade each took their drums off and laid them at their feet. Geetock stepped forward, withdrawing a waterskin. He pulled the stopper and poured the water over Rondee's face. It splashed and trickled down the sides. Geetock said, "Keldot te fesh. We baptize you into the next realm." He placed the waterskin nestled in between his arm and body.

Another wild dwarf stepped forward, uncorked his ale-skin, and poured the contents over Rondee's chest. The smell of strong dwarven ale permeated the air. Bubbles of the alcoholic liquid oxidizing his hide armor slowly dissipated as the wild dwarf said in a gruff and deep voice, "Daemosh te kah-doo. We celebrate your victories." The dwarf placed the skin opposite the other, nestled in the armpit and then backed away.

In unison, the entire clan of wild dwarves yelled, "Ki thelos!"

Silence once again enveloped the room. El'Korr took a deep breath, exhaled, and then walked forward, standing at the foot of the altar.

His deep voice echoed, low at first but strengthening after each word, "You have been baptized to enter the afterlife. The finest ale, reserved for kings, has been shared to honor you and in recognition of your conquered enemies in this life you leave behind. A dwarf is naked without his beard and without his weapon, though I have seen you break bones of giants with your bare hands." El'Korr unclipped Rondee's trophy tiny hammer and rested it in his friend's hands and chest. "Thank you for following me in this realm and now it is an honor to follow after you into the next. Selfot te miember, my friend."

"Kheldosh!" all the wild dwarves yelled together.

El'Korr stepped back as Rondee's family and clan held hands and circled his body. They bowed their heads and telepathically melded their minds with one another. Seconds elapsed and there was an energy building in the atmosphere that caused the surrounding dwarves to glance at one another puzzled, aware that something was happening.

A beam of light formed out of each of their chests and slowly wafted closer to the deceased laying before them. It finally connected over Rondee's body, the white and orange swirling light encompassing the fallen hero. The aura increased to the point that caused the others to look away, all except El'Korr, who narrowed his eyes but held his gaze.

A far off rumble, like that of thunder, was heard. The light pulsed and then ended abruptly as a remnant sound of a bolt of lightning faded away. Each dwarf brought their eyes back to the altar to find it empty. Rondee had vanished.

The wild dwarves picked up their drums and began beating them together once again. They marched out of the chamber in single file. El'Korr remained, as did Dulgin. The others slowly followed, none of them speaking to one another out of respect of what they had just witnessed.

Dulgin whispered to his brother, "Where did his body go?"

El'Korr did not respond but held his gaze upon the empty calboar wood bed.

"Come, brother," Dulgin tugged.

"He died heroically," El'Korr said softly.

"The heart of a true dwarf."

El'Korr turned to look into Dulgin's eyes, "He saved my brother."

"He saved all of us."

The dwarven kin embraced one another. Dulgin gently pushed El'Korr's shoulders back after a minute and said, "Come, we have another fallen hero to honor with the rest of the races of Ruauck-El."

Morthkin, King of the frost dwarves, ruler of Te Sond, and protector of Guul-Fen mountains, stood before thousands assembled in the Great Hall. His white robes with gold stitching, and clergy adornments set the ambience for the gathered. A hush fell over the crowd as the dwarf positioned himself to stand in front of his throne. The heroes lined up on the side, shoulder to shoulder. Spilf stood with his parents at the bottom of the steps. Elite frost dwarf guards displaying polished silver shields stood at attention along the walls, their stoic stares cast straight ahead.

King Morthkins's deep voice echoed, "Beloveds of God, today we are gathered here in honor of a great hero, Bridazak Baiulus, the carrier of the Orb of Truth and a friend of God, the one who has brought light back into this darkened world. His sacrifice, his courage, his faith, has been felt within us all." Morthkin paused, then looked at Dulgin and nodded.

The red-bearded dwarf stepped forward and faced the thousands gathered. Dulgin was hesitant at first, not being used to so many people looking at him, but bolstered himself and said firmly, "Bridazak was my friend. He fought with a dwarven heart and spoke as a noble. He now resides in the eternal heaven, and will embrace each of us at the gate of love—this I'm certain. He will forever be in my guarded heart and I'm sure he has snuck into a few other hearts too. There is nothing greater than to lay down your life for another and there isn't a moment that goes by that I stop missin my friend. If I could trade places, I would."

Dulgin gruffly finished and stepped back. King Morthkin continued the service, "Good races of Ruauck-El, we are not mourning this loss today, we are celebrating the freedom he has given us all, by his sacrifice in the defeat of the tyrant oppressor Manasseh, not once, but twice. Look around you brothers and sisters. See the soul that stands next to you. Together, we are strong, and together we will fight against the injustices placed on us, on our friends, and on our families. Too long have we stood idly by as evil has corrupted our lands, our homes, and our people. It is time!"

Xan nudged Dulgin, "What is he doing?"

Dulgin nodded slightly while smiling, "He is getting these armies all riled up, that's what he's doing."

"Do you think that is appropriate right now?"

"Damn right it's appropriate. Bridazak would be doing something. God commissioned us to gather and save the good folk of the realm, and that's what we will be doing."

Xan said no more and raised one eyebrow at Raina who was watching them parlay. Morthkin continued his rally speech, a change in direction from what he initially intended as a comforting message for those mourning the loss of Bridazak.

Raina startled Xan when she whispered in his ear from behind him, "What is wrong, my brother?"

"We need to talk, in private."

"About?"

Xan leaned in close to Raina and said, "Our fallen Bridazak."

Cheers suddenly erupted within the hall, a deafening uproar, as Morthkin closed his message.

Inside a small antechamber just off the main gathering, Xan and Raina were alone.

"What do you mean, he is not dead, Xan?"

"Sister, he mouthed the words, 'I will be back.' That is all I know. What can you tell me of the underworld? Is it possible he could survive?"

"Only the dead survive the underworld. Bridazak made his choice and he is now in the arms of God."

"But what if God told him to go?"

"Go where—the underworld? Why?"

"I don't know why, I'm just thinking out loud."

"It's impossible, Xan."

"But nothing is impossible with God," he countered.

Raina regained her composure. There was a brief lull before she responded, "My dear brother, I think it would be best not to say anything about this to anyone. We do not want our friends, still in deep pain from their loss, thinking that someone can just go tromping off into the murk of Hell to contest Bridazak's actions. We need everyone focused."

"Raina, but what if? Isn't there a way we can find out magically?"

"Xandahar, enough of this. Let everyone move on."

"I can't, Raina. If you know some way, then tell me."

She hesitated, staring directly into his eyes, and then she answered softly, "The only way to view the happening of the underworld is to use Akar's Looking Glass."

"Where is this item?"

"No one has seen it for centuries. What I am telling you is that it is impossible." Raina held her position until Xan relinquished his fighting spirit and sighed. "Now that this is settled, let us join the others and celebrate the life Bridazak lived, not the life he lost."

Xan nodded, feeling a little defeated. Raina exited the room. The door closed, leaving Xan alone. He thought to himself, *"God, what can be done?"*

If Raina was right, then it would be impossible for anyone, including his closest friends, to find out if he was in heaven or in the underworld. He knew his sister would not approve, but even so, he would have to inform Spilf and Dulgin about Bridazak's last words at some point. Just not yet. It was not the time. *"Tell me when, and show me how,"* he prayed.

Falling through the shadow realm and then floating to the pitch black, lifeless and indiscernible ground, Bridazak finally reached the bottom. His magical bow, the Seeker, glowed intensely, as did his entire countenance. The soft white light radiated out twenty feet in all directions, still not giving him a sense of what he walked upon.

"Now what, Bridazak?" His words sounded hollow and distant and were more defined after each echo resounded. The audible heightened and then faded just as quickly. He looked directly up and said, "Well, you brought me here. Care to give me directions?"

Suddenly, Bridazak spotted the shiny reflection of eyes in the darkness beyond. The round grey globes blinked. He withdrew an arrow, but it crumbled into dust before he could notch it. He reached for another and the remaining did the same within the quiver. His dagger was quickly in his palm and the blade corroded instantly, the pommel cracked. He let it go and watched the weapon meld into the rock he walked upon. The only thing that didn't wither away was his clothes and his bow, now useless without an arrow.

Bridazak now saw several pairs of murky reflections staring back at him and quickly realized he was surrounded, as more creatures gathered to the beacon of light.

"I don't want any trouble," Bridazak said.

Strange guttural laughs ignited and echoed all around him, like screams zipping by his ears. A hideous beast entered the outer layer of light. Bridazak squinted to get a better look. Black slime dripped off of its amorphous body as it languidly approached. A strong stench of death caused Bridazak to cover his nose and his face contorted sourly. Hissing sounds, followed by rising smoke, came from the creature as it entered the incandescent area. It repulsed back, screeching painfully away. Others tried to enter the light and fled in like manner.

Bridazak felt the ground rumble and loose rock rattled and shifted on the surface. Before his eyes, just outside the glowing arena he cast, red lines sprouted from the cracks in the earth and soon molten lava spewed out, creating a red luminescence. In the middle of the forming lava pool was a single black rock that slowly rose. Materializing on top of it was the ruler of Kerrith Ravine. The stone shaped itself into a throne he sat upon, while magma bubbled underfoot.

"If I had known you were coming, then I would have prepared for your arrival, befitting of someone as despicable as you. Why do you bring your foul presence here?"

"We never got to finish our conversation in Manasseh's dungeon," Bridazak said, surprised by his own confidence, considering his situation.

"Yes, you denied my promises and chose your foolish path."

"I chose the truth. You offered me lies."

"Did I? Are you certain? You speak boldly, but you should mind your manners, little-soul," his voice sharp and caustic. "What is it you want here?"

"The almighty doesn't know?" Bridazak could feel the hatred, it was tangible. "I have come for Manasseh. Give him to me and we will leave."

"What makes you think you can come to my home and ask for something that does not belong to you."

"I am not asking, I am telling."

Instantly, the creature appeared in front of Bridazak, snarling black teeth, dripping bloody saliva. He roared, releasing breath so foul, it would kill the undead. Bridazak fell backwards to the ground, repulsed and began to puke violently. Green bile splayed across his cheeks and dribbled down his neck as he coughed and gagged. Its hulking black skinned mass hovered over the tiny ordakian, his claws digging into the rock like sand, next to Bridazak's head.

"Your maker might be protecting your soul, but he cannot protect your mind. You will wish for death after walking in my domain. Your freedom will be your nightmare."

The Dark Lord vanished before his eyes, the smell lifted, the staring eyes dissipated, and distant echoes of flames, gnashing of teeth, and screams reached Bridazak's ears as he stood.

"Mental note, Bridazak—apparently he can enter the light. Be mindful of your host." He looked up to Heaven and said, "Thanks for the help."

31

True Intentions

King El'Korr and King Morthkin sat opposite each other at a long, polished ice table. The blue block crafted perfectly and the emblem of a shield embossed on the surface. Plush chairs made from the high altitude trees within Guul-Fenn Mountains, upholstered with furs, lined the outskirts. Each seat filled with high ranking members from both sides. Steins filled with dwarven ale littered the top.

King Morthkin spoke, "The Shield will take as many as she can hold, but we are now having to force newcomers to wait at the base of the mountains. Hundreds show up daily to join the ranks or for protection."

El'Korr responded, "Aye, and not all are ready to fight. We also have women and children mixed throughout. Several brigades of Manasseh's former army have broken off and have vowed to fight alongside of us, but it is hard to discern their true motives, considering their backgrounds of tyranny."

Raina said, "But we must find it in our hearts to have some trust. I am not saying to bring them in with open arms and let down our guard, but we must parlay with them and have someone on the inside of our team to find out the truth behind their actions."

"These are humans, Raina. We will need to have one of their race deal with them directly. I can handle the dwarves, with my brother, along with King Morthkin, the gnomes are settling with Rozelle, the elves with you and Xan, the ordakians have Spilf, but we do not have a representative for the humans."

Her eyes narrowed, "Where is Abawken? He can talk with them."

An awkward silence hit the room. Raina looked at each of them, trying to figure out what she missed. This was her first interaction with the council since the funeral a few days ago.

El'Korr cleared his throat, "Raina, Abawken has taken a vow of silence according to his customs, and has asked us to respect his wishes."

"That is absurd. You allowed him to do this?"

"What were we supposed to do, force him to talk and tell him that his traditions don't matter?"

"Someone should talk with him. Dulgin?" He looked at her stoically, but did not budge. "Spilf? You are his friend."

"I don't know what to tell him. Bridazak was the only link between him and us and I am not familiar with human ways. I just think he needs some time to think things through, is all. I might want to take up his tradition as well."

"Xan?" But her brother shook his head.

She glared at everyone, "Fine, I'll do it. Where is he?"

"He has not moved from the chapel," Xan responded.

Raina hastily turned, her robes fluttering gracefully behind her as she exited the war room. Silence engulfed the chamber. The single reinforced door slammed shut and smiles broke on several faces sitting around the table.

El'Korr said, "That was harder than I thought. She is a tough one to sneak around."

Xan added, "Yeah, I wasn't sure we could pull it off."

"Good luck to the Huey," Dulgin announced as he lifted his mug into the air. Everyone grabbed their own and swung them high in the informal toast, and then took a large swig.

Raina briskly walked down the torch-lit corridor, passing pockets of patrons lingering in the halls, and small units of troops marching to their next destination. She took no notice of the whispers of those she passed by, who gawked at her presence and labeled her one of the heroes of Ruauck-El.

Her intentions were to change Abawken's attitude and get him back to work. To imagine, a noble warrior of his caliber, hiding away inside some chapel with a vow of silence. She could not understand the human's motives, but she was determined to remind him of the great need she, and the others, had of him.

The double doors to the chapel were closed. Two frost dwarf guards stood at the sides and quickly pulled the entry open at her approach. She entered and stopped a few steps in, perusing the ceremonial chamber of prayer. The doors were slowly closed behind her. Extravagant sculptures of past dwarven warriors lined the edges leading to a raised platform of solid blue ice. Hundreds of candles skirted the steps leading up to the dais. Three huge statues stood at the top, representing the last three kings of the frost dwarves, including King Morthkin. Sparkling pillars of mined gems on either side, radiated a soft glow throughout the chamber and a kaleidoscope of colors splayed on the walls from the lit candles.

Abawken was kneeling at the foot of the stairs. A small trail of smoke ascended in front of the warrior and Raina ascertained it was the burnt remnants of incense as the rich aroma permeated the room.

"Abawken, I wish to speak with you," she demanded as she walked straight toward him.

The human did not stand or acknowledge her presence.

"I don't understand your vow of silence. If Bridazak, whom you had sworn to protect, were still here, he would want you to help the people of the land. We need to have you in the council, to help us lead, and to liaise with the humans of Manasseh's former army." Raina was now behind him.

Abawken remained silent, and stood, but did not turn. He wore new clothing, his sleeveless tunic revealing his bronze and toned arms. The light brown hair of the fighter fell to his shoulders, glistening in the light of the room.

Raina, waited, growing more infuriated by his silence, until finally she grabbed his shoulder and forced him to turn and look at her. His head was bowed slightly as he came around. He brought up his clutched hands, not holding incense, as she suspected, but instead a bouquet of wild flowers, which he extended toward her. He raised his head up slowly, calm, confidently, and said, "Raina, you have ended my vow of silence."

"What is going on, Abawken? I don't understand all of this."

His ocean blue eyes bore into hers and she suddenly felt a quickening of her heart.

Abawken answered, "I know, but I will explain, just listen to what I have to say."

"Explain then," she refocused her determined stance.

"Here, these are for you." She hesitated to take the flowers, but he insisted, "Do you know how hard it is to find flowers in such a place as this? I had to...never mind, I am talking too much."

"No, you are talking too little and not about why you are here. Why are you so nervous? What is this all about?"

"Raina, we have built a connection beyond my expectations, and—," he faltered with his words, "I'm sorry. I'm a little anxious now."

"Anxious? What are you talking about?"

"Raina, I love you," he blurted. Her countenance shifted slightly and she waited for Abawken to continue. "We have been to Heaven, we have seen death, but now let us live life, together." Abawken reached out and gently touched the scar on her face, "I want your scars to now be mine, I want us to be written in the books and songs of this entire world as a symbol of true love. Raina Sheldeen, will you take me as your husband and be my friend until my last breath of this life?" Abawken bent to one knee and took hold of her hand while her other hand grasped the bouquet. He looked up into her emerald eyes, relieved that he had finally asked the question that burned in his heart.

She paused for what seemed like an eternity and gave her answer, "No."

Abawken's glint of a smile faded as he slightly gasped and before he could say anything, she pulled him up to stand and said, "It is customary within the Sheldeen elves to marry our own and not intermingle with the other races. I am sorry, Abawken." She turned to walk out.

Abawken shouted before she was at the door, "He said you would say that."

Raina stopped and turned around to look at him, "Who would say what?"

"Your father."

"What are you talking about now and be hasty with your response Abawken."

"I spoke with him."

She walked back to stand face to face with the handsome human, "Don't play games with me."

"I am not good at games, my Raina. I met your father in the Lost City, and asked for his blessing for your hand in marriage."

"You saw my father? I-I," she stuttered for the words.

"You have his eyes and his personality," Abawken continued as more shock registered on Raina's face. "What was the last thing he said to you in Heaven, before we came back?"

She regained herself, "He said to embrace—"

Abawken finished for her, "Change."

"Yes, embrace change, but I didn't understand what he was talking about."

"Raina, it was me. He gave me his blessing. I have lived only three decades while you have lived several centuries. My time as a human is short and though you may outlive me, I want to spend my every waking moment with you. I want us to have children and there I will live on, through them, through you."

She stared at Abawken and watched the human go to one knee once again, "Raina Sheldeen, will you take me as your husband and be my friend until my last breath of this life?"

"No," she paused, Abawken stood abruptly and then she continued before he could respond, "I will be your best friend and lover beyond this life and the next."

Abawken released his held breath, smiled, and then wrapped his strong arms around her, sweeping her off her feet and twirling in pure joy. "I love you. I have always loved you."

She responded, "I admit I wished at times for this, but I did not think it could come to pass."

His mouth opened in shock, but Raina took the opportunity and passionately kissed Abawken. They were lost in one another, finally out in the open with their feelings. They released, she opened her eyes slowly, and saw his still shut, enjoying the kiss he had imagined for so long.

"How do you feel?" she asked.

He smirked and said while still in ecstasy, "I feel elven."

She laughed, "Then you need to finish learning the language, quickly."

His eyes opened, "How do you say, I love you?"

She leaned in and whispered in his ear and then pulled away with a smile.

"Alluve," he said.

The boisterous laughter within the war council abruptly halted when Abawken sullenly entered. Dulgin left his seat and hurriedly approached the human.

"It's okay, Huey. It was a valiant try, lad," Dulgin quietly consoled, patting his friend on the back in pity.

His head hung low, Abawken was ushered to an empty chair. He sat and quietly muttered, "I just can't believe it."

No one said a word, and then Raina re-entered the chamber, a new sense of focus and purpose on her face. Several eyes glared at her for priding herself in crushing Abawken's heart.

El'Korr stood and addressed her directly, "Raina, the meeting is adjourned. We think it would be best to disband and get some rest." The dwarf started to wave the others to go and one by one they caught on and began to stand.

"Wait," Raina halted them. "I have something to say." Everyone froze in place, uncertain if the mystic might blast them where they stood. "We have other planning to discuss, so I suggest each of you take your seats. No one leaves."

She waited for them to find their chairs. Each of them had their heads held low, except for King Morthkin and King El'Korr. Raina smiled once again.

"Now that I have your attention, we need to start preparing for our next adventure."

"Raina, what are you saying? Did you find another Dragon God we need to destroy?" El'Korr chuckled, but Raina ceased his chuckles when she stared at him blankly.

"A vision came into my mind, and what I saw will shock you—will shock you all," she looked to each face at the table, her intense eyes boring into them. A hush fell in the room and El'Korr's brows slightly raised in wonder before he finally broke the uncomfortable silence.

"What did you see?"

"A sacred event in the realm which will most certainly alter the course of history."

The entire room was captivated and waited in anticipation of what she spoke of. The dwarven king stood and Raina quickly approached him. She leaned close to the orange bushy beard of El'Korr and said, "I saw a new union."

El'Korr blinked and stepped back slightly, "Which armies unite against us, Raina?"

Raina laughed, "No armies." She turned and then addressed the entire room, "Abawken and I are to be wedded." The human fighter proudly stood and took her arm. They nestled close, side by side.

The stunned faces melted to joy as they realized the elven Mystic had turned the tables upon them all.

"And you will be leading the service, King El'Korr," she announced.

He looked around at everyone and then said, "Wonderful, a war, a funeral, and now a wedding. Why not?"

32

The Message

Daysho held the iron chest by two rungs on its sides as the massive arched double-door cracked and grinded open. Huge giants pulled the thick rope pulley system to open the gate to Ravana'a castle within Tuskabar. Several black-hooded mystics, hands hidden within their sleeves and faces shadowed, stood on the other side, waiting.

"I have a message for the Horn King," Daysho announced.

Insidious laughter mysteriously and ubiquitously echoed in his ears. Daysho entered the slate floored keep and the doors slowly shut behind him. The robed mages turned in unison and he followed behind them as they walked deeper into Ravana's domain. There were no torches, no sounds, not even the shuffling feet of the ones he trailed, and the walls were bare of any art or tapestries. Daysho's senses within the dark confines navigated him through the corridors. He was led to an open chamber, where the mystics stopped and stood resolute in a bowing posture at the sides to allow him to enter.

Grey marbled pillars lined side by side in the middle of the sparse hall, cascaded toward a vacant throne, fashioned of bones, at the end, upon a dais. Red embers within bucketed braziers, cast an eerie glow with shifting shadows.

"I am here to deliver a message," Daysho repeated himself.

A melodious female voice echoed, "Approach and deliver your precious message, Daysho."

Her voice had a menacing sharpness while smooth and alluring at the same time. He walked toward the throne, not bothering to try to pinpoint the evil West Horn King. Daysho stopped at the foot of the steps, placed the iron box on the ground, and unlatched the hinge. He backed away three steps and waited.

From his left, he heard slithering, but Daysho remained resolute.

The suave voice returned, "What is in the coffer?"

"Your message."

"An interesting way to deliver a message. I do like originality. Open it."

Daysho moved as instructed and flung the chest lid to reveal the bald, tattooed head of Veric, her personal mystic. Daysho backed up to his former position, but bumped into something. A strong reptilian musk smell bombarded his senses and the distinct hiss of snakes sounded around him. The hypnotic sensation of the smooth scales slid on his neck and caressed his scalp.

She whispered in his ear, "Are you looking to be hired, assassin? Why do you bring me this?"

Daysho did not answer and the eyes of the deceased Veric, flared open. An untenable, hollow voice came from the mage, "I wanted to remind you that I have not forgotten, Ravana."

Her green scaly figure came into full view of Daysho as she slithered forward. The snakes snapped at the human as she passed by. The youthful skin on her face was attractive, but the charm quickly evaporated when her vampiric fangs prominently displayed. A mesmerizing rattle followed as her long tail slid behind her.

"It would have been better if you gave me your message personally. I would have enjoyed you," she responded.

Veric's mouth continued to be used by the mysterious spirit possessing his head, "Anything you hold dear, I will destroy, Ravana."

"Oh, was Veric dear to me? He was of some use, but there are others, always others. I must have wronged you somehow. I am a merciful king, tell me what you want and I can help you."

"I want her back, Ravana, and will not stop until you release her to me."

"You are indeed an enigma. I like this game. Give me her name."

"Kiratta Green."

"Oh, yes, a beautiful human, and one who stole the heart of my true love. It is good to hear from you Romann de Beaux. How are you?"

"Release her, Ravana. Centuries have passed and you know my heart still belongs to her. She is innocent."

"Innocent, you say? Not likely. I was merciful to her and to you, my love."

"I am always watching you, and I will live forever until I see your damned heart crushed with my own hand."

"Romann, Romann, you are so dramatic. I am the ruler here and I will rule as I please. Your sweet Pirate's Belly is only allowed to operate because of me. Come home, my darling, and let us rule together."

"Never. My revenge will come someday. The four Horn Kings will fall—one has already. The realm has begun to change, I can sense it. You should be mindful of the recent events. You can't hide inside your tower forever."

"I am not hiding, my dear, I am waiting."

"For what?"

"For you. It breaks my blackened heart that you toss my feelings for you like the waves upon your ship."

"You have cursed us both, Ravana, but I have not turned one soul to a foul being you converted me to be."

"Not surprising, Romann. You were always the hero, never the villain."

"I won't stop until you release Kiratta from the curse of Oculus."

"I wouldn't assume otherwise. Who is your messenger boy? He is cute, can I have him?"

Daysho's heart quickened, but he refused to make eye contact with the medusa-like vampire. He stood his ground, hands at his side. Ravana slid past him slowly and he gulped. Romann did not answer her.

Ravana's voice trailed in the distance behind him, "You may leave, Daysho. Give my best to your master, but be mindful, Assassin. I know where you live."

Daysho did not hesitate and turned to walk out, eyes looking at the ground. His heart stopped when she appeared suddenly before him, blocking his exit.

"Are you forgetting something?"

He floundered in his response, "My apologies, I am uncertain as to what you mean."

"Take what you brought out of my chamber, Human."

"Of course."

"Look at me, Daysho," she commanded.

He paused and shook his head slightly.

She said, "I will not turn you to stone, trust me. After a while, statues become so droll and boring. I want to see your eyes and I want you to see mine. Now look at me!"

Daysho raised his head and his eyelids opened wider, until finally seeing her glowing sapphire orbs.

"Good," she said. "Now we understand each other. I have seen your soul and you have seen mine. You may leave."

He bowed his head, backed himself to the metal chest, closed the lid, and carried it out the way he came in. The doors to her chamber thumped closed.

Daysho stood before Romann de Beaux, aboard his ship, *The Rose*.

"You have done well, Daysho"

"Then you will give me what you promised?"

"Yes, you will be the first that I have ever turned. There is no going back, Daysho. I pray you heed my words and recant your decision."

"No, this is what I want."

"So be it. The rules of a vampire are different than anything you can imagine. Those turned unknowingly, become Vamplings, the weaker of the species, but those turned by their choice retain all of their past skills and become stronger each passing year."

"I understand, my master."

"Once you transform, you know what needs to happen next."

Daysho looked directly into Romann's swirling red and blue eyes, an evil grin on the assassins face, "Yes, you will have your army, that is certain." Daysho tilted his head, revealing his ripe veined neck. Romann stared at the assassin, hesitant to alter the pure life before him. He had strategized year upon year, decade upon decade, century upon century, but no thought of ever transforming a living soul to a foul and lost spirit like himself had ever crossed his mind. He hated what he was, but even more, he longed to be united with his true love. *"There is no other way,"* he thought to himself, *"but to fight evil with evil."* He splayed his fangs and sunk them deep into the human's flesh.

33

The Smell of Lilac

Abawken and Raina strolled arm in arm through a remote section of King Morthkin's kingdom. They were given privilege to enter a sacred hall the frost dwarves called Klusheed.

"We are almost there," Raina said softly.

Raina smiled and Abawken asked, "Are you going to tell me where we are going?"

"Not yet. You will see shortly."

Abawken noticed the lighting in this particular area of the dwarven construction had a faint hue of orange within the blue-iced walls. He wondered what their destination could be as they passed through numerous guards stationed at strategic intervals leading to this section of the mountain castle, but didn't notice much else, other than Raina. They were together, and his world was right.

They rounded a bend on their walk and came to a brilliant gold door, the apparent source of the orange hue reflecting off the ice.

Abawken waited as Raina walked to the door, which magically opened on its own. The human fighter staggered forward as the majesty of the chamber beyond captured his breath.

"Welcome to the Garden of the Gods," Raina said as Abawken, mouth open, eyes-wide, stopped at the doorway next to her.

Numerous trails split off into the immense, cavern-like room, weaving between the brilliant crystals shimmering in colors they had only seen in

Heaven. The floor sparkled like a polished glass mosaic embedded into the ground. The crystalline forest grew in clusters from every surface and in every direction. Reflective images of the couple refracted throughout the chamber, capturing the colors of their clothing and absorbing them into the natural phenomenon.

"It's beautiful," Abawken finally said. Raina grabbed his hand and tugged him inside, letting the gold door close.

Raina's voice glided smoothly, "The wedding is in just a few days. Soon we will be leading a great quest together, you and I. Before the other power-hungry Horn Kings advance on the territories, we will begin to set up leadership in the West. We will defend the freedom we won at such high costs there. My hope is that we will see a new kingdom of freedom born. But before we do all that, we have time for a small trip."

"A trip?"

"Yes. I will summon Zeffeera and take you to a place I'd like to show you," she smiled.

"Are you going to tell me where?" Abawken wasn't too keen for surprises, but wasn't sure if he would explain that to Raina. She seemed so fond of them.

"I will bring you to a place where the flowers sing in joy over the colors they wield. Birds chirp in chorus with the land, and cool breezes that roll over your body heighten your senses and lull you to rest."

Abawken stopped their stroll and looked into Raina's eyes, "Can there be such a place as you describe?"

She lovingly smiled and said softly, "I am taking you to Teras di Kimil; the Lily of the Valley. My home."

"I thought the elven kingdom of the Sheldeens fell in the wars."

"It did, but not my home. Zeffeera is the protector of the hidden valley, along with Neph."

"Neph?"

Raina grabbed hold of his arm and they began to walk again. She smiled as she continued, "Yes, Neph. She was a gift to me and I long to see her again."

"Another secret, my Raina," Abawken toyed.

"Nay, Neph is a dear friend and one that you will need to experience, as any description I offer will not do her justice. Now, tell me about your family and where you come from."

"I come from the province of Zoar in the far east, beyond the borders of the Horn King. The desert folk isolate from the outer lands and live by the rules of the Serriff."

"The Serriff?" she questioned.

"Serriff Shellahk rules Zoar." He waited for Raina to respond, and she did, as quickly as he expected.

"Your father?"

Abawken nodded.

"Then I'm marrying a prince."

"No, you are marrying me, and that is how I wanted it. No titles, just a man, in search of meaning. Offering love."

"What other mysteries do you hold, my prince?" she mocked playfully.

A distinct scent caused Abawken to freeze in place, catching Raina off guard.

"Abawken, what is it?"

"Impossible," he muttered.

"What is impossible?"

"She found me," a stunned expression on his face.

"Who found you?"

"She lets me know she is near when I smell the Lilac."

Raina laughed and walked a few steps away. She reached down between a cluster of purple and red crystals sprouting out from the ground and pulled out a bouquet of wild flowers, pale toned violet petals adorned the white candelions, and she deeply breathed in the smell as she brought it back to show him.

"You mean this? I wanted to surprise you, but it appears my surprise is not working too well."

He sighed, "My apologies. That smell has been a nightmare to me recently."

"Abawken, you are mine and I am yours. I brought us here so we can share our lives, past and present. Our union must begin with honesty."

"My customs teach reservation, and that being outspoken can lead to misunderstanding, so silence and patience is better. We," he paused, "we rarely like surprises, for example."

Raina smiled with understanding. "I see. Then you may count on fewer surprises from me in the future, and certainly from whomever has concerned you so. Remember, we are together. Your friends are now my friends, and your enemies are now my enemies."

"I have a lot to tell you," he resigned.

Devana walked the halls of the Shield, disguising herself as a lost refugee. She passed the sad, but hopeful faces, that slept along the corridor walls. It has been a long journey ever since the Serriff hired her services to bring back his son, but the complications of the matter have developed even further. She would be patient and study these heroes of Ruauck-El, in order not to get herself caught inside their long reaching grasp. The god summoning halfling had fallen, as evidenced by the grand funeral of state, but now Abawken prepared to marry the Sheldeen mystic, which brought another challenge.

She tired of the peasant folk she milled around with in hiding and longed for the posh lifestyle she had become accustomed to. Tomorrow she would start establishing her presence among these adventuring friends of the sheik prince, and garner the information needed to push the stubborn fighter back to the desert of Zoar with the Sword of the Elements. Her reputation was on the line, and failure in her line of business showed others weakness.

Devana crouched onto her meager bedding in the corner of a heavily populated refugee chamber, and turned, laid flat on her back, her hand draped over her forehead, eyes closed. The reek of body odor and unwashed clothes caused her to wrinkle her nose, but the heavy desire to sleep took over.

The beautiful assassin waited at the threshold leading into the stark room. Her bounty, the wayward warrior, stood with his back to her on the far side.

"There you are, Abawken. Your time is up," Devana said, walking toward him.

He did not respond to her as she approached. The room was dimly lit by a single candle; its dripping wax cascaded from its perch within the sconce hanging on the wall onto the wooden floor.

"Are you going to try and resist me? As much as I'm humored by your feeble attempts," she teased him as she reached out her hand to his shoulder. She continued to speak as she twirled him to face her, "But remember, I always get what I want."

Abawken remained silent and stared back at her. Devana noticed a strange confidence plastered on the human fighter's visage.

"Who are you?" Devana backed away.

The tan warrior transformed into a female elf in her elegant lavender robes.

The human assassin recognized her instantly. "Raina."

"Devana," the mystic responded in kind.

"Nice trick, Mystic. How did you get into my dream?"

Raina stood and slowly strolled toward her. Devana backed to the wall.

"This is my world, Raina. Your spells will not affect me here."

"I came to talk with you, and to arrange your boundaries moving forward."

"I have no boundaries, Elf. You have been out of the game for a while; things have changed."

"Being out of the game, as you call it, only means you have no knowledge of my power, maybe rumors but no knowledge. My warning to you: Abawken's dreams are safe; you will no longer be able to see him. I have linked our minds, and we will be together if you ever try to visit him again, in this manner or in any other."

Devana composed herself, the shock of the situation melded away as she walked past the elf. Her back was now to Raina.

"I was hired by his father to bring him, and specifically the sword, back. As soon as he submits, and the soon-to-be-married Prince comes home, then my job is complete."

"Only a job? Yet why do I suspect that your own tortured soul enjoys power over another?"

Devana turned, "Yes, I do admit, I have enjoyed doing my paid duty, to retrieve your future husband." Devana continued, "You should accompany us. His father is very generous, and would love to meet his daughter-in-law."

"We will meet him on our own terms."

"Great feats can be accomplished in such an environment as this, my visitor." Suddenly, two amorphous beings phased in from out of nowhere, standing just behind Raina, and grabbed her arms. The mystic did not resist, but kept her eyes on Devana, who slowly approached.

"Here, my dear Raina, I am the master. I set the rules. I was trained by the Dream Walker Phelbias, in the Halls of Echoes. In this world, you need to show me a little respect. Abawken will be taken back home with or without you. Truly, I prefer without. Less messy that way."

Raina coolly replied, "Have you heard of Tsieken?"

"Should I have?"

"Well, it appears Phelbias didn't teach you much then."

"Don't try to understand my trainer, Raina. You are a mystic; your power lives in the waking hours. Any knowledge you have of Phelbias is only from your precious textbooks."

"I never read about Phelbias, nor heard of him before you."

Devana smiled and was about to speak, but Raina continued, "But Tsieken, which you have never heard of, trained a man named Balhka."

"Balhka? So?"

"Balhka trained Seefa."

"Where are you going with this, Elf? I really have to be off with my bounty."

"I am giving you a history lesson of several generations of Dream Walker teachers. Teachers long before Phelbias." Raina's voice strengthened, and the calm and collected Devana faltered.

"You have no power here, Raina."

The two faceless beings suddenly dissipated, releasing Raina. Iron bars formed all around the assassin, entrapping her inside a cage. Devana grabbed the cold metal in a panic, and looked around for an escape.

Raina circled the perimeter and said, "You are only the master in the dreams you create. This is not your dream, but mine." Realization and concern registered on Devana's face, wondering what the powerful mage had in store for her. Raina continued, "I was trained five generations ago in all the arts of magic, including Dream Walking. I am the Sheldeen mystic, Devana. We are done here." The elf turned and walked toward the exit.

"Wait!" Devana called out, "What about me? You can't leave me here. I will eventually wake."

Raina stopped, but did not face her, "I will release you, Devana, but be very mindful of the boundary I have set in place. You may inform Abawken's father that he will return home, when he is ready."

Devana lurched forward, sitting upright, gasping for air, and sweating feverishly. She caught staring eyes in her direction as she came back out of the nightmare. Her heavy breathing slowed and then almost stopped, when she heard the distant echo of the elf's voice inside her head, *"Well met, Devana."*

34

Destiny

Abawken entered the chapel and stopped in his tracks at what he saw. The entire room had transformed, thanks to the druid, Rozelle. It was as though he was instantly transported to a sylvan forest. Where statues once reigned, there now stood glorious green trees glowing in the warm light of a Summer's dusk. The once stone flooring was now a soft, moss-like grass, dotted with beautiful wildflowers in full bloom—the sensation of rich pollens completed the façade of the outdoors. Across the room an enchanting archway, laced with yellow and orange petals, prominently displayed on top of the former iced dais, now a grassy knoll.

"Do you like it?" Rozelle asked excitedly.

Abawken, mouth open, stuttered, "This is amazing, Rozelle."

"I did my best, asking the other elves and her brother what would look and feel like an elven wedding ceremony. I hope she likes it."

"Raina will be overwhelmed."

"You are too kind Abawken, but I think her eyes will be only on you, and not this trivial magic I've conjured. Now, get out of here and get ready." Rozelle ushered him out the door and she returned back to her work, finalizing the remaining details.

Abawken turned the corner and collided with the young boy, Jack. The fifteen year old had groomed his shaggy brown hair, parting it on the side and his grey eyes sparkled in the torchlight.

The child, short of breath, said, "I thought I could help out."

"I must go get dressed, Master Jack, but you can ask Rozelle," he pointed back into the chapel.

Jack watched the swordsman, whose skills he had often admired, depart, and then he entered the room. He looked around in awe, until Rozelle snapped him back, "Can I help you?"

"Uh, yeah, I thought I could help out with the wedding."

Rozelle chuckled, "You are cute, but I think I have it covered. Find Xan or Dulgin, they might need someone to help them." She returned to her work as Jack backed out of the chamber.

Jack had been struggling for weeks to find his place. During the army's march to the Shield, he hadn't had a soul to lean on. He missed his dad terribly, and every day doubted his decision to leave the Holy City, and his dad, in coming back to Ruauck-El, especially since his hero and only real friend, Bridazak, was gone. He felt out of place amongst all of these heroes. They had rescued him from King Manasseh's castle, but now it seemed everyone was busy with their lives and he had no one. He longed for someone who would spend time with him.

He watched Xan and Dulgin from the doorway, preparing for the grand event, and Jack realized he would not be needed. The boy sighed as he leaned against the door frame, witnessing the hustle and bustle of servants attending to everyone in the room, bringing in garments, drinks, and food. They all had each other and he resigned himself back to his room, carrying his head low.

The beautiful sounds of harps accompanying a choir of elves set the tone for the monumental ceremony. The voices melodically captured the hearts of all in attendance. The smooth, alluring notes and the nature spectacle filling the room enhanced the glorious event.

King El'Korr stood in the center of the flowered archway. A strand of gold-tasseled, entwined rope dangled around his neck and shined with his off-white robes. He beamed broadly as he waited for the bride to enter.

Abawken waited anxiously in front of him, fidgeting slightly as he looked into the crowd of witnesses. His attire was regal but simple. His ivory jacket draped down to his knees, with the tail down to his calves, over his embossed boots. Silver clasps cinched the front together, while gold embroidery laced the edging along the collar and cuffs. Abawken strummed a few loose strands of hair behind his ear and took a deep breath, glancing over to Dulgin who stood beside him. The dwarf winked.

Dulgin's red beard, groomed with three braids, melded into his coppery silk tunic. He smiled as he nudged Spilf, who was looking as serious as he could, honored to stand with his friend.

Three successive knocks alerted everyone that she was coming. The door cracked open. The music stopped and the singers silenced. All faces turned and watched the parade of the remaining Sheldeen elf race enter. Leading them was Xandahar and trailing behind were several attendants, paired up, side by side, all clad in light green, billowy clothes. They stepped in unison and then a song softly ignited. The voices of the women rang out, smooth and haunting. Then the men joined, deeply resonant, all blending perfectly. A candle, cradled in each of the attendant's hands, reflected the sheen of their fabric and enhanced the ambiance. The processional stopped near the end of the path through the trees and parted from one another, creating an aisle. They turned to face each other, and knelt onto one knee.

Raina stood at the threshold as the last elves positioned themselves. The melodic voices peaked to a crescendo as the glorious bride locked eyes with Abawken. Her white dress flowed over her slender frame, and long, billowing sleeves draped at her wrists. She held the same bouquet of flowers Abawken had given her, still alive and vibrant. A silver circlet with stamped intertwining leaves encompassed her head.

Abawken couldn't breathe, caught by her beauty. She slowly walked to the front and stood beside him. They grabbed one another's hand and smiled.

El'Korr began the ceremony, "Today we blend two heritages that the realm has not experienced before. Let it be known this union is ordained by God himself, and has the blessing of the elven father of the Sheldeens. Today will mark a new season of change."

The dwarven king continued the opening speech, while Trillius leaned against one of the trees near the exit, observing quietly. Rozelle joined him and nestled in beside him, "Isn't this great?" she whispered.

"How long are these ceremonies?" he asked.

She rolled her eyes, "Not long. You will be able to get back to your busy schedule soon enough. Such a romantic, you are."

"Well, I can be, if I wanted to."

"Besides your charm, what else is romantic to you?"

"I can always boast how I almost became a god; that should get me far with the ladies."

"That is stupid, you almost died. Really, though. What is romantic to you?"

Trillius paused and then smiled, "I get lost in your eyes."

"That's nice." Rozelle blushed.

Trillius changed the subject, "You are heading out tomorrow for your nature time, right? I think I'm gonna hold up here until you get back."

"Shhhh, they are going to give their vows."

Abawken took a deep breath and began, "My eyes have been opened by our amazing God in the Holy City. I began a journey to fulfill the mission he showed me, and now I am beginning another, not just to live, but to love. I will love you all the days of my life, here, now, and beyond, and will protect you with strength, and serve you with humility, with all the best I have to give—this is my solemn vow."

Trillius quietly yawned midway through, and was elbowed by Rozelle. He furrowed his brow at her, "What did I do?"

"Nothing. That's the problem," she countered.

Abawken placed a blue frosted diamond ring on Raina's finger, "In the province of Zoar, my homeland, we exchange rings to mark our union. With this ring, we are united."

Raina smiled and then in turn spoke, "Learning and garnering deeper knowledge in the arts of magic have always been my greatest passion. I am thankful to you, my Abawken, for now I will passionately study this art of love, friendship, pursuit, and unity. Our legacy of love will be a beacon for all mankind. I take you as my husband from this day forward—this is my solemn vow."

Trillius glanced at Rozelle, "Are you crying?"

"It was beautiful," she was barely able to answer.

He rolled his eyes and crossed his arms, but his interest piqued slightly when Raina produced, out of thin air, a gold band on Abawken's finger.

Raina said, "I honor your ways with this ring. The custom of the elves directs the bride to assign a bond-name to her new husband. Henceforth, you will be known as Leiv Talhor amongst my people."

The surrounding elves whispered the new bond-name, "Leiv Talhor."

El'Korr announced proudly, "The sacred vows these two have exchanged will be forever burned into the Book of Promises, and from henceforth they will be recognized as husband and wife." El'Korr made eye contact with Abawken and he smirked, "It is the human tradition to seal the deal with a kiss." Giggles and whispers echoed behind them in the crowd of guests.

Cheers erupted as the new couple embraced in their first married kiss and then they turned to face everyone. The flower petals on the archway suddenly burst into hundreds of butterflies that fluttered about.

El'Korr yelled, "The two have become one!"

Raina and Abawken were swallowed by the many people coming forward to congratulate them.

Trillius glanced to the door and noticed a young boy, head low, fondling an interesting bauble, catching his attention; a diamond ring, a very large, diamond ring.

Rozelle nudged him and said, "How did you like the butterflies? I added that little effect in myself." She was proud of her work, but Trillius didn't answer and turned to find the boy gone.

"Rozelle, very well done, but I have to go take a tinkle. I will catch up with you later."

He took off, leaving Rozelle, who sighed, "Yeah, such the romantic."

The sounds of the wedding party faded as Trillius stealthily darted from shadow to shadow, following the young human boy. He had not seen this person before, and he couldn't help but be intrigued by the diamond ring the child held in his possession, and occasionally pulled out to look over when he thought no eyes were on him. Trillius was lured by his curiosity. He easily trailed the adolescent, and wondered how he had obtained such a prize—a prize that would soon be his.

They traversed deeper into the frost fortress, in the lower sections, until the youngster entered a room and closed the door behind him. Trillius waited a minute before making his move. *"I'm impressed. This young lad has a giant gem in his possession, and his own quarters. Who does he know, I wonder?"* Trillius thought to himself.

Jack slouched his shoulders as he sat on the edge of his bed. Two lit candles spread their aura around the small bedroom. He twirled the ring, trying to catch the sparkles, when all of a sudden, his door burst open. A gnome rushed in, short of breath, and slammed the door closed.

Trillius leaned his back against the entrance and gasped, "Sorry, I am trying to get away from her."

"Away from who—"

Trillius cut him off, "Shhhhh. Whisper."

Jack brought his voice down, "Who are you running from?"

Trillius didn't answer and instead placed his ear against the door. He turned back to the boy and smiled, "I lost her."

"Who?"

"Oh, just one of the many women who chase after me. It is a tough life, but someone has to do it." Trillius strolled closer to Jack. "My name is Trillius."

"I know, I heard about you. My name is Jack."

"Young Jack, may I stay for a minute?"

"Sure, you are the most excitement I've seen in weeks."

Trillius sat right next to him on the bed. He bounced a couple times, measuring the comfort, and then smiled. "So, where are your parents?"

Jack shifted uncomfortably, "They are not here."

Trillius read his body language perfectly, "I lost my parents too, when I was young."

Jack looked at the gnome, "I didn't know my mom. She died when I was born."

"Mine too," he lied. "You must blame yourself for her death, like I did. It wasn't your fault."

"I know, my dad said the same thing."

"I am sure he is very proud of you."

Jack nodded, "I miss him."

"Oh, he must have passed recently. I am sorry."

"He lives in the Holy City now, with God. I will see him someday."

"Where is this Holy City you speak of? I have heard the others talk of it and I'm not sure it exists."

"It exists alright; I was there."

Trillius coughed, "You were there?"

"Yes, with Bridazak and the other heroes. I got to see my dad and I decided to come back with the others."

"Come back? Why would you want to come back here of all places?"

"To help others know God and to give them hope, I guess. I came back to be a hero, like my dad."

"Oh, I see, so you are trying to keep the good folk of Ruauck-El, like myself, informed of this glorious God that hid away for centuries and left us for dead with the birth of Kerrith Ravine?"

Jack paused at the gnome's blighting accusation, "It's not like that. I don't know, I'm lost right now. It's hard to explain anything."

"I apologize for my triteness. I have lived a long time and heard rumors of this ancient city. I can't argue that you have been there. Perhaps someday I can visit it. Anyway, why are you feeling lost?"

"It just seems that nobody wants or needs me. I'm like a shadow no one notices. I don't have any friends."

"I know what you mean. I'm kind of lost here also, and I miss someone too."

"You miss a girl?" Jack smirked.

"No, not a girl, a dragon."

"Really? I rode a dragon, a bronze one. Did you ride one also?" he excitedly responded.

"Calm down. No, I did not ride one, but had a relationship, a friendship with one. It is hard to explain, but we had a connection. Anyway, Dal-Draydian, he's dead now, but he gave me quite a bit of knowledge about lost treasures within the realm."

"Lost treasures? What are they?"

Trillius grinned and looked at Jack, "You know, Jack, I like you. I think we can be good friends. In fact, if you are interested, I could show you the ropes of a great profession. A very lucrative profession."

"You want to hang out with me? Yeah, I would love that."

"You said you were like a shadow. I can teach you how to have those shadows become your friend."

"What, like a thief?"

"You think of me as a thief? No, what I will teach you is beyond that ugly line of work. Much better... but it will cost you."

"I don't have anything to give."

Trillius waited, staring at young Jack, until finally the boy revealed what he clasped in his hand; the diamond ring.

"My dad gave me this. It is the only thing I have of him. Can I loan it to you until I can buy it back?"

"What a grand idea," Trillius' eyebrows raised.

"I trust you, Trillius. Thank you for being my friend." Jack held out the ring. Jack's innocence pierced into the gnome's conscience.

Trillius hesitated and then sighed, "How about you keep it and then pay me later."

"Really?"

Trillius shrugged, "Yeah, I guess so. Well, listen, I got to get going and make sure that woman doesn't break into my room or something. Let's talk more tomorrow."

"Okay, Trillius. Thank you, for everything. It was really nice talking with you."

The gnome gave a shallow smile and then left.

Jack sat back down and looked at his father's ring and wondered again where he had gotten it. He always imagined it was his mother's wedding ring. Jack smiled brightly and giggled, which wasn't something he had done in quite a while, at the thought of his new friend, Trillius.

Jack suddenly stopped when he thought he heard something. It was a strange voice, it sounded distant. He went to the door and peeked, looking down the hallway. No one was there.

He closed it, turned, and then heard his name called, *"Jack."* The hollow voice echoed within his mind.

"Who's there?" Jack said aloud.

"Jack, help us."

He felt heat coming from the ring in his hand and when he opened to see the diamond, it flared shades of red within the gem, swirling like mist. Jack looked closer and saw blurred faces, weaving in and out of the red smoke.

"Who are you?" he asked.

"The gem will lead you to us. Follow it." Then the diamond returned to its normal appearance, the cloudiness faded. A strange sense within himself pulled him to leave his room. Jack opened the door and left, longing for adventure.

Coming Soon

Book #3 of the Horn King Series
The Vampire King

Jack descended to the lower levels of the frost dwarf castle, where worked stone and ice turned to more natural tunneling. The diamond ring slightly vibrated in his grasp when he came to a fork in the tunnels, requiring a decision. If he chose the wrong way then the gem remained still, but when he chose the correct way, it pulsed. These lower sections were isolated and much colder. He shivered as he watched his breath rise in front of him. The tunnels were dark, but he was still able to see.

He suddenly stopped when the ring vibrated.

"There is only one way to go," he whispered. Jack looked confused as he peered back and forth down the corridor. He leaned against the wall and sighed heavily. The diamond pulsed and a small phrase entered his mind. Jack stood upright and repeated it aloud, "Vemptukai."

Shifting stone sounded abruptly behind him, causing Jack to freeze in pure fright. He quickly turned and stared into a strange hallway that wasn't there before. The ring pulsed. Jack took his first step inside and flinched as torches sparked to life along the walls as far as he could see. Cobwebs dangled from the sconces and a strong, musty smell abounded. Each step he took echoed, melding into the sounds of the flames leaping from the ancient wood dipped in tar.

"Hello?" he asked nervously. He jumped when the secret door closed behind him, sealing him inside the corridor. Jack ran back, but it would not open as he clutched the edges and strained to move it. He calmed himself and began to creep further, following the endless torches.

Hundreds of feet elapsed, until finally, Jack spotted an open room ahead. The light ended at the opening but shadowy illumination informed him of the chamber beyond. He grabbed one of the ignited sticks, sliding it out of the iron sconce and burned away the dusty webs in the entryway.

Jack saw a circular room with twelve stone sarcophagi lining the wall. There were no exits, he noticed as he cautiously entered. The unmarked graves lay eerily still, thick layers of dust covering each one. A stone pedestal with etched runes stood in the center of the chamber.

The mysterious hollow voice returned to Jack's mind, but now stronger and not quite so distant, directing, *"Place the ring on the altar."*

The frightened but determined boy, bent on adventure, did as instructed. The clear diamond abruptly illuminated into a bright light and then slowly faded. Jack investigated his ring, but before he could touch it, a blast of energy shot out at each of the stone lids, forcing Jack to fall to the ground to dodge the beams. He watched from his sitting position as the rays crumbled the covers, revealing the corpses within.

Rotted flesh dangled from their sunken faces, arms crossed over their chests, and a fine dust covered them from head to toe. Their eyes shot open, black as night, and the crack of joints and bone echoed as they took a step out of their graves. Tattered clothing hung from their heightened frames.

Jack scrambled to his feet and clung to the pedestal, trying to distance himself as much as possible from the beings. His shaky voice asked, "Who are you?"

In unison they spoke aloud, their voice, haunting and hypnotic, "We are the Twelve." They stood motionless and resolute, arms still crossed over their chests.

"What do you want?"

"We want you, Jack."

"Me? I'm just a boy. I don't understand. Did the ring call you?"

"Not the ring, but your soul. We walked your realm two-thousand years ago, until we were not needed any longer and here we have harbored ourselves, entombed for all eternity. New evils have surfaced. Darkened hearts have invaded the land once again, but entrapped by our own demise, we are unable to stand against the threats."

"But what can I do? I don't even know how to fight with a sword yet."

"For what we offer, you will not need a blade."

"But why me?"

"Your strength is beyond measure, Jack. We sensed it when you arrived at this place. We used the ring in your possession as a conduit to contact you. Your soul is the strongest we have felt, unlike any before."

"What is it that you want from me?"

"You have been touched by the hand of Adonai and thus your spirit rests in his hands, never to be taken."

"Adonai?" Jack questioned.

"Adonai ha'adonim—the Lord of Lords, God Almighty, Ruler and Creator of all."

Stunned, Jack responded enthusiastically, "You know God?"

"Yes, but it was too late for us. We condemned ourselves to being forever separated from him."

"But why? What did you do? Why are you here instead of—," he paused.

"It matters not, but what does matter is the choice set before you. Remain the child, learning your way until united with God once again. Or help us."

"Help you, how?"

"You can save us, Jack. We have longed to be in the arms of Adonai, but our souls are no longer ours to give to him."

"Who has your soul?"

"We made a deal with darkness. At the time, we were human, living a finite timeline, but we longed to live forever to battle the evil of the land. We were paladins, determined to vanquish all impurities from the realm. We have lived with the regret of making that deal ever since. When we sensed you, we decided to make contact and to give you a choice. Will you help us, Jack?"

"What is it you need me to do?"

"There is an ancient artifact, called the Mirror of Lost Souls. You will need to find it and bring it back to us here."

Jack laughed, "I don't know about these things, and I'm too young and inexperienced."

"We will bestow upon you powers from each of us, but what we give will alter you greatly from what you now know."

"Powers? What kind of powers?"

"Strength, knowledge, wisdom, speed, endurance, and more—but Jack, do not be enticed only by these gifts. Your transformation will be severe and you won't be able to go back to being a child."

"You mean, I will age also?"

"Yes, twelve years added to your life. It saddens us to burden you with the loss of childhood and we will not be angered if you choose to ignore our plea."

Jack paused, thinking and pondering his life thus far. He didn't have his family any longer, Bridazak was gone, and he longed for something more to help those in need. He felt this to be his calling, his time to make something happen.

"I will help you."

ABOUT THE AUTHOR

Brae Wyckoff is an award winning and internationally acclaimed author, born and raised in San Diego, CA. He has been married to his beautiful wife, Jill, for over 20 years, and they have three children. He has a beautiful grandson named Avery. Brae has been an avid RPG gamer since 1985. His passion for mysterious realms and the supernatural inspired him to write The Orb of Truth, the first in a series of fantasy action adventures.

In addition to writing the Horn King Series, Brae is the host of Broadcast Muse blog talk radio program, featuring interviews with authors, artists, and world changers. He is also the CEO of LR Publishing, a one-stop publishing service provider geared specifically for the growing genre of Destiny Action Adventure Fantasy, which brings life, purpose, and ultimately a message of hope.

www.braewyckoff.com

13892017R00168

Made in the USA
San Bernardino, CA
09 August 2014